Dear Reader,

From the moment she arrived at my doorstep—soaked to the skin from the tropical heat, with nothing but a suitcase and the prettiest smile I'd ever seen—I knew she was trouble. But what man in his right mind could turn away a woman like Rachel Chandler, especially if he's pretending to be her long-lost brother?

Rachel Chandler is no more my kid sister than Brigitte Bardot's a skinny schoolgirl. She's all woman, and she's making me lose my cool. I've got to get rid of her, and the sooner the better. If she doesn't go, I might just do something rash....

a.k.a. Emmet Chandler

Hawaii

ANNE STUART
Tangled Lies

Hawaii

Harlequin Books

TORONTO • NEW YORK • LONDON
AMSTERDAM • PARIS • SYDNEY • HAMBURG
STOCKHOLM • ATHENS • TOKYO • MILAN
MADRID • WARSAW • BUDAPEST • AUCKLAND

HARLEQUIN ENTERPRISES LTD.
225 Duncan Mill Road, Don Mills,
Ontario, Canada M3B 3K9

Prologue

December 1969—Cambridge

There was a biting wind ripping through the Cambridge streets, laced with the icy tang of the sea and the Charles River, whipped into stinging pellets of freezing rain that assaulted the back of his neck as he ducked his head down. He brushed past the crowds of people with unseeing hazel eyes trained on the cracked sidewalks, his affable grin absent. Usually he made a concerted effort to look strangers in the eye and smile, but his cheerful friendliness was nowhere to be seen that day. Ducking around a corner, his booted feet moved faster. He hadn't wanted to leave the town house. Second-year chemistry students tended to think they had all the answers. He would have felt safer if they were graduate students. By that time in their studies people knew enough to realize how much more they had to learn.

Charlie's Pizza Palace was a small, funky hole-in-the-wall that served as meeting place, dining hall, and home away from home for their small, dedicated group. Tinny Christmas carols were blaring forth from an old AM radio behind the counter, and some ratty-looking tinsel, spotted with tomato sauce, adorned the seldom-used cash register. The man slammed the door shut behind him as he entered, closing out the biting wind and some of his misgivings, and went to pick up the pizzas.

Three large, with the works, ought to keep them occupied most of the night, until he could make sure they knew what they were doing. He was older than most of them—he felt somehow responsible. A staid, sober influence, he thought with a laugh. Who was he kidding? But the pizzas and the gallon of cheap red wine they'd brought with them when they'd arrived earlier that afternoon served to distract them for a while, and one of those intense all-night arguments on political theory would finish the night. A wry grin lit his lean, youthful face. There'd be no revolution without pizza and cheap red wine to fuel it, he thought, and lots of theory. Bringing out the money, he felt the customary twinge of guilt. Money was too available to him; too many people were in need, and his pockets were always bulging.

"Keep the change." Hefting the three large boxes in his small, strong hands, he headed back out into the Massachusetts winter. Charlie looked after him, wiped his nose, and stuck the fifty-dollar bill in a back pocket before turning up the radio as dogs barked "Jingle Bells."

The pizzas would be cold by the time he made it the four blocks back to the elegant town house that resembled nothing so much as a Haight-Ashbury crash pad right now. Donovan's parents were touring Europe. He could imagine their horrified reaction if they returned early, in time for Christmas, and saw the holiday decorations Donovan and Julianna had fashioned. But Donovan's parents weren't going to return any time in the near future, and Christmas would pass undisturbed and unnoticed.

Not by the majority of Boston, however. Songs about peace on earth blared forth from every radio, interspersed with bulletins announcing the rising death toll and the constant escalation of that nasty, vicious little war. *All is calm, all is bright,* he thought, turning the corner into the wealthier section of Cambridge, where there were neater streets and quieter houses, where the silent weight of wealth and prosperity and capitalism radiated its smug self-assurance to the deliberately scruffy passersby. Peace on earth was a cruel joke, he thought, ducking his head against the stinging sleet. When the most peace-minded people he knew spent the season of joy and hope constructing bombs, and he was a half-hearted patron. Nitroglycerin cost money, which he had in abundance.

Not that bombs, per se, were that bad, he reasoned, the never-ending argument still playing in his head. A nice, clean bombing that destroyed parts of the war machine without endangering human life had a certain anarchistic charm. But could you always guarantee there wouldn't be a night watchman, a student at ROTC studying late, a miscalculation?

Hell, he was borrowing trouble. He'd smoked too much dope before leaving for the pizzas, and it always made him paranoid. Then again, that was another problem. He couldn't quite reconcile the amount Donovan smoked with the needed care for the chemical combinations. Donovan always insisted it made him even more accurate, but he had his doubts.

Still and all, Donovan, for all his youth, seemed to know what he was doing. And the lab was surprisingly efficient, despite its ramshackle air and jumbled components. He wondered how everyone was getting on in his absence, and how far down the wine bottle had gotten. Maybe he should stop and get some more.

No, he was just being overly moralistic and chicken-hearted. Nothing would go wrong—the house was as safe as a nursery school. Donovan was brilliant, in complete command....

The blast rocked the street beneath him, sending him staggering against a parked car beneath a shower of broken glass. The pizzas went flying, and he stared at them for a blank moment, the anchovies mixing with the shattered glass on the hood of the Dodge beneath him. And then he was up, and running, oblivious to the slivers of glass embedded in his scalp, oblivious of the crackle of fire and the distant screams that echoed distantly in his head. People were everywhere; he shoved them out of his way ruthlessly as he raced toward the town house. Skidding around the corner, he careened into a couple of curious housewives. And stood there staring, with horror, at the pile of rubble and flames that had been the Donovan town house.

"Hey, man, you've got to get out of here." An urgent voice penetrated his horrified abstraction, and he turned with overwhelming relief to see a soot-covered Donovan, the gash on his high, intellectual forehead oozing blood. Julianna was beside him, her arm at a strange angle, the whiteness of shock set in her face. "Come on, man. They'll be after us before you even turn around. Get moving."

"Where's—?"

"Gone, man. Julianna and I were the only ones to get out. We only realized at the last minute it was going to blow. Listen, the heat will be here any moment now, and people know you've been seen around here. Get lost, man, and fast." And without a backward glance, either at his friend or at the rubble of his parents' house that now served as a tomb, he took Julianna's good arm and hustled her down the street.

He stared after them, then swung around to watch the flaming pile of debris. The sound of the sirens was growing louder, and so was the deafening panic that beat down around him. Before he realized what he was doing he had whirled around and was racing back down the streets through the shattered window glass. There probably wasn't a window intact in three blocks, he thought dazedly. It was going to be a cold night for a lot of people. He had almost made it to his illegally parked car when the sound of a radio blared out from one broken window.

"All is calm all is bright...."

December 1969—New York
SOMETIMES THE MAN thought New York was the coldest place on earth. He knew it was impossible, of course. He'd spent years in Minnesota, where it regularly dipped to twenty and thirty below zero during the long, hard winters. New York at ten above was still more bone-chillingly cold.

Even the forced gaiety of the Christmas season didn't seem to help. Of course, there wasn't much to be happy about this Christmas. He faced decisions, and none of the answers pleased him. There were times when prison seemed the least of the evils, but he knew he was fooling himself. Even if he could stand it, and he had little doubt he could bear anything he put his mind to, there were others to consider.

Canada was another possibility. It probably wouldn't be much different from Minnesota. The only problem was the inevitability of it. There would be no changing his mind, no turning back, once he went that far. And he didn't fancy being on the run, giving other people that kind of power over his life.

But the third alternative was no alternative at all. Killing was alien to him; his sister always said that despite his hard face he was the sweetest man on earth. He wouldn't go that far, but he knew he didn't want to participate in organized killing, in a war he didn't believe in.

Sooner or later he was going to have to decide. He had till Christmas, a Christmas that was moving much too rapidly toward him. Reaching over, he flipped on the radio; his large, slender hand sped past the omnipresent Christmas carols that had begun to grate on his raw nerves. He wasn't in the mood for the twenty-fifth rendering of "The Little Drummer Boy."

His hand stayed outstretched, motionless, as he listened to the news bulletin. His hand shook slightly as he withdrew it, pulling it back as if burned. He leaned back in his chair and stared with unseeing eyes out the soot-caked New York window. And for the first time in his life he wanted to kill.

Chapter One

With an almost detached glance Rachel Chandler looked down to see her strong, pale hand grip the armrest of the 747 that was gleefully soaring through air pockets and the most god-awful turbulence to the peaceful paradise of Hawaii. *If I hold on tight enough,* she thought in a controlled panic, *then this ridiculously heavy piece of machinery won't fall out of the sky and into the vast, green-blue Pacific Ocean beneath us.*

"First time you've flown?" a deep, sympathetic voice next to her inquired, and she shook her head. The last thing she wanted to do was to encourage the man beside her. She had had time to size him up through her initial wave of panic before the plane took off, long enough to assure herself that she wanted nothing in the world to do with him. He was dressed in a pale silk suit that had doubtless been tailored to his tall, muscular body; his handsome face was perfectly tanned, the blue eyes above the strong, aquiline nose calculatingly warm and flattering. He was just a little too perfect for Rachel's perverse tastes. She had had her fill of handsome, well-dressed, charming men like her ex-fiancé, Ralph Fowler, all surface charm and no depth at all, and the last thing she needed was to arrive in Hawaii with a man hanging over her.

Of course, she was probably having delusions of grandeur, she thought, deliberately trying to loosen her death grip on the armrest and keeping her face turned out into the clouds. She had no illusions about her looks—she knew just what he saw through those beautiful blue eyes. A woman in her late twenties, she had chestnut hair in a thick braid down one shoulder and dark brown eyes, cautiously curious. She wore a white linen-blend suit set off by an aqua-green silk blouse, the straight skirt with the slit halfway up her thigh providing her seatmate with a needless amount of slender, tanned leg. She should have worn jeans, she thought irritably as one of her seatmate's hands reached over to pat the clenched fist that rested nervously on one thigh. She had been in such a whirl of excitement and panic that she'd put on the first thing she could think of this morning, an outfit guaranteed to make her feel good about herself.

With a cool, deliberate stare, Rachel looked down at the encroaching hand. He had too much black hair on the back of his knuckles, and he wore a diamond pinky ring, which immediately rendered him harmless. How could anyone be seriously threatened by a lothario with a pinky ring? She looked up into his blue eyes, which were a trifle closer together than she had first noticed, smiled sweetly, and said, "Take your hand off me or I'll call the stewardess."

He moved his hand away as if burned, an affronted expression on his face. He probably hadn't been turned down in years, Rachel thought to herself, especially not by someone who in a crowd would be a definite second or third or even twelfth choice. A moment later he rose, navigating the aisles with practiced ease in his hurry to get away from her and seek out greener pastures. She had to admire his balance, though nothing would get her to unfasten her seat belt and leave the dubious haven of her seat.

Not even nature, which had been calling her quite adamantly for the last hour. There were three more hours left to the flight, but nothing, absolutely nothing, would entice her out of her seat to brave the dangers of the airborne rest room. Her bladder would simply have to suffer. Think of something else, she admonished herself as her body protested. Think of why you're doing such an incredibly suicidal thing like flying.

By the end of the day, for the first time in more than fifteen years, she was going to see her brother. After six months' time, countless private detectives, a concerted effort on Minnie Masterson's part to have him declared dead, and sheer panic on Rachel's part, Uncle Harris had suddenly, surprisingly, come up with the goods, confounding all the greedy relatives who had hoped to prove her brother long dead. Emmett Chandler had been found, still on the same island in Hawaii where he had last been seen in the late sixties.

Of course, Emmett being found wasn't as simple as it sounded, Rachel reflected. With Emmett it was never going to be that way. First off, there was his involvement sixteen years ago with a bomb factory in a town house in Cambridge. The town house no longer existed, thanks to the bomb factory, but various members of the radical group he'd been involved in still made occasional reappearances. Emmett had scarcely been a ringleader, and it was the accidental explosion that had sent him on the run to Hawaii, but the FBI had still made occasional inquiries of Ariel and Henry Emmett as recently as three years ago. The elderly couple who had raised two astoundingly disparate grandchildren remained ignorant of his possible whereabouts.

It was a good thing only Rachel had known the next stop on his run. A postcard from the island of Kauai was the last direct word she'd heard from him. In retrospect she had little doubt what he'd been doing on the chiefly agricultural island—Hawaii was famous for the potency of its marijuana and the ease of its cultivation. But apparently that wasn't the answer to his problems either, for a few months later Emmett William Chandler had disappeared. Henry Emmett sorrowfully assumed his grandson was dead; Ariel and Rachel refused to accept the fact. That was doubtless why Ariel had left almost all the money to him, Rachel had decided months ago. She'd known that Emmett had as little interest in the Chandler fortune as she had, but if Emmett was the heir to all those millions, someone would have to find him.

Perhaps Rachel had been wrong not to tell Ariel about the packages in the beginning. They began arriving the year Emmett left, regularly as clockwork, a few days before her birthday, postmarked Hong Kong, Macao, Rome, New Delhi, names to fill her imagination and set her mind at ease. There was never any note, but then, there didn't need to be. As long as she knew Emmett was well enough to think of her, to send her a birthday present from his exotic ports of call, then she knew he was all right. And the small porcelain butterfly would join her growing collection, a collection Emmett had started on her fourth birthday.

Henry Emmett had known, of course. Henry Emmett knew everything that went on in the vast mansion north of San Francisco. But he'd never questioned her, never said a word, merely smiled faintly each year when he handed her the well-traveled packages that arrived with strange postmarks and no return address.

And now she was finally going to see her brother again! She could hardly remember what he looked like, it had been so long. He'd seemed very tall to her when she was twelve, though she knew in retrospect that he was less than six feet. His long, sandy-colored hair had hung halfway down his shoulders, though he usually tied it back in a ponytail, and a full beard had obscured his face for three years prior to his disappearance. Would he still have that skinny awkward look? He'd be around forty by now—perhaps he'd be suave and slinky like the man who had sat beside her.

And would he be pleased to see her? Uncle Harris had decreed that none of the pack of ravenous relatives should even think of venturing out to Hawaii to welcome home the prodigal son until the various legal entanglements were settled. It wouldn't do to have the Chandler heir slapped in jail; it wouldn't do to have the Chandler fortune hit with lawsuits by the survivors of the town house blast. Even Aunt Minnie decided to wait, albeit with a great deal of grumbling and almost daily phone calls to Rachel, usually at work. The District Supervisor of the Department of Social Welfare hadn't been pleased with a junior caseworker spending so much time on personal business, but Aunt Minnie, with all the arrogant disdain of the Chandlers, had been unmoved.

Uncle Harris's warning had even extended to her, of course, though he hadn't felt it necessary to lay it on quite as thickly. After all, the entire family knew that Rachel didn't fly, that nothing short of a major earthquake could get her to leave northern California. But he hadn't counted on her lifelong love for her brother, her general feeling of bereavement at the sudden death of the grandparents who had brought her up from infancy, when her flighty mother had died in a plane crash. Emma had been on her way to a party, five weeks after Rachel was born without a father. She had abandoned Rachel's thirteen-year-old half brother, Emmett, to her parents years before. Despite the large difference in their ages, Rachel and Emmett were bonded closer than most siblings.

Uncle Harris also hadn't counted on the defection of the faithless Ralph, and her real, physical need to see her own flesh and blood after more than half her lifetime. She hesitated a full week, building up her courage, took a leave of absence from her job and disgruntled supervisor, and then yesterday morning called the airline.

And even when this sadistic mode of transportation landed in Oahu, her troubles would be far from over. She had to board still another airplane, no doubt smaller and far more dangerous, for interisland transport to the smaller island of Kauai, and then finding Emmett might prove quite a challenge. Uncle Harris was staying in a hotel on one side of the island. Emmett, he'd informed them, lived in a small cottage on the opposite side, on a stretch of land still belonging to the Chandlers, who once had owned huge tracts of the island. If she could manage it, she'd like to bypass Uncle Harris's well-meaning interference. She'd fantasized too long about finally seeing Emmett again to allow Uncle Harris's bleary interference to taint the beauty of the moment.

She could only be thankful her seatmate didn't rejoin her for the harrowing landing three long hours later. It was all she could do to concentrate on keeping her breathing steady, and her mind on Emmett at the end of this desperate journey. Even the bump that tossed her about as the huge plane finally touched down surprised only a quiet moan out of her. With trembling hands she gathered her purse, untouched crossword puzzle, hand luggage, and composure together and headed for an island bathroom.

IT WAS A HOT, sunny day, one of a thousand similar hot, sunny days, with the gentle trade winds providing just enough natural air conditioning to make it bearable. The man calling himself Emmett Chandler propped his long legs up on the railing of the cottage, his large feet encased in ratty-looking running shoes, and opened a beer. He squinted out at the ocean, at the wide expanse of white sand that was his alone, at least for the time being. Paradise had its points, he had to admit, even if its typically sunny, smiling weather reminded him of nothing so much as a simper. But he needed a simper, some warmth and sunshine and saccharine-sweet good weather, to mend the weariness that went bone deep. It had been a long time since he'd been able to sit on a porch in the sunshine, drinking a beer and being gloriously alone, and it was something he reveled in. Even if this entire complicated scam fell through, he would have salvaged something from it. Maybe just a small amount of his peace of mind, returned to him by the Hawaiian god of solitude.

He no longer wondered why he had contacted Harris Chandler, why he had agreed to this idiotic charade. He knew full well why he had done it, and he damn well didn't regret it. It was only at peaceful moments like this, on a silent afternoon with nothing but the sound of the birds and the ocean intruding, the rich salty sea smell and the tangy scent of hibiscus tickling his nose and warring with his beer, that he didn't feel any hurry to get on with the damned mess. He'd walk farther down the beach that evening, maybe make it all the way to the point and back.

It was only a matter of days, a week at the most, before
he would put the second part of his plan into action, and
then there'd be no time for seaside walks, for sitting on
the porch drinking beer and blotting out the unpleasant
realities of life.

But for now there was nothing to stop him. He wondered for a moment whether he'd ever get his fill of the
hot tropical sun. Even now, weeks after that cold gray
prison pallor had darkened to a deep, dark tan, he felt his
thirsty skin drink in the hot rays. Perhaps *simper* was the
wrong word for it, he thought. Maybe it was the warm,
friendly smile of a beckoning sea goddess, giving rest to
a weary traveler. Tipping back the chair, he drained the
Heineken, shut his eyes against the midday glare of the
sun, and thought about the early days with Krissy.

THE SMALL PLANE that handled interisland travel nearly
undid Rachel entirely. She could only be glad that pas-
sengers entered directly from the terminal, so she didn't
have a chance to fully appreciate its flimsy size. By the
time she was buckled into her seat belt by icy cold fingers and had turned to view her surroundings, it was too
late. For a brief moment she considered knocking over
the black-garbed priest who was making a great to do of
settling across the aisle from her, then decided she could
wait another moment until he was out of the way and still
make her escape. Her early years of Catholic training
kept her in place until the middle-aged priest was settled, and then her numb fingers fumbled with her seat
belt. She could always swim to Kauai. Even with sharks
the ocean was doubtless safer than this ridiculously small
airplane.

Her hands were sweating so profusely that the seat belt
proved impossibly stubborn. She was about to call the

stewardess for help when she heard the warning bells with a sinking despair. The engines were rumbling, missing every now and then, and Rachel leaned back in her seat, prepared to meet her doom somewhere over the Pacific. At least there was a priest at hand—maybe she could entice him into the rest room to hear a final confession.

Takeoff passed in a blur of agony and hyperventilation. Rachel didn't dare open her eyes until she heard the small bells ring once again, signaling that smoking could resume and seat belts be dispensed with. Why in heaven's name had she given up cigarettes? They could provide such comfort to a condemned woman.

She felt the eyes on her almost immediately, knew instinctively they'd been watching her for quite a while now, only she'd been too caught up in her panic to notice. Not another swinger, she prayed.

She managed to sneak a quick glance to her right. Straight into the amused but sympathetic eyes of the priest who'd kept her from making her escape earlier.

"I take it you don't like to fly," he murmured as he unfastened the seat belt that stretched across his generous paunch.

"Not much," she admitted ruefully. "I try to avoid it whenever possible."

"I hope it was something good that made you attempt such a hazardous feat?" He had warm, hazel eyes that smiled across the aisle at her, and a balding head with a ring of gray hair that accentuated his monklike appearance, though Rachel could tell that nature, not religious preference, was responsible for his hairstyle. His face and hands were tanned a deep teak color, with paler laugh lines fanning out around his kind eyes, smiling mouth, and double chins, and he could have been anywhere between thirty and sixty. Rachel guessed he was somewhere in between, perhaps his midforties. He must have been in the islands a long time to be that color, she thought vaguely.

"The best," she confided with a reminiscent grin. "I'm going to see my brother."

The priest's cherubic face held an expression of mild interest. The plane was more than half empty, with only the two of them in the back section over the wings. Leaning across his empty seat toward her, he smiled. "How pleasant for you both. Has it been a long time since you've seen him?"

"Fifteen years," she replied. At his sudden arrested expression she hastened to explain. "Not through any fault of our own. Things just . . . got a little complicated with the family for a while. But now everything is going to be just fine," she added, more to herself than the politely interested priest.

"I don't mean to be so inquisitive, Miss—"

"Chandler," she supplied. "Rachel Chandler."

"Rachel Chandler," he echoed curiously. "We wondered whether you were going to show up."

"You did?" Without realizing it, she undid her seat belt, and slid across to the aisle seat.

"You're Emmett Chandler's sister, aren't you? Word had it that you'd turn up sooner or later. But I didn't realize you were expected."

It was Rachel's turn to be startled. "How did you know? Do you know my brother?"

"We haven't met yet, but we're bound to sooner or later. Kauai is in many ways a very small island and gossip travels fast. Your uncle's arrival, searching for the heir to several million dollars, took most people's fancy. And then, having Emmett show up out of the blue was most extraordinary. Most extraordinary. The papers have been full of his family background, including his younger sister. Oh, forgive me, I'm Father Frank Murphy. I've been on Kauai for four years now, and I must say your brother's appearance has been quite a wonder."

"I can imagine."

"I've been meaning to call on him for the last few weeks, but I never seem to make it to that side of the island. Perhaps you'll tell him I'd like to visit?"

"Do you know where he lives?" Rachel asked hastily, immediately picking up on the most important part of the conversation.

"I believe so. He's staying on part of the old Chandler estate, isn't he? On the east side of the island. Haven't you ever been there, Miss Chandler?"

"Rachel," she corrected automatically. "I'm afraid not. I've never been to Hawaii before. You usually have to fly to get here." She made a small, self-deprecating face. "I never had a good enough reason to risk it before." She leaned forward in her seat. "I don't suppose you could give me directions to the place? I was hoping a taxi driver would know, but now I'm not so certain. I could ask my Uncle Harris, but I'd rather not have to see him first." For a moment she wondered why she was telling this affable priest more than she usually confided to her best friends, and then dismissed the worry. Priests were perfect confidants, and trained to be just that. And his sympathetic interest was just what she needed at the moment.

"He doesn't know you're coming?"

"Neither of them do. I thought I'd surprise them," she said ingenuously. "Except that I don't know how to get to Emmett's house."

"Oh, I imagine you'll surprise them," Father Frank mused, a small smile playing about the corners of his mouth. "And don't you worry, I'll drop you by your brother's on my way back home."

Doubt and relief warred within Rachel. "Are you sure it isn't out of your way?" His kind offer certainly would solve a great many of her problems, and even a friendly priest was preferable as a witness to her longed-for reunion than a no doubt slightly inebriated Uncle Harris.

Father Frank seemed to have been blessed with the ability to read her mind. "Not a bit. And I'll save my own visit for another time. I'm certain you don't want a stranger intruding on your reunion."

Rachel, usually a more reserved person, flashed a devastatingly sweet smile at Father Frank's dazed expression. "Father, you're a saint!" she cried happily.

Father Frank Murphy grinned with a touch of wryness. "Not quite, my friend. But I'm trying."

Chapter Two

A light sheen of sweat covered the man's forehead and soaked through the khaki shirt that hung open around his narrow hips, running in rivulets down his spine. Where were the trade winds when you needed them? he wondered, squinting up toward the blinding late-afternoon sunlight. The sand was hot and shifting beneath his bare feet, and the man calling himself Emmett Chandler moved onward back down the beach. He still couldn't seem to get enough of the blazing sunshine, and wondered if he ever would. He might just have to do something to set things in motion, or he could get seduced into spending the rest of a slothful life in the islands. Not that he didn't deserve a few months of sloth, he thought grimly. But now wasn't the time. The itching in his palms, the edgy feeling to the airless afternoon, the restless nervousness that was making him smoke too many cigarettes and drink too much beer, were all signs that something was about to happen. He just hoped to God it would be soon.

Harris Chandler was no help, either, the man mused. That genial old rummy seemed perfectly content to let things take their natural course. "No rush, dear boy," he'd murmured that morning. "Everything in its own time."

But he had never been one to wait on an impersonal fate to decide his destiny. He'd been waiting long enough as it was. Fifteen years, to be exact. He was sick and tired of waiting.

He could feel the muscles in his legs begin to tighten up on him, and the familiar frustration washed over him. Frustration that his body would no longer do what he told it to, was only beginning to regain the strength and dexterity he used to consider his God-given right. It still amazed him, how fast a forty-year-old body could deteriorate during six months in a five-by-eight cell. And how damnably long it was taking to bring it back.

"There you are, dear boy." He could recognize Harris Chandler's portly figure on his front porch by the always immaculate white linen suit. No matter how warm it got, or how many rum and tonics Harris consumed, his attire was always spotless. Whereas the man known as Emmett always felt sweaty and rumpled, two minutes after a shower.

"I told you I didn't like unexpected visitors," Emmett drawled as he crossed the last few yards of beachfront and headed up the steps. They were new, sturdy steps— he'd replaced them last week, along with several of the rotten floorboards on the porch. "This place is off limits to you unless invited."

"Dear me, how inhospitable." Harris fanned his flushed face, dropping dispiritedly into an ancient wicker chair. "If you would bother to get a telephone, I could check whether or not I was welcome. As it is—"

"I thought we agreed a telephone at this point was ill-advised? We certainly don't want my devoted relatives phoning up to see how I am." Emmett glared at him before flinging his tired body into the hammock he'd rigged in the breeze-laden corner of the porch. There were nights when the walls of his bedroom seemed to be closing in on him, when he was back in that tiny cell once more, and he had to be out in the fresh air or he'd suffocate. No one knew of his night terrors, particularly not the sly and devious Harris Chandler, and he preferred it that way.

"Oh, I still agree. I'm just pointing out that you'll have to accept a few surprises every now and then," Harris replied affably, his faded blue eyes surprisingly astute as they surveyed his partner in crime. "I don't suppose you have anything to drink around here? It's a hellishly hot day."

"No trade winds," Emmett muttered, dropping his eyelids over tired hazel eyes that had seen too much in forty years. "There's beer in the icebox. Bring me one while you're at it."

"Beer." Harris shuddered, but Emmett was paying no attention. Sighing, Harris heaved his bulk upward out of the protesting chair, lumbered toward the kitchen, and came back bearing two tall green bottles. Eyes still closed, Emmett held out one well-shaped hand, and Harris slapped the bottle into it.

"You're a damnable man," Harris observed as he took his seat once more. "Beer is uncivilized."

"You mean the aristocratic Chandlers would never sink to such a working-class pleasure?" he drawled. "They're going to have to accept the fact that Emmett Chandler may have changed during the last fifteen years. Including developing a taste for good beer."

"Nothing Emmett does would surprise his family. At least beer is legal," Harris said morosely, staring at the figure draped in the hammock. "How are you feeling?" he added abruptly.

"Just fine, Harris. How are you?"

"Don't mock me, dear boy. I haven't got the energy to deal with it in this heat. Do you suppose you're ready for the next step in our little enterprise? Have you recovered enough from—"

"I'm great, Harris," Emmett snapped, ignoring the cramps that clenched at his calves. "I'm ready when you are."

Harris eyed him doubtfully. "Well, if you're sure..."

"I'm sure. The newspapers next?" Emmett opened his eyes to survey his half-empty beer bottle. For all Harris's complaints, his was already drained.

"Perhaps. I'll file the preliminary papers with the lawyers next week, and then we can decide who we'll tackle next. The entire island knows about your miraculous reappearance from the dead, and nothing's happened. I would think the news needs to be spread a little farther afield." He looked longingly into the dark, cool interior of the small house. "I may have time for just one more beer before I'm due back at the hotel. We're playing bridge this evening. If I win, I'll take you to dinner tomorrow."

"No more beer," Emmett said flatly. "And I thought we decided I shouldn't be seen any more than necessary in town?"

"I thought so too, but I gather you haven't been paying particular attention to that part of our agreement. The young lady at the Floating Lotus is very appealing, if you like that sort of thing...."

"I like that sort of thing," said Emmett. "Melea is none of your business."

"As long as you understand your priorities, dear boy." Harris rose, mopping his brow with a perfectly laundered handkerchief.

A savage smile flitted briefly over Emmett's darkly tanned face. "Never doubt it, Uncle. Never doubt it."

"Is IT ALWAYS so airless, Father?" Rachel pushed a useless hand through the tendrils of damp hair that had escaped the one thick braid. The hot, humid air had assailed them when they disembarked from the small airplane, still miraculously intact. Rachel could only decide that God had chosen to spare the plane because one of his servants was on it.

Father Frank's round face was flushed and damp, the beads of sweat starting halfway up his bald dome and following a trail down to his double chin. "Not usually. That's the beauty of the tropics. We have natural air conditioning with the trade winds." The taxi smelled of old sweat and bubble gum, and the open windows brought little respite from the stifling heat. "It won't be long till we reach your brother's cottage. It's right on the ocean, so I expect a stray breeze will crop up."

"Has he lived there long?" The dampness of Rachel's palms couldn't be attributed to the weather—it was a cold sweat that started at her backbone and reached down to her fingers and toes. After so many years a sudden panic filled her, overshadowing the terror she had endured that day on the plane. What if he barely remembered her, what if he didn't want to see her? She had burned her bridges behind her, and nothing, not even the eruption of the various volcanoes that dotted the islands, would get her on an airplane for a long, long time.

"Since he returned," the priest replied. "I gather the cottage and all the land surrounding it belongs to your family, at least indirectly. Someone told me Emmett lived there at the end of the sixties, and then disappeared. No one ever knew where, and at that time it seemed better not to ask questions." Father Frank's obvious concern filled his voice.

Rachel leaned back against the seat of the taxi, oblivious to the spring sticking into her damp back. "I remember hearing about the place. We had offers to sell it—incredible offers—but Ariel never would. She thought he might come back to it, and he did." The soft note of triumph blended with the barely controlled fear, a fear Father Frank recognized.

"Don't worry, Rachel. Emmett won't hurt you," he said softly. "I've heard that he's a good man, a fair man. You may come as a surprise to him, but I'm sure once the initial shock is over he'll welcome you. And you know if there's any problem, if you need a place to stay, someone to talk to, I'm always available."

Rachel opened her eyes, smiling across at him in gratitude. "You're very kind. But you're right—there's not going to be any problem. He'll be surprised at first, but Emmett and I were always best friends. I loved him more than I've ever loved anyone in my life, and he knows I wouldn't hurt him. It's only natural that I'm a little...nervous. After all, it's been fifteen years, and I was so terribly afraid he was dead."

Father Frank patted her hand, and the warmth of his touch was comforting. "Well, apparently he's not dead, he's very much alive." With a sudden sinking feeling Rachel realized that the taxi had stopped. "And he's not more than a few hundred yards down that path. I'll be more than happy to come with you if you prefer."

Resolutely Rachel shook her head. "No, thank you, Father. I've planned this for years; I'm not going to let an attack of cold feet stop me now. I appreciate all you've done for me." Her icy cold hand reached for the door handle, opening it before she could have second thoughts.

"Wouldn't you like some help with the luggage?" Father Frank stuck his balding head out the taxi window. "I'm sure the driver wouldn't mind."

Rachel shook her head, hefting the small canvas suitcase in one hand, her purse and tote bag in the other. "I'm fine. I'll call, Father, when I get the chance. Don't worry." She managed a creditable laugh at his troubled expression. "I'm going to be fine."

His smile seemed almost an effort. "I'm sure you are, Rachel. Only be sure to come to see me if there's a problem."

She stood there in the sandy soil, watching as the taxi backed around and took off down the rutted road. And then she was alone, surrounded by the exotic sounds of nature, the swish of the palm trees, the not-too-distant rush of the surf, the calls of a dozen strange and beautiful birds. Her white suit was plastered to her lean body, the linen blend that was guaranteed never to wrinkle in a crumpled mess. She could feel her usually sedate hair escaping its thick braid and curling with the moisture, and the first few steps she took along the sandy path almost buckled her ankles beneath her.

"Damn," she muttered under her breath, dropping the suitcase and bags to massage one ankle. She stripped off her thin, high-heeled sandals and added them to her burdens before starting off down the path once more. All her fantasies were crumbling around her: there'd be no beautiful reunion, with her cool and elegant, a sister any man would be proud of. Instead an overheated waif would arrive on his doorstep, and she wouldn't blame him if he viewed her with less than complete enthusiasm. Well, if he refused to let her stay, she could always

find Uncle Harris's hotel. Or Father Frank would provide something. It was comforting to know there was
someone she could turn to if this was a complete fiasco.
God, what was he going to look like after all these years?

A thousand questions rushed through her mind, flitting in and out like the birds through the towering palms
above her. And then suddenly the clearing was upon her,
and she stopped dead, her numb fingers still clutching her
possessions like a shopping-bag lady.

It was a small cottage, much smaller and more tumbled down than Rachel had imagined. The porch showed
signs of recent renovations, the new lumber white-yellow
next to the weathered gray boards. The small porch ran
the length of the front of the house, holding a few com-
fortable-looking chairs, a hammock, and three empty
beer bottles. If there had ever been a drop of paint on the
rough siding it was long gone, and the roof looked in
need of patching. But the windows looking into the house
were spotless, reflecting the bright sunlight like unseeing
eyes, and the shrubbery around the house was trimmed
and neat.

"Lady, what the hell are you doing here?" The voice
came from a little way behind her, and she whirled
around, dropping her bags into the sand, to stand staring, mouth agape.

He took a step toward her, glaring, that offensive tone
still rich in his voice. "I said, what are you doing here?
This is private property; off limits to tourists. Understand? *Comprende? Capisce?*" She continued to stare at
him blankly, and he shook his head in disgust. "Just my
luck, to have a dimwit show up on my doorstep. Listen,
lady, leave. Get out, vamoose, scram!"

Rachel just continued to stare at him, transfixed. He
was both exactly what she had expected and something

far different. He still had blond hair, but it no longer hung in lank curls halfway to his waist. It was cut short, too short, and shaggy, with streaks of gray lightening it. The hazel eyes that stared at her were Emmett's color, but the look of trust and gentle good humor was gone, replaced with a mocking hostility that grieved her. He was taller than she remembered, closer to six feet, and his shoulders had filled out. His legs were long and tanned beneath the cutoff jeans, and the chest exposed by the tattered shirt was muscled and covered with a thin mat of sandy-colored hair.

But it was his face that mesmerized her. Battered, lined, with a blunt nose that had been broken at least once since she'd last seen him, and a cynical, world-weary mouth, he was still far more attractive than she had ever remembered. And more dangerous. Those hazel eyes that looked as if they had seen too much looked straight through her, and his cynical mouth curved in disgust.

"Listen, lady, am I going to have to remove you forcibly? Believe me, I wouldn't have any qualms about it. So, if you don't want a few bruises on that pretty white skin, I suggest you hightail it out of here."

That threat, absurd though it was, managed to galvanize her. Not that he wasn't capable of violence—it only took one good look at him to recognize him as a man capable of whatever was needed to get the job done. But he also wasn't the sort to beat up on a lone woman lost on the beach. She found herself smiling, with sudden relief and joy. This was her Emmett.

The smile didn't escape him. "Lady, are you out of your mind? I'm threatening you and you just stand there grinning like an idiot. If you aren't going to go away, then why don't you tell me who the hell you are and what you want?"

Rachel's smile moved from her mouth to her entire face, filling it with a light that made Emmett draw a sudden, startled breath. "I'm Rachel, Emmett. Your sister." And she ran into his arms.

Chapter Three

Emmett had taken one look at the slim, rumpled, undeniably feminine figure in white who stood staring at his
cottage and muttered a pungent curse under his breath.
This was the last thing he needed—another idiot tourist
lost in his backyard. He had pushed himself too hard and
too long today. Harris's unexpected visit had banished
any last trace of weariness, filling him with a nervous
energy that made it impossible for him to spend the afternoon lying in a hammock and drinking beer as he had
planned to do. He had jumped up the moment Harris
had left, pushing his protesting body further still, forcing the cramps in his legs to loosen up, making another
mile down the beach and back in the still, humid air. At
that moment there was nothing he wanted more than to
stagger to the refrigerator, grab another beer and col-
lapse into the hammock. He wasn't in the mood for another unwanted visitor.

And then she had turned around at the sound of his
voice, and for a very brief moment any claim to rational
intelligence left him. Those huge brown eyes staring up
at him in shock in her pale, sweat-streaked face, the
rumpled white suit that almost disguised the clean,
strong, feminine lines of her body, the astonished mouth

that looked as if it ought to be kissed, and often. Emmett stared back, taking a moment to marshal his defenses.

"I'm Rachel," she had said. "I'm your sister." And the feel of her hot, strong body in his arms, the scent of jasmine on her slender white neck, the tremors that shook her as she wept against his shoulder made his arms tighten instinctively around her, holding her closer. This was one thing he hadn't anticipated, and a small groan escaped him.

Rachel was laughing and crying in his arms, her fingers clutching his shoulders in disbelief. Now that she could see him, touch him, hold him, it was like coming home. It hadn't taken long for her to recognize the haven he represented, and she didn't even stop to wonder if he was glad to see her. He felt strong and alive beneath her clutching fingers, and he smelled of hot sun, sweat, and beer. She felt his arms tighten around her, felt rather than heard the small groan, and in sudden self-consciousness she moved away, backed out of his arms, with a light, nervous laugh. Looking up into the face she had waited so long to see again, she couldn't make out a thing from his expression. The hazel eyes looking down at her were unfathomable, the cynical mouth was a thin, straight line, and his whole body radiated extreme wariness.

Rachel ran a nervous hand through her rapidly escaping hair. "I guess I surprised you."

He continued to stare at her. "You could say so."

"But you and Uncle Harris couldn't think I'd just stay in northern California? Not when you finally showed up? I couldn't, Emmett, I just couldn't." His stillness as he watched her added to her nervousness, and she rubbed her fingers against her damp palms. This wasn't going the way she'd so often imagined it; she was somehow making a mess of it, and she didn't know how to remedy the situation.

"I thought you were too terrified of airplanes to ever fly?" he drawled, and Rachel flushed.

"I am," she admitted. "But I had to do it. It's been fifteen years, Emmett. I haven't seen you since I was twelve years old; I barely remember you."

The wary look around his eyes dwindled somewhat. "If you've waited fifteen years, don't you think you could have waited a few weeks longer?" He watched that hopeful expression on Rachel's face begin to crumple.

"I'm sorry," she murmured. "Don't you want me here?"

Once a sucker, always a sucker, he told himself in disgust. "It's not that. You just came as a surprise. Where are you staying?"

She looked up at him, her crushed expression warring with the faint stirrings of hope in her deep brown eyes. "Here?" she said softly.

This time Emmett didn't hide his reaction. "Damn!" The expletive was muttered under his breath, and Rachel flinched.

"I don't have to stay here," she said hurriedly. "I could always find someplace else. Perhaps with Uncle Harris, or the local priest said he could help me. I wouldn't want to inconvenience you."

"You could go back to the mainland." He tried to steel himself against the barely hidden pleading in her face.

She shook her head stubbornly, and for the first time he saw a trace of the strength of will that had driven her family crazy on more than one occasion. "I'm staying here. I have no intention of getting on another airplane until I recover from my last trip."

A curious resignation filled him. "Why?"

"Because I want to be with you. I won't bother you, I promise, Emmett. But I've missed you so much, and I need you." Her voice shook an infinitesimal amount, and with sudden self-consciousness she cleared her throat. "You're the only family I have left."

"What about our thousand and one aunts and uncles and cousins?" He was stalling, and he knew it.

"You don't remember very well if you think there's much family feeling in them. You and I were always outsiders. Please, Emmett."

He stared down at her for a long, meditative moment. "I must be out of my mind," he muttered, reaching down for her suitcase. He hefted it easily, shooting her a curious glance. "Is this all you've got? It's not very heavy. How long were you planning to stay?"

"Until you're ready to come home." She was still unsure of him. "I figured I wouldn't need much—just some bathing suits and shorts and stuff."

"Great," Emmett growled, picturing that strong, lithe body roaming around the tiny cottage in nothing more than a skimpy bathing suit. Someone up there took sadistic pleasure in trying his endurance. Melea had only begun to take the edge off a six-month hunger; it was just his luck that this beautiful, shyly sexy creature would turn out to be Emmett Chandler's sister.

"Come on, kid." With a jerk of his head he signaled for her to follow him as he made his way back to the cottage. She scrambled after him, her bare feet silent in the sand. He stopped on the wide porch, dropping the suitcase unceremoniously and turning to look down at her. "I suppose we'd better try and let Uncle Harris know you're here. We'll have to drive over there; I don't have a telephone." He hesitated a moment. "We may as well wait till after dinner. Are you hungry?"

Rachel considered it for a moment. On the one hand, her stomach was in a complete knot from nerves and apprehension, on the other, she wanted to delay as long as possible his ejecting her. "How is Uncle Harris?" she queried, stalling for time. Maybe she could pretend to sprain her ankle, making it impossible for her to go to the hotel tonight. It had been such a long time.... She didn't want to lose him so quickly.

As swiftly as the thought entered her mind she banished it. She had never been a devious person, and that would have been a rotten way to renew her relationship with her long-lost brother. "I'm more thirsty than hungry," she said truthfully, her eyes still watching him as if they couldn't get enough.

There was a strained silence between the two of them, only the sound of the surf breaking on the sand filling the humid air. "I imagine you'd like to wash up," he said finally. "Your room is on the right. We'll have to share the bathroom—this isn't the Hilton, you know." He grabbed her suitcase and disappeared into the cottage, almost as if he was afraid he'd change his mind.

Rachel stared after him for a moment, disbelief and joy filling her. And then she rushed after him.

For a moment the darkness of the room was blinding after the bright sunlight. He was standing in a doorway, staring at her. Without a moment's hesitation she ran to him, flinging her arms around him.

"Thank you, Emmett," she babbled happily. "I promise, I won't get in the way, and I'll cook for you, and clean for you, and won't ask any questions that you don't want to answer."

He suffered her embrace for a long moment. She felt him withdraw a moment before his strong hands came up and unclasped her arms from around his neck. He put her away from him, firmly but very carefully. "I don't need you to cook or clean for me, Rachel," he said gently. "I can take care of myself—I have been for years. And you can ask all the questions you want; if I don't want to answer, I won't. And one more thing..."

"Anything," she said rashly, smiling up at him starry-eyed with happiness.

"You've come as quite a surprise to me. I think it would be a good idea if you didn't make a habit of hugging me all the time—at least not until I'm used to you. It's going to take a little while to realize that my baby sister has grown up into a lovely young woman." His voice was surprisingly gentle, but Rachel flushed anyway.

"Of course, Emmett." She met his wary gaze straight on, smiling. "I'll do anything you want me to."

His cynical mouth curved in a smile that didn't reach his eyes. "Sure, kid. In the meantime why don't you clean up, and I'll meet you on the front porch in a few minutes with a beer. That is, if you haven't developed your uncle's patrician disdain for beer. 'Cause that's all that's here and cold."

"Beer would be great." She watched his retreating back for a moment, her eyes filled with tenderness. He was limping slightly, and she almost called out to him with sudden concern. At the last moment she stopped herself. There would be time enough for all her questions, she realized, turning into her room and shutting the door behind her.

The room was small and spotlessly neat. The narrow bed was covered with a rough cotton bedspread and the rag-rug on the unfinished pine floor was a bright splash of color. The small sturdy dresser would more than hold the little amount of clothing she had brought with her. There was only enough room for a small rocker besides the bed and dresser, and moving around would be more than a little cramped. No curtains were on the window to keep out the lush greenery surrounding the house; there was no closet to hang her one dress. The only other door led to the bathroom she'd be sharing with her brother.

Her brother, she echoed to herself, smiling dreamily. She was finally here with her brother, and she had him all to herself. As she moved to unpack the suitcase that Emmett had dumped on the bed, she found herself humming softly and happily under her breath. She felt happier than she ever had in her entire life, she realized. Like a girl on her first date, like a bride on her honeymoon, like a woman who's just discovered life.

She didn't stop to recognize the danger of those comparisons. Still humming, she headed for the bathroom, her bare feet silent on the rough wood floor.

Emmett stood in the kitchen, two open beers in his hand, listening to the sound of her moving about her room, the quiet sound of her humming. Moving toward the porch, he caught sight of himself in the mirror, recognized the look of expectation on his own battle-worn face. He stopped for a moment, staring into his reflection. "You're a damn fool, you know," he said softly. The man in the mirror nodded his agreement, and then he headed out onto the porch.

Chapter Four

Emmett might announce he could cook, but in at least that one area he was less than truthful. Rachel dutifully took another forkful of the dried-out hamburger, still doing her best to avoid the soupy instant mashed potatoes and the canned peas that had been cooked almost beyond recognition. Even the beer that accompanied the meal was warm. Emmett had eaten quickly, with the no-nonsense attitude of one performing an unpleasant duty, and after one taste Rachel could understand why. He now sat, tipped back against the wall, drinking his third beer and watching her out of hooded, unfathomable eyes.

She had spent as long as she had dared on her appearance that night. The cool water she had splashed on her flushed face would have to suffice—she didn't want to risk the time to take the shower that she longed for. Brushing out her silky mane of hair, she considered leaving it hanging around her shoulders, then discarded the idea. The air was still hot and heavy around them; if Emmett saw her with a thick curtain of hair down her back, he'd think his sister was playing with not quite a full deck. Resignedly she rebraided it in one thick plait, pulling out a few softening wisps to frame her high forehead. A touch of mascara and clear lip gloss and she would have to do, she thought critically, surveying her reflection in the small, slowly unsilvering mirror that hung over the bathroom sink.

What had Emmett called her? A lovely young woman? He must have been possessed of more brotherly feeling than he gave himself credit for—no one in his right mind could have called her lovely, she thought critically. Her eyes were brown, her hair was brown, her figure neat but undistinguished, her features even and boring, boring, boring. No high, luscious cheekbones—they were right there in her face where most people's cheekbones were. Only her mouth could claim distinction, being slightly too large for her face. Not the best choice for a distinctive feature: in her early twenties she would have given anything for an aristocratic, aquiline nose with a genteel little hook in it. Anything to give her face the character she thought it lacked.

Rachel hesitated for a moment over what to wear. She had only brought one dress—a bright yellow sun dress with thin spaghetti straps—but the occasion deserved her best. After all, her first dinner with her brother after fifteen years should be something to celebrate.

She had practically raced out of the bedroom, still in bare feet, terrified that he might have changed his mind, might have decided to send her packing to Uncle Harris's after all. But he hadn't said a word, handing her a Heineken with an unreadable expression on his face.

Rachel broke off another piece of overdone hamburger, bringing it to her mouth gamely. Emmett obviously hadn't considered the occasion worthy of celebration: he was still wearing the same disreputable clothes, although he had shoved his feet into a ratty-looking pair of sneakers and buttoned a few buttons on his worn khaki shirt. Several days' growth of beard still adorned his chin, and he made no attempt at dinner conversation. He just sat and watched her, drinking his beer.

He was watching her now with hooded eyes and what looked suspiciously like the beginning of a smile hovering about his mouth. "You can stop now," he said suddenly, and the sound of his voice in the stillness startled her into dropping her fork with a noisy clatter. "You don't have to eat any more to prove you're a good sister."

"It's very good," she lied, washing down the last dried-out piece that still stuck in her throat. "It's just that I'm not very hungry after all the excitement."

"It's edible, but that's about all," he stated flatly. "Are you any good as a cook?"

"Pretty good." Sudden hope flared in her. "I like to cook, and if you do something you like, it's easy to be good at it. I'm not a terribly efficient housekeeper, though," she added doubtfully, aware that this was a mild understatement. If she didn't allow herself the sinful extravagance of having someone come in and clean her cluttered apartment once a week, she'd live in complete chaos. "I could try, though."

"That won't be necessary. You can take care of the cooking; I'll do the cleaning. Sounds like a fair division of labor to me," he drawled.

She held her breath. "Does that mean you want me to stay?"

He shrugged, his eyes still watching her flushed, eager face. "It's up to you. I imagine you'll want to get back before too long."

"Not without you. I'll stay until you're ready to come back with me," she said firmly.

"Won't you miss your friends, your life back there? I don't suppose you have a job you have to get back to, but I expect you'll tire of paradise long before I do."

"I took a leave of absence from my job," she replied diffidently. "You're all I care about, Emmett. All I have. Wherever you are is paradise to me."

He pushed away from the table with a sudden, abrupt motion, taking his beer and moving across the room. He was still limping somewhat, and Rachel stole a covert glance at his tanned, muscled legs in the cutoffs, searching for a scar, some sign of what caused the limp. Nothing was visible, just tanned, strong flesh, and she quickly raised her eyes upward to his back.

"Are you always this open, Rachel?" he said suddenly from his position by the window, his back still toward her. "Aren't you afraid you might get hurt?"

"Not by you, Emmett." She rose and followed him. She wanted to reach out and touch him, to put her hand on his arm, to put her arms around him and rest her head on his shoulder the way she used to years ago. But she stopped a foot away, afraid to crowd him. "You wouldn't ever hurt me, not if you could help it."

He cast a quick glance down at her. "You think just because I'm your brother, you're immune?"

"Not entirely. I'm a fairly good judge of character." The sudden memory of Ralph Fowler entered her mind, and she amended her statement. "At least, I usually am. And I know you wouldn't want to hurt me—that's not the kind of person you are." She allowed herself to take one step closer to him, still lost in the glorious realization that this was really her brother after so many years. "I don't understand what you're so worried about, Emmett. All I want to do is be with you and love you. It's not really very complicated."

He turned back, staring sightlessly out into the darkening shadows. "Did you ever consider that I might not be worth loving?"

A feeling of unbearable sadness filled her, and then she reached out a hand, tentatively placing it on his arm. He didn't flinch, didn't move, didn't look at her in the stillness.

"Emmett, I don't..."

"Yoo-hoo, dear boy, are you home?" Harris Chandler's delicately slurred tones echoed through the night. "I made an absolute killing at bridge, and I've come to celebrate. I've even brought you beer, and something more civilized for myself." He clattered up the steps, flinging open the screen door with a self-satisfied expression on his florid face. "There you are, my boy. Why didn't you answer...?" His voice trailed off as he took in their motionless figures, and his face fell in an expression of ludicrous dismay.

"Good god, is that you, Rachel?" he gasped. "How in the world did you get here?"

"I flew," she said simply, reluctantly moving away from Emmett to plant a dutiful kiss on her uncle's flushed cheek. "How are you, Uncle?"

"Surprised," he said, sinking into the nearest chair. He looked more stricken than surprised, but Rachel was still concentrating on the silent Emmett and didn't notice.

The man beside her moved then, reaching forward to pluck the six-pack of beer and the whiskey bottle from Harris's limp hands. "I'll get you a drink, Harris," he said blandly. "Do you want something 'more civilized,' Rachel?"

"Beer would be fine," she replied, turning her attention to her uncle. "Are you feeling all right, Uncle Harris? You don't look well."

"I'm fine," he said with a trace of uncharacteristic irritation. "It's just this damned heat." He took a spotless white handkerchief out of his pocket and mopped his brow. "What I want to know is what you're doing here, after it was agreed that the family would stay away for a while? Give Emmett a chance to get accustomed to things."

"You may have agreed; I never did. Emmett's my brother, Uncle Harris, my closest relative. I certainly wasn't about to sit around waiting for you to take your own sweet time in coming home." Her voice was calm and reasonable but Harris was having none of it.

"Do you have any idea how inconvenient this is? I sincerely doubt there'll be any space at my hotel—things are pretty well booked up right now. Well, not to worry. We'll find you a bed for the night, and then you can head back to the mainland tomorrow with your mind at ease."

"I'm not going back," she said with quiet firmness. "I'm staying right here until Emmett's ready to come back."

"Don't be absurd, my child. Did you ever stop to realize it wasn't me who said the family should keep away? Emmett's the one who needs peace and quiet, time and solitude, to adjust to civilization once more. You'll just be in his way, dear heart, no matter how much you want to help. Even across the island at my hotel would be too close."

"I'm not going to stay in the hotel, Uncle. I'm staying here. With my brother."

"Nonsense, child. He doesn't want you here—he can't have you here."

Emmett reappeared, a dark amber drink in one hand and two Heinekens in the other.

"Emmett, tell this girl she's out of her mind. You can't have her here." Harris took the drink with desperate hands, downing half of it in one gulp.

Emmett's mouth curved in a cynical smile that Rachel was rapidly learning was characteristic of him. "I told her she could stay as long as she wanted," he said, handing her the cold beer.

"Are you out of your mind!" Harris exploded, and Rachel stared at him, amazed at his reaction.

"Easy, Uncle," Emmett said gently. "You're making problems where none exist. My sister has come to visit, and it will give me a chance to catch up on family gossip and to get to know her all over again. Sort of a dry run before we head back to California."

Harris drained his drink, holding it out for a refill with a shaking hand. "I think you're both crazy. At least let me see if there's a room for her at the hotel. This place is too small for the two of you."

Emmett had the foresight to bring Harris's bottle with him, and he tipped him a generous amount. "She stays here." His voice was flat, brooking no opposition, and Rachel found herself staring at him in grateful amazement.

There was a long, stubborn silence between the two men, a clash of wills that Emmett was bound to win. "Very well, my boy," Harris said finally. "It is, after all, your life. But I do think it's a needless complication."

Emmett smiled faintly, stretching his tired body out in the corner of the battered sofa. "Rachel won't complicate matters, Harris. Will you, kid?"

She took the other corner of the couch, keeping as close to him as she dared. Tucking her bare feet up under her, she smiled. "I'll be no trouble at all," she promised, starting in on the beer. She wasn't used to drinking quite so much, and the day had been long and tiring. Not to mention she was suffering from jet lag. She leaned back, watching Emmett's battered profile with lazy affection. If only Uncle Harris would finish his drink and leave, she thought dreamily. She wanted to have her first night alone with Emmett, wanted to find out what he'd been doing for the last fifteen years. Something had kept her from asking questions so far—a fear that he'd throw her out if she became too inquisitive—but she was rapidly losing any reticence. She was also rapidly losing consciousness, she realized with a flash of humor. It had been a long day.

"You'll find your sister has grown up into quite a determined woman," she heard Harris grumble.

"I've already discovered it," Emmett's lazy voice responded, and Rachel smiled dreamily as she drifted further and further away. She was a very determined woman, especially where loved ones were concerned. And there was no one she loved more than Emmett; the more she saw of him the more she knew it. This was going to be a golden time, she thought, resting her head against the sofa and closing her tired eyes. When she looked back to pick the happiest times in her life, this would be one of them. If only it would last forever. If only Harris would go away and leave them alone. If only...

The quiet sound of their voices barely penetrated. "I think my little sister has fallen asleep," Emmett said with a trace of amusement.

"Are you absolutely out of your mind!" Harris hissed. "What the hell do you think you're doing? She can't stay here."

"She can and she is." The voice was so cold and icy that in her sleep Rachel didn't recognize it.

"We have to talk, Nephew." There was an odd emphasis on the last word, but Rachel was drifting deeper and deeper into sleep.

"Fine with me, Uncle. But I'll put my little sister to bed first."

"I'm sure you will." Harris's voice was heavy with sarcasm, but Rachel didn't notice. Strong arms were reaching under her, lifting her up against a hard chest and cradling her there. She snuggled up against him, blissfully secure. When she was little he used to carry her up to bed, and this was one more tie with the past. She only wished she could wake up long enough to enjoy it.

Her room was dark when he carried her into it. Laying her down carefully on the bed, he reached for the light cotton blanket to cover her. Rachel opened her eyes for a moment, smiling up at him in the moonlit room. "I guess you can't put me in my pajamas like you used to," she murmured sleepily.

An answering smile softened his face. "I guess I can't." He turned to go, but her voice stopped him.

"Would you kiss me good night, Emmett?"

He hesitated, but only for a moment. On silent feet he moved back to her bedside, leaned down, and kissed her lightly on the cheek.

"That's not right," she mumbled, feeling childish and cranky and self-indulgent. "The way you used to."

"The way I used to?" he echoed.

"Our special way. You used to kiss me on the forehead, the nose, and the lips. It was our special way," she insisted sleepily.

"I'd forgotten," he said softly, and the answer satisfied her. Leaning down again, he brushed his mouth gently against her brow, then the tip of her nose, and then feathered her lips in a gentle, brotherly kiss.

"Good night, kid," he said, straightening up.

"Good night, brother mine. I'm glad I'm here."

He hesitated for only a moment. "So am I, kid. So am I."

Chapter Five

He had spent more comfortable nights in his time. There was something to be said for the confines of a five-by-eight cell: When another human's noise carried to your sleepless ears, you knew it was someone equally scruffy and unpleasant. You weren't tormented with the image of Rachel Chandler's long, clean limbs stretched out under that cotton bedspread; the feel of her soft lips didn't linger against your own. All you could think of was your own misery, and how soon you would get out of this hellhole.

He had gotten used to doing with only a few hours sleep, gotten used to waking with the sun. He was out on the porch at just past six, eyes bleary from lack of sleep, another day's growth added to his scruffy beard, a cup of wickedly strong coffee in his hand. He rubbed a lazy hand across his chin. Shaving might wake him up, but he was damned if he was going to bother. If Rachel Chandler didn't care for her brother with several days' growth of beard, that was her problem—he wasn't going to change his life to accommodate her patrician tastes.

Now, where did that chip on his shoulder come from? he wondered, tipping his chair back and squinting at the early morning haze. She hadn't done anything to rouse his ire; just arrived on his doorstep, pretty and innocent and sweet-smelling, with those big dark eyes that looked so trustingly up into his. Couple that with the fact that she was supposed to be his sister, and it was little wonder he was in a foul mood. Didn't she know she shouldn't go around trusting every man she meets, no matter who he says he is? That blind innocence and faith infuriated him, and for the hundredth time he told himself he was a damned fool for letting her set foot inside the cottage.

He'd have to get rid of her, of course. He'd realized that somewhere in the dark restless hours between midnight and dawn. The sooner the better, much as he hated to admit that Harris was right. There was no room in their complicated scheming for an ingenue, no room at all. He'd take her to Lihue Airport that very afternoon in his battered four-wheel drive, and then swing by and see if Melea could get off work early that night. He felt no qualms about using her: Melea made no bones about her interest in him. They had suited each other perfectly.... His mind caught the past tense, and he swore out loud, softly, his voice quiet in the early morning stillness. He was old enough to know better, old enough not to fall for a pair of trusting brown eyes. Hadn't he learned anything in the last six months?

He could, of course, always revise his plans. Rachel Chandler could be viewed as a gift from the gods, the means to an end that would be even more effective than he had originally planned. But he didn't think he could do it. Some last shred of decency still remained embedded in his tough old carcass, stubbornly clinging. He couldn't deliberately harm an innocent, no matter how much circumstances called for it. The fallout would be enough as it was. He'd take her to the airport, whether she liked it or not, and forget about her. With luck his plan would come to fruition long before he had to join the bosom of the Chandler family back in California.

In the meantime, though, there would be nothing wrong in making her one day on Kauai a pleasant one. They could drive along the coastal highway to the northwest end by the towering Na Pali cliffs, maybe even have a picnic on Lumahai Beach. Or he could head in the opposite direction, show her the Menehune Fishpond, reputedly built by Hawaiian leprechauns centuries ago. He had a feeling his unwanted houseguest would be enchanted. Even an old cynic like himself was tempted to believe in the little people. The last plane out was scheduled for late afternoon; if she didn't spend the entire day in bed, he could play the kindly big brother, show her the sights, and send her on her way with a charming show of reluctance. Would she be convinced? It depended on just how gullible she really was. He had the unpleasant feeling that apart from her obvious adoration for a prodigal older brother, she was more than a little astute. How much would her familial devotion blind her? He swore again, softly, rubbing his beard once more. He might as well shave; it was too hot to grow a beard here, so he'd have to do it sooner or later. Might as well be now.

Rachel opened her eyes hesitantly, focusing her gaze on the room with the slow-motion wariness of someone who had forgotten where she was. She was still in her sun dress, with the thin cotton blanket pulled across her bare shoulders. Hawaii, she remembered suddenly. And Emmett.

The small bathroom was deserted, the water liberally splashed over the sink and the floor attesting to its recent occupant. Rachel surveyed the male artifacts with fondness and an eye toward the future; for the first time in years she would have a man to buy presents for. His birthday was only a few months away, and then there'd be Christmas, and all the other holidays she'd have with him. The very thought made her almost dizzy with happiness, and she sang in her clear, warm contralto as she showered the stickiness from her skin.

There was a pot of coffee on the stove, still warm, but no sign of Emmett. She poured herself a cup, controlling an anticipatory shudder at its muddy blackness, and strolled out onto the porch. He didn't see her coming, didn't hear her, and she allowed herself the luxury of standing there in silence for a moment, watching him.

"I've changed my mind." He didn't move, didn't turn his head to acknowledge her presence, but she realized he had always been aware of her, probably from the moment she left her bedroom. "I think it would be better if you returned to California today. Harris was right: I still need some time to myself to get used to things."

Rachel was unperturbed. She moved into his range of vision, taking the seat beside him and staring out at the ocean. She took a sip of the coffee, stalling for time, and nearly spoiled the effect by choking on the devil's brew. She was dressed in shorts that showed off her long, winter-pale legs, and an old clinging T-shirt, and her wet hair was tied back loosely, the drying curls framing her face. A face that had just the barest hint of a smile. "No, Emmett," she said, firmly, kindly, and took another sip of coffee.

He turned his head slowly, majestic with outrage, and his hazel eyes would have chilled a lesser mortal. *"No?"* he echoed. "Listen, kid, you don't tell me no. I'm the older brother here—what I say goes. And I say you go."

"No, Emmett," she repeated serenely. "What would you like for breakfast? I saw some eggs and cheese in the fridge; I can manage a decent omelet, if you'd like.

You're out of bread, but we can do a little shopping later today.''

''I'll pick some up on the way to the airport.''

''No, Emmett.''

''If you say 'No, Emmett,' again, I'm going to beat you,'' he growled, and was rewarded with an unperturbed laugh.

''You certainly would not. You never hit me when I was a child, and I certainly deserved it. You didn't even spank me when I destroyed your beloved baseball jacket. So you aren't about to start hitting me now.''

''You're a hell of a lot more frustrating than you were at twelve,'' he grumbled.

''I thought we worked this out last night,'' she said mildly, watching his expression out of the corner of her eye. He'd shaved, and his clean jawline lessened some of his world-weary, battle-worn look. He was quite handsome, she realized with sudden surprise, if only his eyes weren't quite so wary and his mouth didn't curl in that cynical droop. ''I can cook, you can clean; I can ask questions, you can ignore them. It should work out fine.'' Bravely she took another swallow of coffee. ''Speaking of questions, I don't suppose you'd feel like telling me where you've been for the last fifteen years?''

''Trying to get away from you,'' he snapped, his gaze still trained on the ocean, missing her sudden, unexpected withdrawal.

She recovered quickly, used to low blows. Besides, he hadn't meant it. He couldn't know that she'd suffered for years with the fear that everyone she cared about had abandoned her, starting with her parents right on through to her erstwhile fiancé. ''A little drastic, don't you think?'' she returned, her voice slightly husky.

He did look at her then, not missing the subtle nuance in her voice. "Fifteen years is a long time. Do you want dates and places; a job résumé?" The edge in his voice was softened slightly.

"Just a summary would do fine," she replied. "You can give the dates and places to the lawyers."

He shot her a suspicious glance, but she continued to smile sweetly at him. He might almost have imagined that raw note of pain in her voice a moment earlier. Well, now was as good a time as any to try out the elaborate tale he and Harris had concocted. Of course Rachel, for all the intelligence that shone out of those warm brown eyes, was more than a little biased, but still, it would serve as an initial test. "It seemed a good idea for me to leave the country for a while," he said diffidently, stifling the sudden, almost forgotten flash of pain at the cause of that defection.

"I remember," Rachel said softly, recognizing but misinterpreting the look of pain in his eyes. "You were involved with some of the student radicals in their bomb factory in Cambridge. You were there when the place exploded, right? It was years before the men stopped coming around the house, looking for you."

He squashed down the sudden surge of anger that filled him. He could remember it as if it were yesterday—the acrid smell of smoke, the rubble of the small, elegant town house that had housed the tiny, inefficient bomb factory. "I was close by," he replied in a flat, cold voice. "And I wasn't in the mood to go into explanations to the powers that be. Hawaii seemed as good a place as any to hide out in for a while."

"And support yourself growing dope." There was no judgment in her voice, just a simple, cool, statement of fact.

"There was that, too," he admitted. "Hawaii's got a great climate. But things started getting a little complicated, and I decided it might be time to see the world. You don't really expect me to go into details, do you? They include several years in an ashram in India, some time in the Middle East, even a stint in South America."

The old Emmett would have been at home in an ashram; she wasn't too sure about this cynical new one. "And what made you decide to return home?"

He turned, giving her his best, most charming smile, one liberally laced with cynicism. "For the money, of course. Surely you don't think Aunt Minnie's myriad charms would entice me?"

"Imagine your remembering Aunt Minnie. She is pretty unforgettable at that," Rachel mused. "What about Ariel and Grandfather? Didn't you think they deserved some word, some sign that you were still alive?"

Emmett shook his head. "Too much time had passed. I figured I was better off dead to all concerned. After all that time I figured I didn't owe anyone anything."

"Not even me?" There it was again, that damnably plaintive note that she so wanted to avoid. "Then why did you keep sending me birthday presents?"

There was a long, strained silence. "I guess because I'm sentimental at heart," he said finally. "But not sentimental enough to let you stay here."

"Tough." She rose with one fluid gesture, stretching her long limbs into the sky. "You aren't getting rid of me, Emmett; you might as well accept the fact and stop fighting it. I'll be making two omelets—it's up to you if you don't want to eat one."

She could feel his eyes following her as she headed back into the house, though there was no way she could guess his thoughts. His voice trailed after her. "Make them scrambled."

Without turning back, she grinned. "You got it."

HARRIS CHANDLER didn't look the slightest bit surprised at Emmett's approach that afternoon. He did raise one aristocratic eyebrow at his apparel. The chinos were neat and clean, the chambray shirt relatively untattered, and he was clean-shaven for the first time in what seemed like weeks.

"Turning over a new leaf, my boy?" he murmured, carelessly pulling out a chair for him with one foot and signaling for the waiter. "Perhaps having Rachel here wasn't such a bad idea after all."

"It was a damnable idea," Emmett snarled, leaning back in the uncomfortable chair that Harris's inn seemed to specialize in. Or perhaps he just hadn't regained enough extra flesh to cushion him from the elegant ironwork. The bar was empty at that hour, but he hadn't even bothered to check Harris's room first. A few months' acquaintance had taught Emmett all he needed to know about Harris's habits.

"I'll be gentlemanly enough not to say I told you so," Harris said with a smirk. "Though I'm surprised disillusionment has set in quite so quickly. She hasn't even been here a full day and already you're climbing the walls. Tsk tsk, my boy. Still and all, it is a a treat to see you in decent clothes."

"Say one more word, Chandler, and I'll strip them off and walk naked back to the cottage," Emmett growled.

"Dear me, are you sure you're not actually my nephew? He's the only person I know who might have actually done such an outrageous thing."

'You know damned well who I am, Harris,'' he said in a low tone, reaching for the Heineken that the waiter, who knew him from experience, had placed in front of him. That wasn't precisely true, of course. He had told Harris as much as he felt he needed to know and nothing more.

Harris smiled faintly. "Do I, dear boy?" He took a delicate sip of his rum and tonic. He didn't start his serious drinking till after the dinner hour; at this time in early afternoon he was still on his maintenance dosage. "So what are you planning to do about dear Rachel? A sister at a time like this could be damned inconvenient."

"Have you any suggestions?" Emmett stared morosely into the dark green bottle.

"None that you'd like. You could always bring Melea back with you tonight. I don't think Rachel would like that very much at all."

"Damn it, man, the girl's supposed to be my sister."

"That's what she thinks." Harris nodded. "But I've seen the way she looks at you; it's not going to be long before that poor girl has the most crushing case of incestuous longing. You could circumvent such an unpleasant experience and drive her out quite effectively with a little strategic jealousy. Or you could have a drunken binge."

"That's more your style," Emmett snapped.

"Now, now, there's no call to be rude," Harris replied, unaffronted. "I'm only trying to help. Have you simply told her she has to leave?"

"I tried to first thing this morning. I got exactly nowhere." Emmett shook his head in disgust. "She's about as tractable as a bull elephant."

"I could have warned you about that."

"You could have warned me about a lot of other things," Emmett shot back. "She gave me quite a turn when she told me I'd been sending her birthday presents every year since I'd been gone. How did that little bit of information escape you?"

"What?" Harris paled beneath his thin layer of tan. "Are you serious?"

"Do I look like I'm in a joking mood, Chandler?" Emmett shot back. "Emmett Chandler has been sending his sister presents every year for the past fifteen. I only hope I can find out what they are before I make some mistake so bad that even a trusting soul like Rachel will see through me."

"Oh, I have great faith in you, dear boy. You won't let a little thing like that trip you up." Harris waved his doubts away with an airy hand, and Emmett found he had to agree. When the time came that he couldn't out-think the opposition with both eyes shut, the time had come for him to retire. But since when was Rachel the opposition? Since he had gotten into this, and the sooner he remembered it the better. Whether he liked it or not.

"But do you realize the ramifications of all this, dear boy?" Harris was continuing, his face flushed with excitement.

"I'm way ahead of you. It's proof positive that Emmett Chandler is still alive, and reasonably aware of what's going on in his family. Unless, of course, some well-meaning friend or relative has been taking care of the presents for the last few years as an act of kindness."

"You haven't met the Chandlers, nephew, or you'd know that none of them is motivated by acts of kindness, with the rare exception of Rachel. And I'm afraid it's unlikely to be friends, either. Rachel has never been one for casual friendships—she's always been rather shy and reserved. Very bright and capable, of course, but essentially wary of entanglements. The only person she ever really cared for deeply, apart from her grandparents, of course, was you. I beg your pardon, but you know who I mean."

"Thanks a lot," he drawled. "You've really made me feel a lot better about the whole thing."

"Now is hardly the time for a guilty conscience, my boy. We're too far along for that. Just keep in mind that you aren't planning to hurt her but are merely helping us flush the real Emmett out of the woodwork."

"And if Emmett never shows?"

"Then there'll be a tragic accident, and you'll start a new life with a substantial sum of money, and Rachel will get the chance to formally mourn her missing brother. It'll give her a nice sense of completeness, which experts say is so necessary in resolving relationships."

"Hmph. And if Emmett shows up, how do you think the Chandlers will view the impostor?"

"*Impostor* is too harsh a word, dear boy. They'll take my word that you were my assistant, and we knew all the time that Emmett would return. And you'll still be possessed of a comfortable sum of money. Which is why you got involved in this in the first place, isn't it?"

Emmett ignored that comment. "What makes you so sure that the real Emmett would turn down the bequest? There aren't too many people who'd turn down millions of dollars for a principle." Especially not dope-growing, bomb-making Emmett Chandler, he thought viciously.

"Of course he will. He always hated the money as much as Rachel did. The sooner he divests himself of it the happier he'll be, and he won't think twice about passing it on to the next in line. Mainly his aunts and uncles, your humble servant included."

Emmett immediately jumped on the most important part of the conversation. "Rachel hates the money?"

"Hard to believe, isn't it? She turned it down; otherwise she would have inherited some of it, I expect. She only accepted a small trust fund left by her mother, and then she went ahead and traded all those nice, sound, blue-chip stocks in for the most ridiculous things. Solar companies, medical research, the like. Nothing with a decent profit to their names. I doubt she makes a quarter of the interest she should. Father is probably turning over in his grave at the thought. No, she hates the Chandler millions with a passion—only wants what she earns herself. So you see, you two are completely ill-suited. Here's Rachel who turns down a fortune, and you who'd do anything for one." There was no condemnation in his voice, more a distant respect. Harris Chandler could understand greed; principles were a little more foreign to him.

Emmett rose to his feet, looking down at his fellow conspirator out of hooded eyes. "Any more surprises, Chandler? I don't like working in the dark."

"I've told you everything I know, my boy. I only wonder if you've been equally frank with me."

Emmett's smile was an unpleasantly cynical curve to his world-weary mouth. "Sure I have, Chandler." He strode out of the bar, leaving the older man to stare after him out of troubled, slightly bloodshot eyes.

"I wonder," he said again. And signaled for another rum and tonic.

Chapter Six

Several days later Rachel had to admit that things were not going as she had planned. Emmett had been drawlingly, studiously polite, eating the food she cooked, answering her questions, initiating her into the mysteries of the ancient and crotchety Land Rover that served as transportation. The rest of the time, when he was there at all, he spent sitting on the porch, drinking too much beer, smoking too many of the dark, strong cigarettes he preferred, and watching the ocean. Shutting her out, politely, effectively, and completely. And there was absolutely nothing she could do about it but try to be patient.

Rachel tried to reach him through cooking, but half the time he wasn't even there for meals. She'd go out to the porch to call him, and there'd be no trace of him—just a smoking ashtray and a few stray beer bottles. He never seemed to get drunk from all the Heineken he put away—just more and more remote, watching her out of those wary, cynical eyes as she wandered along the beach. If he did stay for dinner, he'd disappear soon afterward, returning some time in the middle of the night, long after she'd fallen into the deep, dreamless sleep the fresh air and hot days blessed her with. But he was always there in the morning, sitting on the porch with his long legs propped up on the railing, a cup of his perfectly vile coffee in his hand.

She had been there three days when she decided on a more positive approach. One of her happiest memories from childhood had been Emmett's twenty-first birthday. It was just before he'd dropped out of college, and Ariel and Henry Emmett were at their usual doting fondness, the four of them a tight-knit, happy family for the last time in Rachel's memory.

Rachel had always remembered the food from that night: Emmett's favorite, *cioppino,* a savory seafood stew that had originated in San Francisco. It should bring back memories of home as nothing else could. Determined for one last try, she took the car when Emmett was out on one of his interminable, solitary walks, and bought all the ingredients, including cake flour and bitter chocolate. Her memory was good enough to reconstruct the dinner, with the added help of a *Joy of Cooking* dated 1942. If she ever had to deal with a sugar and egg and butter shortage, the book would come in very handy, she thought, losing herself in the war-time recipes for a good hour while the *cioppino* simmered and the cake cooled. She could only hope Emmett wouldn't return too swiftly—she wanted it to be a surprise.

She was startled out of her cookbook reverie by the realization that it was past six and Emmett still hadn't returned. Heaven only knew when he would. In the meantime she had better take advantage of his absence and take a long, soothing bath, put on her freshly washed sun dress, and use every artifice of makeup in her repertoire. By hook or by crook she'd seduce him into paying more attention to her, or die trying.

Feeling a slight bit of discomfort at her inadvertent use of the word *seduce,* Rachel pushed her wicked thoughts out of her head. It was only a figure of speech, anyway. But heavens, her brother was being the most stubborn man alive. And he used to be such a sweet, amenable creature. Almost too amenable, Ariel used to say, blaming that quality for most of Emmett's troubles. Well, he'd certainly cured himself of that particular failing, she thought with a wry smile.

The bathroom was filled with the scent of jasmine and the steam from her lengthy, heavenly bath as she carefully applied her makeup. The first, gentle layers of tan had warmed her face, turning it from pale to a soft golden color. The sun had already lightened her chestnut hair with a few streaks of blond. With a critical eye she surveyed her body, clad only in a lacy, peach-colored bra and wispy bikini panties. Breasts too small, she decided, hips just a tiny bit too big. But the legs were long and turning a delicious tan, and her stomach was just slightly rounded. Not a ten, mind you, but not bad, either. Too bad it was wasted. If only there were some gorgeous man, looking enough like Emmett to make it interesting. . . .

"What the hell . . . ?" The door to the bathroom was flung open, letting out the steamy, scented air, framing the astonished figure of her brother. He stood there for a moment, the wariness gone from his eyes as he took in her slender, rounded figure clad only in the silky underwear. "Lord!" he swore loudly, slamming it shut again. "Can't you lock the damn door?" he shouted from the room beyond. Rachel stared blankly at the wall, too startled to even protest that there wasn't a lock. It would have done her no good: The sound of his heavy footsteps, followed by the roar of the Land Rover told her soon enough that he'd gone again.

With a sigh she turned back to the mirror and picked up her eye pencil with a shaking hand. She hadn't had room to pack a robe in the small suitcase she'd brought. Maybe she ought to go buy one tomorrow, and be sure to wear it at all times. Emmett certainly was getting prudish in his old age, though. They used to go skinny-dipping together when they were younger, and the underwear wasn't much more revealing than the bathing suits she'd worn the last few days. Well, there was nothing she could do but apologize when he returned, and promise to be more discreet. The dinner should go a long way toward placating him. She smiled back at her reflection, and her eyes were shining with anticipation.

Five hours later she was sitting alone on the porch, in Emmett's customary position, her long, bare legs stuck out in front of her, one of his horribly strong cigarettes in one hand, a glass of Harris's whiskey in the other. It was her fourth drink, straight, and she didn't much like it. Leaning back, she drew in on the harsh black cigarette, stifling the sudden urge to choke. As long as she stuck to Emmett's brand, it was highly unlikely that she'd get hooked again. So far she hadn't been able to finish one; the cottage was littered with barely smoked remains of a pack.

When would she ever learn? she demanded wearily of herself. She was a fool to have expectations, when nothing ever came of them but disappointment and disillusion. Emmett, despite the blood tie, couldn't care less about her, wanted her away from here. And after tonight she would go. She loved him enough to leave him alone, if that's what he really needed. And it seemed he did.

The last candle of the dinner table flickered and went out in the living room, and Rachel gazed idly into the room. Wax had dripped onto the whipped cream icing of the mocha cake, flower petals had fallen into the *cioppino,* and the chilled butter had melted and run all over the folded white sheet Rachel had used for a table-cloth. Well, Emmett had said he'd take care of the housekeeping—it would be up to him to clean up the mess of the meal he hadn't bothered to return for. Maybe the shock of seeing his sister in her underwear had been too much for his delicate sensibilities, Rachel thought with a wryness that barely masked her pain. Maybe during those interminable fifteen years he'd spent time in a monastery and forgotten that women's bodies existed.

And then she remembered the intent light in his eyes, the mocking curve of his mouth, and the way he moved, and she knew that he was a man who would always know far too much about women's bodies. The problem was simple and already clearly stated: She had forced herself on him, and he was doing the best he could to avoid her. There was nothing she could do but brave the terrors of aviation once more and return to California. Maybe by the time Emmett was ready to come home, he'd also be ready to be her brother.

Draining the whiskey with only a small shudder, she stubbed out the cigarette and pulled her tired, slightly inebriated body out of the chair. Suddenly her bedroom seemed very far away indeed. Especially with the hammock so close. She had always liked hammocks, and she didn't hesitate for a moment. The night was warm; she didn't even need a light covering. Kicking off her sandals, she climbed up into the hammock with only a modicum of difficulty. The sound of the ocean was a soothing melody in her ears, lulling her into a sleep she needed. Her last conscious thought was of Emmett, and she contemplated crying herself to sleep. She was dead to the world before the first tear could fall.

THE MAN calling himself Emmett Chandler was not enjoying himself. He had smoked too much, and the inside of his mouth felt like mattress stuffing. He had drunk too much, just enough to make himself contentious, not enough to make himself oblivious. Which was just as well, since he belatedly discovered that he had no desire at all to spend the night with the more than willing Melea. He wanted to be back at the cottage, watching Rachel move with that damnable, unconscious grace of hers, her voice low and soothing as she told him ridiculous stories about their supposed eccentric relatives. He wanted to talk back to her, tell her about the lost years, the horror of the last six months, the need that drove him relentlessly and would cause her nothing but pain and despair. . . .

"You're getting sentimental," he muttered to himself under his breath as he drove slowly back to the cottage. "Must be a midlife crisis. Leave the kid alone." But she wasn't a kid, and well he knew it. He called her that on purpose, and she seemed to like it well enough. It was his way of reminding himself that she was supposed to be his sister, and that she was thirteen years younger than he was. And no matter what he wanted her to be, her allotted role in his life was that of unintentional victim. He didn't want to hurt her any more than he had to, and the only way he could think to avoid it was to keep his distance, ignoring the expression in her soft brown eyes. Damn it, and her, and everything.

He swerved into the drive behind the cottage, trying to drive the memory of that body, wrapped in steam and jasmine and lace, out of his stubborn, frustrated mind.

Why the hell hadn't he stayed with Melea? But he knew perfectly well why he hadn't—Melea was no longer enough for him. He wanted more than physical oblivion. He wanted Rachel, and had from the first moment he'd seen her.

And that was just something he was going to have to come to terms with, he thought as he moved slowly up the front path to the steps of the cottage. Wanting something he could never have. He should be used to it by now—life was filled with choices, and he'd made his years ago. He couldn't let a momentary desire for a vulnerable young woman stop him.

He halted on the porch for a moment, listening intently. It was after two in the morning; Rachel would have been in bed for hours. There were no lights left burning for him in the cottage, an unusual occurrence, and the smell of a smoldering cigarette teased his nostrils.

Immediately alert, he pivoted in his tracks. Rachel didn't smoke; they must have had an unexpected visitor. His eyes narrowed against the darkness; he peered around, ready for anything. Had the real Emmett finally responded to his challenge? Was he waiting somewhere out there in the bushes, or had he already disillusioned Rachel about the silent man she'd been living with for the past three days?

There was no sound but the ocean breaking in gentle waves on the beach. And a sudden, sighing sound from the hammock.

Emmett hadn't regained all his strength and agility, but enough of it had returned to assure him that hand to hand, the real Emmett Chandler wouldn't have a chance against him. Few men would, he knew, without pride or doubt. He had been trained years ago, and that training had come in handy more than once during the last decade. And might come in handy again tonight.

As his eyes grew accustomed to the darkness, rather like a cat's, he realized there was a body in the hammock. One solitary glass with the dregs of very dark, straight whiskey rested on the table beside it, and an ashtray full of half-smoked cigarettes still smoldered. He moved to stand over the sleeping Rachel, staring down at her for a long, contemplative moment before reaching out a gentle hand to shake her awake. The rough, callused skin touched the warmth of her bare shoulder, and the scent of her jasmine perfume floated to his nostrils. The last thing in the world he planned to do was carry her to bed. He'd done it once, and that was his limit. He'd hate to imagine her reaction if her beloved brother Emmett climbed into bed with her.

"Wake up, Rachel," he said gently, and was rewarded with her dark brown eyes staring up at him. "You should be in bed." His hands were impersonal as he helped her from the hammock. "You must have fallen asleep."

Sleepily she shook her head, the unbound chestnut hair a tangled curtain around her face. "I drank too much," she whispered.

"I'm ashamed of you," he chided gently, steering her into the darkened living room, his hand lightly possessive on her waist. "A sister of mine, falling prey to demon rum."

"Demon whiskey," she murmured, leaning against him. The scent of jasmine was just slight enough to drive him crazy, but he didn't push her away, didn't pull her closer. He just stood there and endured the torment. "I was mad at you," she added dreamily.

"Why?" By its own volition his hand came up to caress gently the cloud of hair away from her face, and sleepily she nuzzled at that hand.

"You didn't come home for dinner. Didn't even tell me. I cooked your favorite things, Emmett."

Out of the corner of his eyes he saw the table with its guttered candles and wilting flowers, the food still sitting there, untouched. "I'm a thoughtless bastard," he said, and she nodded in solemn agreement.

"I forgive you, though," she added, smiling dreamily.

"Exactly how much whiskey did you drink?" he inquired as he continued heading her in the direction of her bedroom. She was moving very slowly, and he couldn't say he really objected.

"Whatever was left in Uncle Harris's bottle."

"That was a hell of a lot, little sister. You're going to have some headache tomorrow." *Sister,* he reminded himself grimly as the feel of her warm body was having a predictable effect on him. *She's supposed to be your kid sister.*

"That's all right," she murmured as they reached her door. "It was worth it." She turned around and twisted her arms up around his neck. He could feel her body pressing against his, and thanked God she was too drunk and too sleepy to recognize what her nearness was doing to him.

"Good night, Rachel," he said firmly, reaching up to unclasp her hands from behind his neck. "Go to bed."

"Aren't you going to kiss me good night?" she pouted, holding fast.

"Not tonight," he said firmly, resisting temptation. "You're going to bed and sleep it off."

He could have detached her clinging grip if he'd really wanted to, he knew it full well. He told himself he didn't want to inflict even that small amount of pain on her, and he knew he was lying.

Rachel was undaunted. "Well, then, I'll kiss you," she said simply, standing on tiptoes to reach his forehead. Her aim was slightly off, landing on the bridge of his nose. The next wasn't much better, her soft lips brushing against his cheekbone, but the final one was dead on target, her lips pressing sweetly against his, clinging as her arms clung to him, soft and ready to open for him at the slightest pressure.

He did hurt her then, his fingers biting into her wrists and pulling them free from around her neck. She didn't even seem to notice the pain, falling back from him with a dazed expression on her face. "Go to bed, Rachel," he said again, and this time she obeyed, stumbling from him and closing the door behind her with a silent click.

Emmett stood staring after her, his entire body aflame. It was a long moment before he turned to survey the room, the remnants of the meal still sitting on the table. Picking out the hibiscus petals, he stood there and ate more than half of the seafood stew, realizing belatedly that he hadn't eaten since breakfast. The stew was cold and delicious, and he turned to the cake, eating three pieces, waxy whipped cream and all, before putting the remnants in the huge refrigerator that was the only modern piece of equipment the kitchen boasted. He moved silently, so as not to wake up the doubtlessly sleeping Rachel. If she made another appearance, he didn't know if he could resist such delicious temptation. Not in his current condition.

Casting one last look at her closed bedroom door, he moved on silent feet out to the porch. It had to be getting near dawn, he thought, kicking off his running shoes and moving onto the sand. With no other thought in mind, he stretched out on the beach, cradling his head in his hands, staring up into the inky dark sky dotted with stars. A moment later he was asleep.

RACHEL, HOWEVER, wasn't quite so fortunate. For a long time she lay in her bed, staring out her window, her mouth still tingling with a forbidden longing. And when she fell asleep this time, she was crying.

Chapter Seven

Rachel opened her eyes slowly, wincing as the blinding sunlight shot a shaft of pain through her cloudy head. Her eyes felt sandy, her arms and legs tied down with lead weights, and her mouth tasted like an old ashtray. But the pain was by far the worst symptom. She groaned, very quietly, and the sound sent another streak of anguish soaring across her nerve endings. In complete, careful silence she turned her face into the pillow and longed for a swift, merciful end.

Suffocation was not much of an improvement, and her stomach was beginning to resemble nothing so much as a cement mixer. The smell of frying bacon didn't help, nor did the disgustingly cheerful sound of someone whistling. Until Rachel realized who had to be whistling.

It took all her meager supply of energy to drag her body out of bed, when she realized with an abstract air that she was naked, her clothes strewn from one end of the room to the other. The events of last night were unclear; she remembered finishing Uncle Harris's bottle of whiskey, sitting on the porch and watching the ocean while she felt sorry for herself. Emmett hadn't bothered to come home last night, and therein lay the problem. But he had come home at the last minute, hadn't he? Or was her memory at fault?

The only other thing she remembered from last night was her determination to fly back to the mainland today, to stop imposing on the unwilling and morose Emmett. She didn't seem capable of cheering him up; the least she could do was to leave him in peace. There might even be a boat, a nice, slow, luxurious ocean liner to take her back to California. If she had to go by way of the Atlantic Ocean, it would be small price to pay for the relative safety of sea travel.

In her current foggy state she couldn't even begin to think of getting dressed without a long, hot shower. She yanked the sheet from her bed, leaving the bedspread and thin cotton blanket in a heap on the floor, and draped it around her like a toga. She didn't want to risk stumbling in on Emmett without the proper amount of clothing on her poor abused body.

But the bathroom was blessedly empty. Dropping the sheet on the floor, she headed straight for the sparsely provisioned medicine cabinet. She spilled three aspirin into one shaking hand, tossed them down, and followed them with warm, rusty water from the sink. The aspirin stuck on the way down, leaving a chalky white trail down her mouth and throat, and she shuddered, shaking all over like a wet dog. The shower was next, hot streams of water pouring over her, washing away most of the cobwebs and gritty feeling from the night before. By the time she stepped from her bedroom, dressed in an old pair of shorts and an oversize cotton shirt, she felt almost human, and almost ready to face the day and her unwelcoming host with a modicum of equilibrium. She'd be very cool when she told him she was leaving, she told herself, and she wouldn't cry at his expression of profound relief. If she really cared about him, she could spare him that much.

"I was just about to wake you up." Emmett was standing in the doorway of the kitchen, looking disgustingly fit and cheerful. Rachel stared at him in befuddled amusement, accepting the proffered cup of coffee numbly. He had shaved, and his khaki shirt, if not ironed, was at least freshly washed, and the faded jeans boasted fewer patches than usual. The running shoes were still the same ratty pair, and the lines around his wary hazel eyes belied his early morning bonhomie. But he was actually off the porch and viewing her with something less than his usual distance. "How's the head?" he added with a surprising solicitude only slightly marred by the faint trace of amusement that lingered about his wide mouth.

"Better," she murmured, bracing herself for her first sip of the thick, bitter coffee he usually produced. To her amazement it was very good, and she took another, deeper drink, feeling the caffeine flow through her veins and open her eyes.

"I'm sorry I missed dinner last night." The words came out almost hesitantly, and Rachel knew instinctively that this new-found brother of hers was a man no longer given to apologies. The words were gruff, graceless, but Rachel accepted them gladly.

"That's all right. I should have told you I was planning something special." She continued to stand there, only a foot or two of the cottage separating them, unable to break the uneasy atmosphere. She was conscious of a nagging feeling that had been plaguing her since she woke that morning, a sense that something wasn't right. At first she'd attributed it to her hangover, but as her alertness was increasing and her headache dissipating, the sense of something guilty and wrong nagged at her. She wanted to take a step or two backward, away from Emmett. He was standing there looking at her out of those fathomless hazel eyes, and for the first time she was uneasily conscious of his body, the aura of a sort of tough strength and grace that stirred something deep within her.

And then he smiled at her, a sweet, singularly innocent smile that lit the dark contours of his face and flowed to her with a gentle warmth. It was the first time he'd really smiled at her since she'd arrived so precipitously, the first time she truly felt welcome. If there was a knowledge lurking behind those eyes, a wisdom that saw her confused unease and recognized its cause, she ignored it.

"I thought I could make up for it," he continued easily. "You haven't seen much of the island yet. Why don't we take a picnic lunch and go for a drive down to a small private cove I know of? Some of the best snorkeling is there, and you haven't spent enough time in the water."

"I don't know how to snorkel," she stammered, this time taking a small, hesitant step backward. For a moment she wasn't quite sure she could trust his sudden affability.

"I'll teach you."

"I don't think so. I'm still afraid of the water. There are nasty things lurking in there—sharks and jellyfish and piranhas."

She sensed more than saw the instant alertness in his body. "You're still afraid?" he questioned softly.

She managed a shaky smile. "I didn't have you around to help me get over it. I used to try to remember what you told me, about not being afraid of it, but I never could seem to manage it. I'd think about you, start sinking, and panic."

His eyes were clear and warm as they looked down into hers. "I won't let you sink, Rachel," he murmured in the sudden stillness. And then he smiled, his old, self-mocking smile. "Come on, kid, I'm calling a truce. I'll keep all the man-eating jellyfish away. Are you with me, or have I managed to drive you back to California with my bad temper?"

A nagging feeling of guilt still tugged at the back of her mind. Without hesitation she squashed it down, smiling up at him with blinding happiness. "I'm with you," she said recklessly. "Just give me time to pack a lunch."

"Already taken care of," he said. "All you need is your bathing suit." Plucking the now-empty coffee cup from her, he placed a hand on her shoulder and whirled her around in the direction of her room. "Go ahead and change and I'll meet you in the Land Rover."

It was a good thing her back was to him. The touch of his hand, heavy on her shoulder, had brought back her memory of the night before with a resounding force, and with it embarrassment mixed with guilt. For a brief moment she had forgotten who he was, forgotten he was her brother. She couldn't afford to let that happen again if she was to continue living in such close quarters with him. Brother or not, there was no denying he was a very attractive man, with a sort of world-weary air that made a person want to wrap her arms around him and cradle him against her breast. Maybe she should go back to California, despite this sudden thawing. But as she stripped off her clothes and tugged on the sleek black-and-red striped maillot, she knew she was staying right where she was. For as long as he'd let her.

It was a perfect day—all that paradise had to offer—and Rachel found herself opening up to it with a wholehearted abandon that swept away early morning doubts and hangover-induced guilt. The small private cove was as beautiful as Emmett had predicted, and the water warm and crystal clear beneath the deep blue of the sky. She couldn't quite remember when she had ever been as happy, she thought, stretching out on the sand, the hot sun baking into her bones, the bones Emmett had insisted she cover with a thick sunscreen. He hadn't offered to help with her back, and for that she was perversely disappointed. And grateful.

She stuffed herself like a pig, still amazed at Emmett's provisions. Deviled eggs, cold fried chicken, sliced ham and cheeses, and crusty French bread filled the basket, complemented with a chilled white wine instead of Emmett's usual Heinekens. He partook sparingly of the wine, and smoked far fewer cigarettes than usual, seemingly content to just lean back against an outcropping of rock, his eyes closed, his long legs stretched out in front of him, at peace with the world. Rachel knew without asking that those moments of peace were few and far between, as they were for her, and she wished there was some way she could prolong the moment, the day, the time of resting.

Rolling over on her stomach in the sand, she watched him out of suddenly curious eyes. Up until now she had avoided looking at him, kept her eyes averted like a chaste maiden, she thought with sudden self-disgust. The sound of his heavy, even breathing told her he was asleep, and pushing her sunglasses up on her slippery nose, she allowed herself to stare at the sleeping Emmett, looking for faults.

There were a surprising number of them, she thought with wry amazement. He was forty years old, and he looked as if he'd lived every year of those forty to the fullest. His legs beneath the swimming trunks were admittedly long and tanned and muscled, the thighs firm and lightly covered with hair. His shoulders were neither too broad nor too narrow—slightly bony, they had an inherent strength in them, a strength that traveled to his arms and that Rachel had felt more than once. His chest was the chest of a forty-year-old, still firm enough, with a light matting of sandy blond hair that trailed in a V down his stomach to disappear beneath the waistband of his trunks. The hair was a new addition; in his twenties Emmett had still been smooth and hairless. All in all she liked the hair, she mused, digging her toes into the soft white sand. And she liked his body, tired and slightly beaten-up looking and a far cry from Ralph Fowler's California beach-boy perfection. She liked the way the gray mixed with his shaggy blond hair, the way his mouth curved in that cynical, world-weary smile, the way the lines crinkled around his wary hazel eyes. The eyes that were now open and watching her with barely suppressed amusement.

She could always hope the flush that mounted in her face could be mistaken for sunburn. But she had already discovered that Emmett wasn't often mistaken about anything. "Find anything interesting?" he drawled, unwilling to let the embarrassing moment pass.

Rachel grinned reluctantly. "I was trying to see if I could remember you from fifteen years ago," she admitted with a rueful laugh, ignoring any other reason for her interest.

"And you don't?" He seemed no more than casually curious.

"'Fraid not. But then, I was only twelve; I wasn't used to paying a lot of attention to you. You were just my brother—there when I needed you." *And gone when I needed you most,* she thought, then banished that old pain with sudden decision. "Where did you get that scar on your shoulder?"

Emmett made a face. "A bullet from a stray war."

Rachel's eyes widened behind her dark glasses. "And the one on your stomach? I hope you're going to tell me it was something like an appendectomy?"

"That scar is lower," he murmured, and watched, fascinated, as her color deepened again. "I'm afraid the one on my stomach came from a knife fight. In a bar in Nicaragua. The one on my chin was from Beirut."

Rachel pulled herself into a sitting position, shivering despite the blazing tropical sun. "I guess I'm lucky you're still alive."

"I don't know if you're lucky or not." He was reaching for his cigarettes, his eyes abstracted. He took as long as he could in lighting the dark, strong cigarette, then turned his fathomless eyes on her. "I've told you before, Rachel, I'm something of a bastard. No fit brother for you, when it comes right down to it. You'd be far better off with some nice guy who'll care about you instead of hanging around with a brother who doesn't care about anyone but himself." He blew out a cloud of smoke, watching it curl up against the sky with an intense gaze.

Rachel pushed the dark glasses up on her forehead, squinting at him through the bright sunlight. "You're wrong," she said abruptly, with a certainty that brought a reluctant smile to Emmett's face.

"Wrong about what?" he countered. "Wrong about being a bastard, or wrong about you needing a nice guy who cares about you?"

"Wrong about both." Her voice was firm. "If you really don't care about anyone but yourself, how come you've let me stay with you when you'd obviously rather be left alone?"

"Maybe I have my reasons," he drawled, that mocking smile that was uncomfortably close to a sneer playing about his mouth.

"If you do, I certainly can't imagine what they'd be. There's no way my presence at the cottage could benefit you." He didn't bother to deny it, just kept watching her out of unreadable eyes. "And you're wrong about my needing some nice guy to care about me. I don't like nice guys, I don't trust them. I prefer people like you."

That surprised a laugh out of him. "Thanks a lot, kid."

"No, I mean it," she said earnestly, edging closer to him across the sand. "I've been surrounded by nice guys most of my life; I've gone out with them, gone to bed with them, even almost married one of them. And they've all been so nice, all smiles and surface charm, and nothing underneath but a well-hidden cruelty that can break your heart. Everyone's got some goodness and some meanness in them; I prefer people with their meanness out in the open for everyone to see, rather than those who reveal it as a nasty surprise later on."

She was close enough to touch him, but she kept her hands at her side, her fingers trailing loosely in the sand. It was Emmett who reached out and touched her, his fingers brushing the side of her face in a soft, tender caress. "It sounds like my little sister hasn't had too easy a time of it in the last fifteen years," he said gently. "Or maybe you've just been choosing the wrong nice guys."

She smiled. "It's been okay. Getting hurt is part of life. But I've missed you, Emmett, missed you even more than I realized. It wasn't until I saw you that I knew just how much you meant to me. I took one look at you and felt like I was coming home."

His hand pulled away as if burned. "You're nuts," he said abruptly, jumping to his feet. Rachel stayed where she was, looking up at him, small, graceful and very vulnerable. "And you're also going to learn how to snorkel."

The moment had passed, safely enough, it seemed, and Rachel let out her pent-up breath. "No way," she said, rising to her feet in one graceful motion.

"For a woman supposedly devoted to her brother, you don't seem very eager to please him," he drawled in challenge. "Can't face a little shallow water?"

"Of course I can," she shot back, following him down to the shore. "It's the creatures I don't like. Besides, I don't see why I have to try it."

"To prove something." The snorkeling equipment was in a canvas bag by the edge of the water, and he squatted down, rummaging around in it, keeping his face averted from hers. There was no way she could see his expression, no way she could know whether he was serious or not. She reached down a hand to touch one tanned, bony shoulder, then drew it back.

"Prove what?" she stalled, looking at the mask and breathing apparatus he held in one large, well-shaped hand, looking at the clear blue ocean that could close over her head and suffocate her, that was no doubt teeming with dangerous livestock.

"That you trust me." He was looking up at her, and his eyes looked almost green in the bright sunlight.

She stared down at him for a long moment. He needed her trust, for some obscure reason it mattered terribly to him; she could read it in his eyes. Well, she had faced the terrors of aviation for him; she would face certain death in the blue, blue ocean with even greater equanimity. She held out her hand to him. "Lead on, Macduff." And as his warm, strong hand closed over hers, the last trace of panic vanished.

Chapter Eight

The feel of the water filtered through her semi-conscious mind, rocking her as she lay sweltering among the clean white sheets of her narrow bed. She could still feel the pull of the undertow, the buoyancy of the salt water, the gentle rolling motion haunting her as she lay there, drifting in and out of sleep. If she allowed her mind to wander, she would find herself floating facedown in the incredible blue ocean, Emmett's hand steadying her as she faced the fear and the wonders of the world underwater, could relive the hours she lay there, cushioned by the warm Pacific, her body drifting against Emmett's as they floated together, legs brushing, arms touching in an unconscious ballet that was only rendered innocent by the warm water surrounding them.

It was too hot to sleep, she grumbled to herself, turning over in the narrow, tumbled bed and punching the pillow, too hot and humid. The restlessness was eating away at her until she thought she might scream. It was after two in the morning—for once Emmett had gone to bed when she had, and he was doubtlessly sound asleep. If only Rachel could say the same for herself.

Rolling over again, she finally pulled herself into a sitting position, wrapping her arms around her long legs and staring out into the tropical darkness. Perhaps she was just too happy to sleep. It had been a perfect day; Emmett's truce had extended through the evening. He had set himself out to charm his little sister, Rachel thought, and had succeeded far better than even he would have guessed. Not that Rachel was fooled by the charm he obviously had in abundance. She could still see the traces of shadows in his hazel eyes, feel the fleeting moments of wariness as he watched her. He wanted her to trust him, and she did, implicitly, with all the faith and love that had been shunted aside for years. But why couldn't he trust her?

There was a sudden, muffled sound in the night, and Rachel was instantly alert. Only silence answered her questioning ears. Was someone outside, wandering along the beach, skulking through the bushes? The sound came again, a crashing sound, followed by what sounded ominously like a groan. It couldn't be Emmett—she knew for certain he hadn't left his room. Did he sleep so heavily he couldn't hear the creature crashing about outside, waiting for his chance to rip her into shreds?

Stop it, she ordered herself sternly. There's no need to be such an abject coward. All you have to do is turn on the light and go wake Emmett. He'll check and make sure everything is all right. If you can survive airplane flights and snorkeling, you can survive things that go bump in the night.

Climbing out of bed, she moved as silently as possible, so as not to alert their nocturnal visitor. It had been too hot for nightclothes, and she stopped long enough to pull a light, seersucker nightdress over her nude body before stepping into the hall in silent bare feet. Moonlight illuminated the cottage, the ramshackle chairs and sofa silent sentinels in the night stillness. Crossing the rough pine floor on bare feet, she stopped outside Emmett's door and tapped softly. "Emmett," she whispered.

There was no answer, and for a moment Rachel dealt with the panic that he might have left after she had fallen asleep, might have gone into town to the bar once he'd gotten his innocent young sister settled for the night. Leaving her all alone with the monster that groaned and crashed . . .

Another groan and crash, this time from directly behind Emmett's door, wiped out the last of her indecision. The doorknob yielded easily to her fingers, and she stepped into the room, trying to accustom her eyes to the darkness. "Emmett?" she said again.

He was lying angled across the bed, and Rachel thanked an impartial God that he was still wearing his cutoff blue jeans, though nothing else. As far as she could tell he was sound asleep, but his big strong body was covered with a film of sweat that had nothing to do with the warmth of the night, and he was wracked with tremors that shook the sturdy double bed with their force. He muttered something that sounded like, "No, don't," and thrashed his head back and forth against the rumpled sheet. The pillows had long since been discarded, the covers a heap on the floor, the room dark and silent like a tomb. There was no question but that the thumps, groans, and crashes she had heard had come from his nightmare-ridden body.

"Emmett, wake up," Rachel said in an urgent undertone, moving uncertainly into the room. Still caught in the middle of his nightmare, he continued thrashing, oblivious to her presence. She tried again, raising her voice, but he paid no attention. Rachel paused there by the door, halfway in the room, halfway out, wondering whether she should leave him, whether she should shake him awake or if he needed to dream the dream through.

And then he sat up, his eyes sightless and staring in the darkened room, looking straight at her but through her. "Oh, God, please don't," he whispered in a voice full of such pain and torment that the last bit of wisdom left her, and she ran to the side of the bed, climbing up and taking his trembling body into her arms.

He started violently at her touch, then subsided as the night terrors began to leave him. His breath was still coming too rapidly, but he allowed her to cradle his body in her arms, his head resting against her soft breasts, as she crooned to him soothing, meaningless words that she wished someone had crooned to her when loneliness and terror had overwhelmed her. "It's all right, Emmett, I'm here," she whispered, rocking him gently, her hand brushing the sweat-dampened hair from his face. "It's okay, Emmett, everything's fine." Meaningless, stupid words, but the sound of her voice seemed to calm him. She could feel the tension drain from the strong, hot body in her arms, and she wished more than anything she could see his face, see whether he wanted her there or wished she were on the other side of the world.

His voice broke the stillness, hoarse and whispered. "Don't leave me," he said against the warmth of her breasts.

Relief and love flooded her, and she tightened her hold on him. "I won't," she promised. "I won't ever leave you, Emmett," she murmured. He needed her, wanted her, for the first time in a long time she mattered to someone. She could feel him relax further in her arms, hear the steady rhythm of his breathing deepen, and realized, to her absolute amazement, that he had fallen back asleep, this time without the horrifying dreams that had tormented him.

Of course, there was no telling if those nightmares would return later in the night. Rachel had promised him she wouldn't leave him, and she would keep her promise, even if it meant a sleepless night for her. She would watch over him, keep the night terrors at bay. But what in the world lurked in his past, that would crop up in the vulnerable hours of sleep to torment him so? She wouldn't ask; she could wait for him to tell her, if he ever wanted to. It was enough that he wanted her with him, needed her.

With a sigh of pure happiness she leaned back against the tumbled sheets, her arms still cradled around Emmett's sleeping body. As a matter of fact, she'd prefer not to sleep. These moments of closeness were precious and few, and she didn't want to waste them sleeping. Once more she was filled with the indefinable feeling of having come home, and she smiled into the darkness. A moment later she was asleep.

WHEN EMMETT AWOKE hours later the faint smell of jasmine tickled his nose. He was used to that—all his waking and sleeping hours seemed to be haunted by Rachel Chandler. It was little wonder he imagined her distinctive scent.

But was it imagination? Something warm and soft and heavy rested against his chest, something that stirred when he moved, emitting small, sleepy sounds. It was with a real effort that he silenced his groan of despair as he realized he wasn't alone in the big old bed. Rachel was lying beside him, her dark eyes closed, her body curled up next to him, lost in a dreamless, innocent sleep.

Damn, little sister, he thought in a kind of exasperation. What the hell are you doing in my bed? I can't do this to you—you're too vulnerable. I don't want to hurt you any more than I have to, and God knows, if I wake up and find you in my bed, I'm not sure I can keep my hands off you. And even if I know it's not incest, you won't. And I'm not sure I could stop long enough to explain.

He was off the bed in one fluid move, so fast and graceful that Rachel only stirred for a moment before sinking back into sleep. He stood there, staring down at her: the soft determined line of her jaw, the eyelashes that feathered across her tanned cheek, the thick braid of hair that was just beginning to come loose. Memory was returning to him slowly. It had to have been another one of his nightmares. It would be a long time before he would forget those months in that tiny cell, forget the sounds and screams in the night, the last time he had seen Delaney....

And Rachel had come to comfort him. Somehow the thought brought him no comfort at all. She lay there in all her trusting innocence, ready to give him anything he wanted. If he were as big a bastard as he sometimes suspected, he could even get her in bed without telling her the truth. Little matter that she would think she was committing incest; that would be her problem, not his. He knew women well enough to know that she wanted him, even if she didn't quite realize it yet. But she would, sooner or later. And when she did, would she run away? Or would she begin to suspect that he might not be her brother after all?

He couldn't take that risk. He'd taken too many as it was, letting her stay, opening up to her more than he'd opened up to a woman in years. Maybe he was getting confused too, he thought wryly. Maybe he was thinking Rachel Chandler really was his baby sister, come back to life. And then he dismissed the thought as swiftly as it had come. He knew full well that his feeling for Rachel Chandler was far from brotherly. And yet, damn it, it wasn't the simple physical desire he felt for Melea and dozens like her. Rachel was special; no matter how much he tried to deny it, that thought remained festering in his mind. If he didn't watch it, he'd find he was abandoning something he'd planned for over fifteen years. And all for nothing. Once Rachel Chandler discovered the truth, as she was bound to eventually, she'd feel nothing but ha-tred for him.

Well, there was nothing he could do about it, nothing that could change the situation. He could enjoy it while it lasted, enjoy watching her move around the cottage with her long legs and small, high breasts and that half-shy, half-naughty expression that flitted back and forth over her expressive face. It wouldn't be much longer; it couldn't be.

He saw the white-suited figure sitting on his porch as he walked slowly from the ocean. The early morning swim had done its customary job of clearing the cob-webs from his brain—the coffee he had started before going out would finish the job. He wasn't in the mood to deal with Harris Chandler this early in the morning, and his glare as he mounted the front steps of the cottage was distinctly unwelcoming.

"What are you doing up so early?" he growled. Harris had appropriated the most comfortable chair, and he was now leaning back, a mug of coffee cradled in one slightly trembling hand, his usually ruddy face still pale around the gills, his eyes bloodshot, a grin lighting his face.

"''Morning, nephew,'' he said affably. ''Would you mind not dripping all over me? I just had this suit cleaned. Don't you believe in towels?''

"No." Collapsing into one of the weaker chairs, Emmett took the cup of coffee Harris proffered. It was pale beige and thickly sweet, when Emmett preferred it black, but he stayed put. Anything that got Harris Chandler out of bed before noon had to be worth hearing. "What are you doing here, Chandler?"

"Such a welcome," Harris chided mournfully. "I heard some news last night, my boy. Quite fascinating news that I could barely wait to share with you. I have no doubt you'll be as interested as I was. Where, by the way, is the little sister?"

"Rachel's still asleep," Emmett said briefly. "What news?"

"I happened to notice her bedroom door was open and the bed empty," Harris continued, unfazed. "Where does she happen to be sleeping?"

"None of your damned business."

"Dear me, I hope you haven't forgotten yourself entirely, dear boy. Rachel is a very attractive girl, but she does happen to believe she's your sister. Unless you've been indiscreet enough to tell her otherwise."

"She still thinks I'm her brother," he said tersely, choking on the thick, sweet coffee.

"Thank heavens for that. Then where is she sleeping?"

Emmett met his red-rimmed gaze blandly. "In my bed. Any more questions?"

Harris had run into that tone of voice before, and being a devout coward, immediately backed down. "Very well, my boy. It is, after all, your business. I just hate to see Rachel hurt any more than she needs to be. She hasn't been particularly lucky in love. Too trusting, I suppose. I hate to see her trust betrayed again."

"You're part and parcel of that betrayal, Chandler," Emmett snapped. "I'm asking you again, what news?"

Harris hesitated for only a moment. "Emmett Chandler's been seen on the island. The real Emmett Chandler."

He was immediately alert. "By whom? Is the source reliable?"

"The most. Apparently there's a priest who—"

"Good morning, Uncle Harris." Rachel stood in the door, sleep-tousled and cheery in the early morning sunlight. There wasn't a trace of embarrassment or unease in the bright, loving smile she flashed at Emmett. "What's all this about a priest?"

Chapter Nine

Harris Chandler greeted his niece affably, not a shadow crossing his florid complexion. "Good morning, darling. I must say, you're looking entirely fetching this morning. Hawaii must agree with you."

Rachel smiled, moving across the porch on her long, tanned legs to sit on the arm of Emmett's chair. "Being with my brother agrees with me," she corrected cheerfully. "The coffee's terrible again," she informed Emmett. "How anyone can brew something so ghastly in the land of Kona coffee is beyond me. And yesterday's was so nice. I thought you'd turned over a new leaf?"

He smiled up at her lazily. "My new leaves don't last very long, kid. Maybe you'll have to get up earlier and make the coffee yourself."

Rachel shuddered dramatically. "A decent cup of coffee isn't enough to make me rise at the crack of dawn. Maybe I'll buy some instant."

"Now, I am offended," Emmett drawled. "No matter how bad my coffee is, it's certainly better than instant."

"A matter of opinion," she returned, leaning back against his shoulder. "So why are you up so early, Uncle? I thought you had the Chandler weakness for sleeping late.''

"I think my relatives are less than respectful," Harris mourned. "That's exactly how your brother greeted me this morning. I don't always sleep until noon."

"You would if you could," Emmett said lazily, drinking in the scent of the jasmine that lingered in the tangled mop of chestnut hair that grazed his face. "Harris was just trying to convert me. He hasn't been to Mass in probably twenty-five years, but he still thinks I should return to the Mother Church. I've told him to mind his own business, but he ignores me."

"It would be one thing, Rachel dear, if he were just an agnostic." Harris leaned forward, warming to the tale. "But after all those years of pagan religions—ashrams in India, chanting in the jungle, South American rituals— the boy's soul is in a lot more mortal danger than someone who simply hasn't gotten around to church in recent years."

"The boy will be just fine without your interference," Emmett stated. "I don't want to go to church, I don't want to meet this priest, I don't want to do a damn thing but lie on the beach with my kid sister."

Harris glared at him, but Rachel was too busy smiling beatifically down at Emmett to notice. "I've met Father Frank, if that's who you're talking about," she said. "He's really very nice; he's the one who dropped me off here."

"Really?" Harris was suddenly more alert. "That's quite interesting. Where did you meet him?"

"On the plane from Oahu. He said he'd stop by and visit eventually. He was very interested in my prodigal brother, but I guess he hasn't had the time yet. I thought

I might drive over there and see him. I promised him I'd keep in touch."

Emmett and Harris exchanged bland glances. "That sounds like an excellent idea, Rachel," her uncle said. "As a matter of fact, I've come to fetch your brother for the day. There are various legalities we have to work on. Boring stuff, I'm afraid, and nothing that concerns you. Why don't you take the Land Rover and visit this priest, maybe do a little sight-seeing, and then meet us for drinks at the hotel bar around seven?"

"Oh, I don't mind coming along with you," she protested. The last thing she wanted to do was leave Emmett. She had had him for so short a time now, she wasn't ready to surrender him for even a few hours if she could help it. "Father Murphy can wait; I'm sure the island grapevine has let him know I'm just fine."

"The island grapevine, as you call it, is very effective," Harris said grimly.

"Not effective enough," murmured Emmett. "I think you ought to go visit this Father Murphy. Maybe if you put in a good word for me he'll save my soul in absentia."

"That kind of flippant attitude won't get you very far in the Catholic Church, Emmett," she warned.

"I'm counting on your good graces, kid," he drawled. "But you'd better put on something a bit more demure—I don't want you distracting the good Father from his holy vows."

Rising, she stretched against the sunlit sky, unaware of the almost painful hunger in Emmett's eyes. "I don't think I'm likely to do that; Father Murphy is a pussycat, but not what you'd call a sex symbol. I think we'll manage to keep our hands off each other. Are you sure I can't go with you?"

"Positive, kid. You'd be bored silly. Just be sure to watch the sun if you go out on the beach. You may have several layers of tan, but you could still get quite a nasty burn if you don't watch out."

"Yes, sir," she murmured docilely, leaning over to kiss him lightly on the cheek. The skin was warm beneath her lips, smelling faintly of lime-scented shaving cream and the ocean, and she could see his eyelashes close for a moment. "See you at seven."

The two men watched her move back into the cool confines of the cottage, both intent on their own thoughts. Finally Harris spoke. "Do you think that was a particularly wise idea, my friend? Sending her into the lion's den, so to speak?"

Emmett stretched out his legs, staring thoughtfully at the ocean. "Was it the lion's den? Apparently this priest has seen Emmett recently? Emmett, not your humble servant?"

"That's the word. He's not talking, of course. Sealed by the confessional and all that. But the cousin of the bartender works at the church, and he heard the priest talking to some man called Emmett. Tom Moko saw the man, and said it wasn't the *haole* who meets me occasionally in the bar. Though he did look like you, I guess."

"And you can trust the bartender?" Emmett was very calm. Something had finally happened. He could have wished it had happened sooner, before Rachel Chandler had appeared to complicate his life, but he wasn't about to be distracted at this late date.

"As well as I can trust anyone," Harris replied, draining his coffee with a shudder. "You know, she's right. This coffee is ghastly."

"Tough. And I think sending Rachel over there was a very good idea," he added as an afterthought.

"You do? Why?"

Emmett swiveled around in his chair to stare at Harris. "We do want to find the real Emmett, remember? I think Rachel might do a very good job of flushing him out."

"You're a cool customer, aren't you? I thought you were beginning to care for your kid *sister.*"

"She's okay," Emmett snapped. "Money's better."

"You could have fooled me. And if it's the money you're so concerned about, and I assume it is, then have you ever stopped to consider that it might be better if Emmett Chandler never makes a reappearance? If he's still alive, he must have his reasons for lying low. It would make things so much easier if you died a nice cut-and dried death. No hassle with a seven-year waiting period to have the real Emmett declared dead, no hassle with trying to convince an aging hippie that the money should go to his relatives and not some home for Krishna consciousness? Maybe we should drop our inquiries, continue on as if you're the real Emmett, and send you over a cliff in a few months?"

"No." His voice was adamant.

"Why not? It seems an admirable solution to all our problems. Particularly since you don't seem to have any qualms about sacrificing Rachel."

"It's too late for that decision. There's no longer any question as to whether Emmett Chandler is really alive. He's sent Rachel birthday presents for the past fifteen years; he's been seen recently. He's going to make an appearance, Harris, and we'd better be ready for him."

Harris looked doubtful. "Perhaps. You forget, I knew my nephew, you didn't. I'm not convinced he's going to show up, not convinced at all. He's just as likely to stir up a bit of trouble, just to spite us all, and then disappear."

The front legs of Emmett's chair slammed down on the porch. "If he knows about us, don't you think he'll know his sister is here too? In our evil clutches? Don't you think that will make him show his face?"

"I doubt it. I told you, the Chandlers don't put themselves out for their relations, and Emmett, much as he disliked the idea, was very much a Chandler. I think he'll be just as willing to sacrifice Rachel as we are."

Emmett closed his eyes for a long, pained moment. "Poor Rachel," he murmured.

"She'll survive. She's survived worse in her time," Harris said coolly. "How long will it take you to get ready?"

The look of disgust Emmett flung at him would have penetrated even his thick hide if he'd happened to see it. But Harris was too busy flicking an imaginary piece of dust from his spotless white jacket. "Don't worry about it, Emmett, my lad. Your tropical idyll isn't over yet. Rachel will doubtless find another innocent excuse to crawl into your bed again, and then you can decide how gentlemanly you really want to be. I must say," he continued, sauntering down the front steps, "I'm surprised at my little niece. I wouldn't have thought her capable of that sort of perversity. She always seemed like such a sweet, shy creature. I don't know what Ariel would have—" Harris's spotless figure went sprawling into the sand, his mouth filling with the wet grit. Emmett stood over him, his face an expressionless mask that was far more frightening than any look of rage would have been.

"Don't you ever," he said in a deceptively mild voice, "say anything like that about your niece again." There was no threat following the statement; there was no need for one. Very carefully Harris Chandler picked himself up, spitting sand from his mouth. His freshly laundered suit was a mess. He brushed at it with ineffectual hands.

"How very clumsy of me," he murmured, his eyes shifting away from the man standing dangerously close to him. "I'll meet you at the car."

Emmett stood there for a long moment, watching Harris's now-rumpled figure shamble across the sand toward the large, air-conditioned Lincoln that served him as transportation around the island. Slowly he unclenched his hands, taking several deep, calming breaths. It had been a long time since he'd been that angry, a good long time. The intensity of his fury surprised him, surprised and disturbed him. There was no room for that kind of uncontrolled passion in his undertaking. He'd have to remember that, or risk everything. And he'd come too far to risk it all for a pair of brown eyes and the sweetest mouth he'd ever tasted. Somewhere he was going to have to reassume his usual cold-blooded attitude. Unfortunately Rachel Chandler had a disturbing facility for heating up his usually icy hemoglobin.

He moved silently into the house, hoping not to disturb Rachel. His bedroom was empty, and he threw on clean clothes swiftly, keeping his gaze averted from the rumpled bed, in his mind's eye still seeing Rachel lying curled up against him.

Without a backward glance he turned and ran down the front steps to the ostentatious car. There was no room for second thoughts, no room for Rachel Chandler, not now, not ever. He'd better remember that.

Harris leaned out the passenger's window. "You drive, my boy. I'm a little shaken up."

Emmett grinned then, a feral, almost frightening smile that failed to reassure Harris even a tiny bit. "Good," he said, sliding into the driver's seat. "Stay that way." And he backed away from the cottage.

Chapter Ten

"This is one of the oldest churches in the islands." Father Frank surveyed the ancient, whitewashed structure with justifiable pride. The church was small, plain, and undecorated, and yet Rachel felt closer to God there than she had in a long time. "It's been rumored that Father Damien spent time here before going to the leper colony on Molokai. I'm very lucky to be here," Father Frank said simply.

Rachel smiled. "I think I agree with you. It's very peaceful here."

"Are you in need of peace, Rachel?" he questioned softly. Father Frank was looking much as she had last seen him, his round face florid in the heat, his rounded stomach pushing against the plain black shirt, his bald dome glistening with the sheen of perspiration.

Rachel laughed, a small, uneasy laugh as she pushed a hand through her hair. She'd made the mistake of letting it hang down around her shoulders, and her neck was suffocating. "How did you guess?"

"It's my job to be observant. You looked more troubled than when I last saw you. Are you?"

"Perhaps." There was a sudden, furtive movement toward the back of the church, and Rachel broke off, startled. "Who was that?"

"Just one of my helpers," the priest said blandly. "Why don't we go out into the garden, where we can have some privacy? Unless you want to make your confession?" He gestured toward the confessionals with one small, plump hand, and Rachel shook her head hastily. She doubted she was ready for quite the intensive soul-searching confession would require of her.

"I'd love to see the gardens," she murmured, casting one last, curious look in the direction of the intruder. There was no sign of him as she followed Father Frank's portly figure out into the shady garden, and she dismissed it, still caught up in her own problems.

"Tell me, Rachel, did your brother send you here to me?" he inquired once they'd seated themselves beneath a shady candlenut tree.

"Whatever made you think that?" Rachel was startled. And even more startled to realize that Emmett, in fact, had done just that.

"Just curious. Did he?"

"He suggested I might stop by here on my way around the island," she replied hesitantly. "Did he have any special reason to send me here? I thought you didn't know him."

"I don't. Is he the reason you're here?" Leaning back in the wicker chair, Father Frank resembled nothing so much as a benevolent Buddha, and Rachel felt her misgivings melt away in the warmth of his concern.

"Yes, and no. I didn't come because he suggested it— I've been meaning to be in touch ever since you dropped me off, but I've just been too busy."

"Getting to know your brother all over again," the priest supplied, nodding. "I understand. And is it working out well? Is he the way you remembered him?"

"No," she said instinctively, then recovered herself. "I mean, it's working out well...far better than I could have expected. But he's not at all the way I remembered him. Of course, it's been fifteen years since I've seen him, and I was only twelve at the time, more interested in movie stars than my own brother. But there's something... different about him, something that almost frightens me. And yet it pulls me too, Father. And that's what worries me."

"Worries you? Why should it?" His voice was soft and soothing, inviting confidences, and Rachel's final doubts left her.

"I love him," she said simply. "More than I've ever loved anyone, though I can't really say why. We don't have anything in common, except a few ancient memories, and he's a cynical, closed-up man. I suppose it must be the blood tie that makes me feel so close to him."

"Perhaps. People have been trying to define what love is for centuries, and I don't know if anyone has succeeded yet. Love can exist with absolutely nothing in common, and of course the opposite is true. Quite often what people dislike most in other people are their own characteristics." He leaned forward, putting a gentle hand on her arm. "So what are you worried about, Rachel? Why are you worried that you love your brother?"

"Do you suppose... Is it possible that I might love him too much?" she questioned softly.

"I don't know that someone can love too much," he mused. "Are you afraid you'll suffocate him with your affection? Demand too much of his time and attention?

If you truly love him, you can be wary of being too demanding; give him the room he needs.''

"That's not what I mean," she said quietly. "I know to give him enough space." She steeled herself. "No, I'm afraid of something quite different. You see, Father, I have no interest in other men right now. The very thought of my ex-fiancé or any man touching me gives me the shivers. I don't want to be around any man, I don't want any man touching me. Except my brother." There, it was out in the open, spoken, and the world hadn't collapsed. She stole a glance at Father Frank's moon face, expecting shock, disgust, and condemnation.

Instead she saw compassion and a blessed hint of amusement. "In other words you're afraid you've got an incestuous longing for your brother. You're afraid that you don't just love your brother, you're in love with him. Is that it?"

"I was trying not to put it quite so bluntly," Rachel muttered, her face red to the roots of her hair.

"But why not? You can't free yourself of these worries unless you face them, Rachel. Not that I think you have a thing to worry about," he added.

"Why not?" She was more than willing to take any kind of assurance, even vague ones.

"It's only natural for you to be temporarily obsessed by your brother. He's your closest relative, and he's been gone from your life for fifteen years. Didn't you tell me that since your grandparents died you've essentially been alone? No one to care about, no one to care about you? It's only natural that you'd fall upon the reappearance of your brother like a starving man falling on a feast. It will pass, Rachel. Any stray feelings of physical longing will dissipate as time passes and you become accustomed to having him back with you. That is, if he's planning to stay around."

"Of course he's planning to stay!" Sudden panic filled Rachel at the thought that Emmett might just suddenly disappear once more, wander off into the tangled jungles of Kauai without a word to anyone. She didn't think she could bear it if that happened again, not after having found him. "What makes you think he wouldn't?"

"Well, Emmett Chandler hasn't got the reputation of staying put for very long. Of course, he stands to inherit quite a sum of money.... Perhaps that will help him put down roots."

"I'd never even thought of the money," Rachel mused. "I can't imagine that Emmett would really care one way or the other about it."

"Most men care a great deal about several million dollars," Father Frank observed. "Isn't that why he decided to reappear?"

"That's what he said," she replied uncertainly. "I suppose the money will keep him around." She raised unhappy eyes to Father Frank's benevolent hazel ones.

"And that will give you plenty of time to get used to his presence and turn your attention back to eligible young men around you. A time of physical and social celibacy spent tending to your brother will most likely prove very beneficial."

"And what if it doesn't feel celibate?" she whispered, closing her eyes, the image of Emmett's tough, strong body flitting through her mind.

Father Frank patted her hand again. "Take my word for it, Rachel. Don't worry. You're not going to commit any mortal sins with your brother. The sooner you relax about this, take it in stride, the sooner it will pass."

"I suppose so," she said doubtfully, wanting to believe him but not quite daring to.

"In the meantime I think you should spend some time by yourself. Go for a drive out by Haena . . . sunbathe on the beach . . . meditate. Meditation can do wonders for a troubled spirit."

"Now you sound like my brother," she laughed. "He was into things like meditation long before they gained popular acceptance. And I plan to spend the day exactly as you suggested, lying in the sun and clearing my mind of everything but how beautiful Kauai is. Does that meet with your approval?"

He nodded benevolently. "An excellent plan. But watch our hot sun—even with a tan you can still get badly burned."

Rachel laughed, rising to her full five feet six. "Between you and Emmett I don't have to worry about myself at all. He practically forced sunscreen on me before I left. I promise, I'll take care of myself."

"You do that. And come back and see me before I go."

"Before you go?" she echoed, startled.

"I'm being reassigned. Something I've wanted for a long time, I'm happy to say. I'm being sent to El Salvador." He sighed. "It's been a dream of mine for longer than I can say. Life will be very simple there, even primitive."

"And dangerous?" Rachel found herself asking.

"Possibly," Father Frank allowed, unmoved by the prospect. "I'd like to feel you were settled before I went, Rachel. It won't be for a few weeks, I expect. You'll be feeling positively blissful by that time. If you're not, you send that brother of yours to me, and I'll sort him out for you."

"I doubt you could," she replied wistfully. "Emmett's more than a match for anybody."

"Oh, I might have a few tricks up my sleeve," Father Frank said serenely. "Priests are required to come equipped with an ace in the hole on occasion." He rose, taking her hand once more. "Take care of yourself, Rachel."

Acting on sheer impulse, Rachel put her arms around his rotund figure, hugging him tightly. Unlike Emmett, he didn't pull away, shocked. He returned her hug. "Go in peace, Rachel," he whispered.

THE BEACH at Haena was a marvelous expanse of thick white sand, dotted heavily with tanning bodies. Rachel had considered going back to the small private beach she'd shared with Emmett yesterday, then thought better of it. Much as she wanted to continue exploring the marvelous underwater world of snorkeling, the thought of swimming alone had been a deeply ingrained tabu. Besides, Emmett had kept the wildlife away; alone she just might become shark bait.

She did what she promised Father Frank she would do, clearing her mind of all the bitter entanglements that twisted through her coiled emotions. She would do as he suggested, simply relax and love her brother to the best of her abilities. Those small, strange, unbidden longings were simply a matter of hormones, a normal enough reaction when two virtual strangers were sharing a small space and an intense emotional relationship. The less she worried about it, the safer she'd be. Wouldn't she?

She could have done a little bit better in obeying Emmett's and Father Frank's instructions concerning the burning power of the sun. She covered herself dutifully with sunscreen, but the Hawaiian rays proved more than equal to that feeble defense. She'd only been lying on the clean white sand for a few hours when the skin on her back began to tingle and burn.

Swinging into a sitting position, she pulled an oversize shirt across her shoulders, a sudden determination filling her. Despite Father Frank's assurances, that nagging guilt pulled at her, destroying her peace and her happiness with her brother. It would be a simple enough matter to relieve that guilt and anxiety, scratch an itch she hadn't even realized existed. If it was just a simple matter of hormones gone awry, she could find someone safe to help her relieve her frustration. She would do what she had never done before: Find the most attractive, single man at the hotel bar and set her sights on him. A one-night stand should provide her with more than enough animal lust to keep her mind off her brother.

Of course, there was the depressing thought that doubtlessly the most attractive single man at the hotel bar would be Emmett. She'd simply have to settle for second best. Though how she was going to manage it with any kind of savoir faire was another matter. Her sexual experience consisted of some adolescent fumblings, a restrained graduate student at Berkeley, and Ralph's athletics. She hadn't even been in a singles bar, didn't know the first thing about picking someone up.

Well, it was about time she learned, both for her sake and Emmett's. It would do them both good: Maybe she could even find someone for her brother. He hadn't struck her as someone who went without feminine companionship for long. Her first step would be to stop in town on the way to the cottage and buy something to wear, something appropriately flattering and "come hither," with a neckline down to there. Heavier makeup, perhaps a flower in her hair.

Sternly she squared her shoulders as she headed back to the Land Rover. If she felt more like a virgin sacrifice than a woman anticipating a night of carnal pleasures, she had only herself to blame.

Chapter Eleven

The bar was crowded, a blur of noise and light, when Rachel made her appearance. She paused on the threshold long enough for the mostly male customers assembled to get a good look at her before she headed toward the Chandler table. If she felt like a prize heifer up for auction, there was nothing she could do but throw back her head and ignore it.

The dress had been a great piece of luck. It had been the first thing she'd tried on, and she'd immediately fallen in love with it. The deep yellow-gold brought out the warm tones of her tanned skin, the latest bit of sunburn only giving her a more burnished, tawny look. The neckline was deceptively demure: her small, firm breasts pressed enticingly against the thin material, their tops just barely visible, and the straight skirt had slits halfway up her long, leggy thighs. She'd even bought a pair of high heels to show off her admittedly good legs and let her thick mane of hair hang in an unruly curtain around her burnished face. Her eyes were artfully made up, with shadows of gold and green, the eyeliner giving her a sooty, sultry gaze, and the lip gloss was Passion Peach. She'd even taken the time to paint her nails, her toes peeping out of the spiky sandals in a way calculated to drive some poor man wild.

Not that she was in the mood for a foot fetishist, she thought with a grim attempt at humor. Just someone marginally attractive, with enough sex appeal to drive forbidden thoughts out of her mind.

As she threaded her way through the tables she could feel the eyes on her, knew that all her work hadn't been for nothing. Even Emmett was staring up at her, those hazel eyes of his dark with something indefinable. Or perhaps it was something she didn't dare to define. He watched her in silence as she slid into a chair, his wide, cyrnical mouth snapped shut disapprovingly.

"On the prowl, little sister?" he murmured, leaning back and toying with the dark amber drink in his hand.

"Now, Emmett, don't be such a disapproving old sod," Harris reproved. "She looks quite lovely tonight. Pay him no mind, Rachel dear. He's just jealous because you don't dress up like that for him. He's a demanding older brother."

It took Rachel a moment to regain her equanimity. Harris's words had struck a responsive chord, and she realized instinctively that despite her determination to seduce some hapless soul, her dress, her makeup, her come-hither look had subconsciously been designed for Emmett. She managed to smile composedly at her uncle, keeping her eyes averted from Emmett's glower.

"I thought it might be time to sample some of the social pleasures the island has to offer," she murmured. Emmett set his glass down on the table with a bang.

"Excellent idea. No need to immure yourself in that cottage just because your brother has chosen to be antisocial. A girl your age needs eligible male companionship. I'd be more than happy to introduce you to some of the young men I've met here. I must say, I'm glad to see you've decided to come out of mourning for that scoundrel, Ralph. He was never worthy of a Chandler, anyway. I'm sure if we just look around we'll find someone more suitable.'' He signaled for the waiter. "Take that group of men at the bar. I've played golf with them.... All excellent fellows. Charming, well-bred. You could go a lot farther and do a lot worse, my dear.''

"I never knew you had a secret ambition to be a pimp, Uncle." Emmett's voice was dangerously cold, and Harris gave him a suddenly nervous smile.

But Rachel wasn't about to be deterred at this point. Emmett might not recognize the danger in her absorption with him, and thank God he didn't. But it was up to her to do something about it before the situation turned into Greek tragedy.

She turned to look at the three men sitting at the bar, not the slightest bit troubled to find them eyeing her with avid interest. She lazily crossed one leg to give them a better view of the tanned expanse of thigh that she knew was her chief attraction, and considered the possibilities.

They were all handsome, tanned, blond. Two of them were probably in their late twenties, the third was older, possibly a few years older than she was. He was less pretty than the other two, with a ready smile and frankly avid eyes that held just a trace of coldness. It took her a moment to realize he reminded her of Emmett, and without considering the consequences, decided on him.

"Who's the man on the left?" she whispered to her uncle, reaching with one slender hand for the sweet rum drink he'd ordered her. Emmett said nothing, just continued to glare.

Harris swiveled around to intercept the lascivious look from the man. "Stephen Ames," he said shortly, some of the enthusiasm leaving his voice. "I think you could do better, my dear. He's charming, of course, but he has a somewhat unsavory reputation...."

Better and better, she thought. Emmett had an equally unsavory reputation. Stephen Ames would prove an admirable substitute. "Could you introduce me?"

Still Emmett said nothing, watching her out of still, basilisk eyes. Harris cast a nervous glance at him, almost as if he were asking permission. He got no response. "I suppose so," he said finally.

"What does Rachel's young swain do for a living?" Emmett drawled suddenly.

"I don't really know.... He seems to have plenty of money. He plays golf for large sums and wins consistently. He may possibly have some...ahem...agricultural interests."

A faint look of contempt passed over Emmett's face. "Sounds likely."

"You used to do the same thing," Rachel said hotly, guilt and apprehension tightening her nerves.

He looked at her then, his eyes playing over her burnished face, the low-cut dress, and the soft, tremulous mouth. "That doesn't make it a good thing."

"But—"

"I hate to interrupt, Chandler," a smooth voice broke in, and Rachel turned to see Stephen Ames leaning over her in a perfect position to look down her dress. "But I couldn't miss the chance to be introduced to this stunning creature. I thought I knew all the beautiful women on the island."

"Stephen Ames, my niece, Rachel Chandler. And this is her brother, Emmett."

Stephen smiled, his raft of perfect teeth dazzling in his tanned face. "The mysterious Emmett Chandler! And you're this young lady's brother. I must say I'm glad to hear that. I was afraid you'd be something inconvenient like a husband or lover."

Rachel was afraid she did not like Stephen Ames. For one thing, his voice was hoarse, with a hint of a whine in it, and possessed of an urban accent that grated on her nerves. For another, his heavy-handed charm made her uncomfortable, particularly combined with those avid eyes which seemed to burn her skin. She smiled back. "Only a brother," she said in a dulcet voice, the inviting tone just slightly forced.

"Then I don't have to ask his permission to take you out," he said, smiling with too many teeth. He had rested one hand on the back of her chair, and his fingers were stroking the bare skin of her shoulder blade, out of sight of Emmett's hawklike eyes. Rachel pulled away abruptly, then forced herself to lean back, ignoring the pain of her sunburn. Stephen's laugh was smug, offensive, and she was about to tell him to go drown himself when she looked across at Emmett.

His face was set in a grim line, his mouth was twisted in that cynical curve she disliked so much, and his eyes were hot and hostile as they met her quizzical look. He'd changed to a white, collarless shirt: the long sleeves had been rolled up to expose tanned, muscled forearms, and the first three buttons left undone to expose a tanned column of chest, sprinkled lightly with sandy-colored hair. A wave of longing, as intense as it was unexpected, washed over her, and she shut her eyes for a moment to blot out the sight of him.

"What do you say about day after tomorrow, Rachel?" Ames was saying. "I could show you things about this island you didn't even dream existed. A woman like you shouldn't be wasted on a brother and an uncle.''

Where had he perfected that line? she wondered dimly. It must have worked before, though how any intelligent woman could have fallen for it was beyond her comprehension. Opening her eyes, she avoided looking at Emmett, smiling up into Stephen Ames's undeniably handsome face. He really was much better-looking than Emmett, and he had the perfect body seldom seen outside of underwear commercials. If he'd just keep his mouth shut, she'd manage it, and in doing so blot Emmett out of her mind. "That would be lovely," she agreed serenely, feeling the waves of anger radiating from across the table.

That encroaching hand made another foray across her exposed skin, and for a brief moment she imagined it was Emmett's hand. No, not Emmett, she cried inwardly. Some man that looked like him, talked like him, but wasn't her brother. A small burning knot of desire began to flame down low, and she allowed the fantasy to take hold for a brief moment. "I'll pick you up at seven then," he murmured in that hoarse voice. "Harris, you'll give me directions, won't you?"

Harris was looking uncomfortable. "Of course, dear boy. I'm sure my niece could do with a little diversion for a change."

"Oh, I'll divert her all right. And that's a promise." The hand was removed from her naked back, and he sauntered, no, swaggered back to his barside companions. Harris turned an apologetic face to Emmett, but he was already on his feet.

"We're going," he announced abruptly, his hand closing over Rachel's forearm. It wasn't a light grip, it was a hard, bruising, angry clasp, and she felt herself yanked to her feet unceremoniously. "I think my little sister has accomplished what she set out to do."

"But I haven't finished—"

"Believe me, you've finished." His entire body was rigid with rage as he began dragging her toward the door.

"I'm coming," she muttered hastily. "Stop dragging me—everybody's staring."

"I wouldn't think you'd mind making a scene," he shot back, his grip never loosening as he hauled her out on the front porch. "You certainly came dressed for attention."

She stumbled slightly as he pulled her across the sandy drive toward the Land Rover. "I don't see what you're in such a fit about," she argued lamely.

"I don't particularly like watching my sister act like a tramp." He thrust her into the passenger seat, moving around to climb behind the wheel, his face still a mask of fury.

"I wasn't acting like a tramp," she defended herself hotly. "I just thought it might be a good idea.... I mean, I thought I might like to go out on a date."

He laughed unpleasantly. "A date? Is that what you call it? It seemed more like you were setting an appointment for stud service." He pulled out of the hotel drive with dangerous speed, taking the corner rapidly. Rachel clung to the frayed seat of the Land Rover with clutching fingers as he took off down the road with a speed she hadn't realized the old vehicle was capable of.

And then suddenly she was very calm beneath the twilight skies as a feeling of intense joy filled her, even if it was tempered with despair. "You're jealous, aren't you?" she said quietly.

"*Jealous?*" He didn't bother to move his eyes from the road, something she could only be grateful for, considering the speeds at which they were traveling. "Rachel, I'm your brother, for heaven's sake. Why should I be jealous?"

Why, indeed, she thought. "Just because you're my brother doesn't mean you wouldn't want my complete attention. I would think you'd enjoy being loved the way I love you."

The headlong pace of the Land Rover was slowed perceptibly; the grim set of his mouth relaxed a tiny bit. He still didn't look at her, but his hands no longer seemed to clutch the steering wheel so tightly. They were beautiful hands, she noticed for the first time. Long-fingered, with well-kept nails; strong, capable-looking hands. Funny, she had never remembered Emmett having such large beautiful hands. But then, there was a lot about the man beside her that she didn't remember.

"You love me, do you?" he drawled, and some of the tension drained from Rachel's sunburned shoulders. It was a dangerous subject, but in her relief at the sudden disappearance of his temper, she ignored the risks.

"Yes," she replied. This would be the only time she'd tell him. In a couple of days she'd be caught in a torrid affair with Stephen Ames, and Emmett would once more be nothing but a cherished brother. She turned to watch his profile, and her voice was earnest. "I love you more than anyone I've ever loved in my life. I can't imagine why, when you're such a pig to me, but I do love you, Emmett. Anyone else I choose to spend time with is only a second choice."

There was a long silence. "Is that why you honed in on Stephen Ames, Rachel?" His voice was low in the gathering darkness, low and caressing.

Panic clutched at her. "What do you mean?"

"You know exactly what I mean." He paused. "All right, Rachel, go out with him. But I suggest you be careful. I don't think he's quite the knight in shining armor you seem to think he is."

"I'm not planning to marry him, Emmett." She tried to inject a caustic tone into her voice.

"No," he agreed. "Just exorcise some demons." Before she could respond to that provocative statement—not that she knew what to say—he had pulled up beside the darkened cottage. "Why don't you go on in? I'll probably go for a walk, maybe drive back into Lihue."

"What for?" she asked, not moving.

He looked at her then. The moon was rising across the sea, sending a silver-white shaft across the water, gilding her hair, reflecting in her eyes. "Did it ever occur to you I might have my own demons?"

There was nothing she could say. Opening the door, she slid out of the Land Rover, slamming it shut behind her. Her spiked heels sank precariously into the deep sand, and he watched as she delicately slid first one, then the other from her slender feet. She moved gracefully across the sand to the front steps of the cottage, and he could tell by the set of her shoulders that she was using all her willpower to keep from turning around to look at him.

She was more beautiful than ever to him, silvered by the moonlight, that damnably provocative dress clinging to her slender, rounded body. The ache that was never far from him nowadays seemed to increase. Two could play at her game, he thought grimly. Melea was a lot warmer and more accommodating a lover than that brainless jock at the bar could ever hope to be. With a sudden, violent motion he spun the wheels in the soft sand, backing out of the drive with the same furious speed that had hounded him earlier. Out of the corner of his eyes he saw Rachel turn on the porch to watch him. And it was probably only sheer romantic fancy on his part that made him think the reflection of the moon caught a faint silver trickling of tears across her cheeks.

Rachel waited until the Land Rover disappeared from view, racing down the road at breakneck speed, before continuing on into the house. With a surreptitious hand she brushed away the damning tears, and her shoulders cried out in agony. All evening she'd tried to ignore the pain of her overindulgence in the strong Hawaiian sun, but it was finally catching up with her. Well, at least it would keep her mind off her troubles, she thought with a grim hopefulness. If her back hurt too much she wouldn't be able to think about other aching parts of her body.

She turned on a light against the encroaching darkness before heading into the kitchen in search of baking soda. It was an old remedy for sunburn, tried but true: A nice cool bath with baking soda to soothe the injuries of the day. She should have known Emmett wouldn't have any such thing.

The bathroom cupboard was equally bare, and she stared at the empty shelves in frustration. The skin across her back felt tight and stiff with pain, though her reflection was deceiving. The deep, reddish hue beneath the golden tan would only be discernible to an experienced eye—Emmett's, perhaps? It was just as well she hadn't turned her back to him in the bar.

At least she'd had the foresight to pick up some Vitamin E cream when shopping earlier. That would have to do, as long as she could reach the afflicted area. If she couldn't, she would simply have to suffer in silence. She certainly wasn't going to ask Emmett to smear the cream on her naked back. If he even bothered to return before morning. She had the strong suspicion that he had no intention of doing so, and she accepted it stoically. More stoically than she accepted the sunburn.

There was no way she was going to be able to wear even the lightest of nightgowns. Stripping off the new dress, she dropped it over a chair, tossed her underwear after it, and turned off the light. She was too tired to cream off her makeup, too tired to do anything more than find her way to bed and try to will sleep to come. She hadn't been sleeping well the last few nights; last night in Emmett's bed was the closest she'd come to a sound sleep since she'd arrived in Hawaii. That, of course, was no longer an option. She would simply have to lie on her stomach and think of something cool and soothing. And hope she didn't hear Emmett when he chose to return.

Moving across to the bed, she ran into the chair, stubbing her toe painfully. Suddenly a very short, obscene word broke the inky stillness. That word had come from her own mouth, and sudden tears of pain and frustration followed it.

"Are you all right?" Emmett's voice startled her into a panic as it came from the living room, and without hesitation she dived into the bed, pulling the covers up over her nude body.

"I'm fine," she called back. Her voice was still husky with unshed tears, and she sounded anything but fine. A moment later the door opened, and Emmett stood there, the light from the living room a halo around his shaggy blond hair. She couldn't see his expression against the light, but she huddled deeper into the bed, her raw shoulders scraping against the sheet. She gave an involuntary moan of pain, and he moved into the room, switching on the overhead light.

"I wasn't expecting you back so soon," she stammered, for lack of something better to say. She felt impaled by the cool intensity in his eyes, like a butterfly caught on a pin.

"I changed my mind," he murmured, moving closer. "What's wrong, Rachel?"

"Nothing..." she began, but the scowl deepened on his face. "Nothing much," she amended. "I just got a little sunburned today. And don't say 'I told you so'—I know you did. I guess I wasn't paying enough attention."

He stared at her for a long, silent moment. "Do you have anything for it?"

"Just some Vitamin E cream, but I—"

"Where's the burn?"

"On my back, but I—"

"Could you reach it yourself?" His voice was cool, unmoved, as he reached for the tube of cream that lay unopened on her dresser. "Obviously not. Roll over, Rachel, and I'll put it on for you."

Deep color suffused her face, deep panic filled her heart. "Emmett, I really don't need it. Besides, I'm not wearing anything."

"Why not?"

"Because it hurt too much...." She let her voice trail off in the face of his knowing expression.

"I repeat: Roll over." He moved closer to her, his movements slow and deliberate, and determinedly she moved her gaze past his strong, lean body to his face.

"Emmett, I told you, I'm not wearing anything," she protested breathlessly.

"Rachel, you haven't got anything I haven't seen many times before." There was a hint of amusement lurking in those hazel eyes.

She glared at him, affronted. "I don't care. I happen to be modest, and you happen to be my brother."

"Yes, I am, aren't I?" he said gently. "Well, why don't you wrap the sheet around you, roll over, and then push the sheet down to your hips? Your modesty will be intact, I'll be able to put this cream on your back, and then we can both get a decent night's sleep. Though I do think it's a little early."

"I was tired," she said, sniffling just a tiny bit. The tears had dried up at his unexpected invasion, but the burning misery still hovered just behind her large brown eyes.

"Are you going to do as your big brother says or will I have to turn you over myself? I might be tempted to administer a good spanking at the same time. You strike me as someone who didn't get enough spankings when she was young."

Rachel's embarrassment fled her for a moment as she looked at him curiously. "Don't you remember what you did when Cousin Harold tried it?"

Emmett just returned her gaze blandly. "Nothing more than he deserved," he hazarded. "Turn over, Rachel."

With a sigh she did as she was bid, rolling onto her stomach, her naked breasts pressing into the rough cotton sheet. A moment later she felt his hands on her: cool, gentle hands, pushing the top sheet down around her hips, exposing the narrow, delicate curves of her back. She felt the bed sag beneath his weight, felt him move the heavy curtain of hair away from her neck. A moment later the cool, soothing cream flowed onto her painful back, the fingers feather light as they smoothed it into the injured flesh.

"You don't have anything more effective for sunburn?" He queried in a low, soothing voice.

Rachel had closed her eyes, reveling in the soothing, peaceful movements of his hands on her skin. "Vitamin E's wonderful stuff," she murmured hazily.

"You're even more of an aging hippie than I am." The amusement in his voice was tempered with a tenderness that pulled at her. "You should have bought some nice, clean chemicals."

"Peasant," she murmured. "Natural medicines are always preferable."

"I don't know if I agree with that," he said, and his voice was low and seductive. The hands were moving over her back with a devilishly skillful touch, the fingers light and sure and knowing. He was very good at this, she thought sleepily. He knew just how to touch a woman, just how to move her. She could picture those hands, the fingers long and tanned as they moved across her back. She wanted to roll over on her back, feel those clever, clever hands do their magic on her breasts. A sudden wave of horror washed over her, horror and guilt. But no revulsion. She still wanted what she wanted, even if it was wrong, terribly wrong.

"Why did you tense up?" Emmett's voice was no more than curious as his hands left her. "Doesn't the cream help?"

She managed a nod. "I guess I'm just overtired. Thanks, Emmett." She didn't dare look at him, couldn't look at him. If she did, she was sure he would see the shameful longing in her vulnerable face. "I'll see you tomorrow."

He didn't move for a moment, just sat beside her. She wondered what he was thinking as he looked down at her. But he didn't say a word. She felt the cotton sheet drift lightly down on her back, and then he rose. "Good night, Rachel." A moment later the light was off again; the door closed quietly behind his departing figure. Rachel raised her head then, staring through the darkness at the closed door. The pain in her back was nothing compared to the pain in her heart.

"Damn," she whispered, her voice thick with tears. "Damn, damn, damn."

Chapter Twelve

Her bedroom was dark and gloomy when she finally gave up the fruitless battle for sleep and dragged herself from her bed the next morning. For the first time Hawaii was in shadow, the palm trees swaying in an angry wind, the tangled underbrush whipping against the house. The tiny cottage was almost unpleasantly cool, and she dressed in old, faded jeans rather than the shorts she'd been favoring, pulling on a long-sleeve cotton overshirt and a sweater against the unexpected chill. Last night's makeup still lay on her face, and she scrubbed it away with more vehemence than necessary. For a moment she regarded her reflection in the bathroom mirror. The intense scrubbing had reddened her cheeks, and the dark brown eyes looked out at the world with troubled solemnity. She looked about fifteen, she thought, braiding her hair in two thick braids to accentuate the effect. *Think young, think prepuberty. And maybe it will all go away.*

Squaring her shoulders, she moved out into the shadowy living room. Emmett was staring out at the ocean, his broad back at her, and she watched him longingly for a moment.

"What can I make you for breakfast?" she called out briskly, rubbing her hands together in nervousness and chill.

He turned slowly, and his wary eyes seemed to impale her across the length of the room. There was an uneasy silence in the room, and then he seemed to rouse himself. "Nothing." He turned back to stare at the angry waves that were pounding on the beach, much closer than usual, even at high tide. "I've had coffee."

"Yuk. I know your coffee." She shuddered dramatically. "Come on, that stuff will curdle your stomach if you don't let me make you something to cushion it. How about scrambled eggs? Or toast, at least."

"Nothing, Rachel." His voice was low, abstracted, and he kept his gaze out the window. For some reason she didn't like him calling her by name. *Kid* was so much safer than the gentle, loving sound of her name on his lips.

"You never used to be so disinterested in food," she joked, moving closer to him. "I remember you were already growing a little bit of a paunch when you were twenty-five. Ariel always used to warn you you'd get fat if you didn't watch it."

"I guess I took her warnings to heart the last fifteen years," he murmured. She was standing directly behind him, and he turned to stare down at her then, his eyes bland and unreadable. "We're due for a storm."

Now it was her turn to look away. She moved beside him, staring out at the high waves crashing onto the beach. "It looks like it," she said inanely. "How bad is it going to be? Are we in any danger down so close to the water?"

"I don't expect so. I'll check with Harris—he'll have heard the latest weather reports. We don't usually get hurricanes out here; I imagine we'll just have a bad blow and then it will all die down. Are you frightened of storms?''

She laughed then, the sound slightly rusty in the late morning stillness. "How did you guess?"

His reluctant grin answered her, and she allowed her tense shoulders to relax slightly. "I know, I know, I'm a devout coward. I think I'm scared of just about everything."

"You're not that bad," he said soothingly, that rough voice of his curiously caressing against her shattered nerve ends. "You just have a few phobias."

"That's putting it kindly indeed, brother dear." She used the title deliberately, to remind herself of what she didn't dare forget. "I'm afraid of flying, of the ocean, of storms, snakes, love, and death. Not necessarily in that order."

He remained very still beside her, and she could smell the strong, rich smell of coffee on his breath, feel the body heat emanating from his lean, tough body. "What *aren't* you afraid of?" His voice was soft and low.

"I'm not afraid of you, Emmett," she said softly, keeping her face, like his, directed out at the stormy sea. They stood like that for a long moment, shoulder to shoulder, not another word passing between them. And then Rachel stirred herself, moving away in a deliberate effort to break the hypnotic mood that seemed to spin out from him. "More coffee?"

"What?" He seemed startled by the mundane question, and the hazel eyes that turned to look at her seemed out of focus for a moment. As if he were looking far, far away, a long time ago. "Oh, no thanks. I need to stretch my legs. I'll be back in a while." Setting the empty mug down on the windowsill, he headed for the door.

"In the rain?"

"It won't rain for hours yet, Rachel. I've been here long enough to read the weather pretty well—the storm shouldn't hit until sometime late this afternoon or early evening. Plenty of time to batten down the hatches. You'll be all right." He stopped his forward stride for a moment. "Won't you?"

Fixing a bright smile to her face, she waved airily at him. "Of course. Go ahead." There was a definite air of escape to him as he took the front steps two at a time. Rachel moved back to the window, watching him move down the beach at a rapid pace. He had demons too, he'd said last night. Looking at him now, she could readily believe it. But were his demons hers?

The day moved at a snail's pace, the hours crawling by as the weather worsened. For two hours Rachel walked the floors, longing for Emmett to return, too edgy to settle down for more than a couple of minutes at a time. By the time he finally did return, windblown and even more taciturn, her nerves had only shredded further; she felt ready to scream with frustration and tension. The heaviness of the air, the approaching storm, the steady, nerve-wracking whoosh of the wind, combined to give her an unreasoning sense of doom. Disaster seemed about to befall her, that wretched Greek tragedy that she so wanted to avoid.

She spent more than an hour sitting in the living room across from Emmett, watching him out of the corner of her eyes. Not a word was exchanged. Emmett, always slightly taciturn, had become monosyllabic, leaning back in a straight chair and keeping his cool, wary gaze on the book in his lap. During the hour they sat there she never once saw him turn a page.

The house was getting darker and darker, but neither of them made any effort to turn on a light. The wind was picking up in force, and Rachel could barely restrain a tiny shudder of apprehension. The tense atmosphere of the room only added to the clawing panic that was building inside her, but she wasn't going to ask Emmett for help this time. She was going to keep as far away from him as possible until some semblance of sanity returned to her enfeebled brain.

To her amazement Emmett finally turned a page in the thick, hardcover thriller he was ostensibly reading. That studied, deliberate movement was the last straw, and Rachel knew she couldn't sit still a minute longer without going out of her mind. Jumping to her feet, she knocked over the glass of iced tea that had balanced, forgotten, on the armrest. Emmett looked up, absolutely no expression on his face, watching her as she made an ineffectual effort at mopping up the tea that spread in a puddle over the rough pine floor.

"I think I'll take a nap," she said breathlessly. She had to get away from him, away from those wary hazel eyes that looked right through her, away from that tanned, compact body that she should have been scarcely aware of. She didn't dare go for a walk; with her luck she'd be just out of reach of the cottage when a tidal wave would hit. The open Land Rover was equally suspect, and the kitchen provided little protection.

"Good idea," Emmett growled, turning back to his book. "I'll be going out for a couple of hours; we can have dinner when I get back."

"You're . . . going out?" She couldn't keep the forlorn note out of her voice, and almost against his will a smile curved Emmett's cynical mouth. "Could I go with you?" Being trapped in the narrow confines of the Land Rover with him was the last thing she wanted, but she was even more frightened of the incipient storm than her incomprehensible longing for her brother.

"'Fraid not. I've got too much to do in too short a time, and I can't have my kid sister tagging along with me." His voice was cool, almost bored, and implacable. For the first time she began to feel like a kid sister, importunate and in the way.

There was no way she could continue with her pleas. "All right." Her tone matched his for coolness. "I assume you'll come rescue me if a hurricane hits?"

"You assume right. Go take a nap, Rachel. You probably won't even know I'm gone, and you might possibly sleep through the storm, if you're lucky."

"You mean you'll be gone during the storm?" It came out in a panicked shriek that she couldn't help.

Emmett closed his book with a sigh, looking across at her in the darkening room. "I'll be back, Rachel. Nothing's going to hurt you."

"You promise?" She was unconvinced.

He hesitated for a long, uncomfortable moment, and she had the impression he was weighing his every word. "I'll do the absolute best I can not to let you get hurt, kid," he said finally. He opened his mouth to add something, then closed it abruptly.

He should have followed it with his customary instruction, "Trust me." But he hadn't; something had stopped him, something that Rachel couldn't begin to fathom. She hesitated, then offered it unasked. "I trust you, Emmett."

Was it pain that darkened his face for a moment? She couldn't tell in the shadowy room. "Go take your nap kid," he said, dismissing her. With a small, lost shrug, she went.

A nap might not have been the best possible idea either, she realized forty-five minutes later, lying flat on her back on her narrow bed. The sunburn had lessened enough to make that position comfortable, and staring at the ceiling was definitely preferable to staring at her rumpled pillow. Emmett had left a few minutes ago—the noise of the Land Rover starting up had wrenched her out of the first few moments of the sleep that had so stubbornly eluded her. There was no way she would get back to sleep, she thought wearily. The wind around the cottage was picking up, the waves had crescendoed to a muffled roar, and she was alone and lonely, and quite as miserable as anyone had ever been. There was nothing she could do but lie there and wait for a sleep that wouldn't come. At least it would keep her free from disturbing dreams. She could concentrate on what she was going to do when she got back. This extended holiday was all well and good, but she had a living to make. If the idea of returning to her job was less than enthralling, those were simply the breaks. A few days of hearing people with real problems would soon wipe out her self-indulgence.

There was Mrs. del Gado, with thirteen children and advanced breast cancer. There was Marty Halprin, so prone to destructive rages that he hadn't been able to hold a job for more than three months in all his forty-five years. And there was Robbie, young-old Robbie, abused by her father at age five, a runaway at ten, a prostitute at twelve. She was fifteen now, and worn out by life's battles. The very thought of her made Rachel shrink in shame.

All her problems were of her own making, and she could damn well unmake them. She had been a coward too long—it was past time for her to face up to the mess

she'd made. And she would, just as soon as she caught a
little bit of sleep. Turning into her pillow, she closed her
eyes for a brief moment as the storm raged outside.

He was there with her, as she knew he would be once
she fell asleep. He looked like Emmett, talked like Emmett, but he wasn't her brother. Of that she was irrevo-
cably certain. He was leaning against the foot of the
narrow iron bedstead, and his hazel eyes were no longer
wary or unreadable, and those hands, those large, beautiful hands that could never belong to a Chandler,
reached for her.

He was hazy and insubstantial as he stretched out beside her, a demon lover come to claim his earthbound
bride. He kissed her, but she couldn't feel his mouth on
hers. Her clothes were gone, yet she hadn't felt him remove them. She was alone with him, at his mercy, lying
on the bed aching for him to come to her, but the slow,
sensuous touch never connected with her hungry skin.
Wrapping her in his arms, he cradled her against him,
and still she was lost, lost in a cocoon of emptiness.
"Please," she whispered against the strong neck she
could see but not feel.

"Please what?" She knew his voice, strong and rough
and strangely tender.

"Please," she begged again. "I need you. I can't feel
you, can't touch you. Please, let me."

His lips brushed hers, maddeningly, and she thought
she could just begin to taste their warmth. "Please,
who?" he prompted in her ear. She could feel his breath
hot on her, but his mouth still seemed locked away.

"No," she moaned. "I can't."

"Yes, you can, Rachel. Tell me who it is you want. Say
my name, Rachel, and I'll be there." The lips brushed
hers again, maddeningly, and she could feel him parting

her legs. But she couldn't feel him, his hands, his strong tanned body, his mouth.

"No," she said one last time. He was the demon lover, come to claim her, and if she spoke his name out loud her soul would be lost.

He drew himself up, looming over her, dark and mysterious, yet someone she knew so well and loved so well. "My name, Rachel," he demanded in a strong, husky whisper, and she could feel the tension trapped in that voice. And suddenly it no longer mattered; she had to shatter the invisible barrier that kept him from her, and if she lost everything in the doing, it would still be worth it.

"Emmett," she whispered, her voice filled with love and longing and unshed tears. "Emmett, love me."

Suddenly the tiny bedroom exploded. A bright flash of light illuminated the room; the rumble of a hundred angry gods deafened her. She sat up, screaming in panic, to stare at her darkened room. She was fully dressed, alone, and shattered. Another flash of lightning streaked across the black landscape, followed by the roar of thunder far too close for her peace of mind.

"It's all right," she said out loud in a shaking voice, hoping vainly that the sound of her voice would banish some of the panic. "It was only a dream. The storm woke you up. It was only a dream." Balancing on one trembling elbow, it was all she could do to reach over for the light. There was a soft click and absolutely nothing happened.

For a moment Rachel stared at the light numbly. The power must have gone off, she thought dazedly, climbing out of bed. She would have to find candles, matches, some way to keep the darkness at bay. Where was Emmett when she needed him?

It was warmer now, and the jeans were clinging humidly to her long legs. Stripping off her clammy clothes, she pulled on the faithful yellow sun dress, its soft cotton folds settling loosely around her fevered body. The air was thick, hot, and damp; the incipient violence of the weather hung heavy in the air.

The living room was only slightly lighter than her pitch-dark bedroom. She had no idea what time it was, didn't really care. All that mattered was that she was alone in a rickety old cottage during what sounded to her frightened ears like a typhoon at the least, and she could rely on no one but herself. A little light would help, she thought, keeping her eyes averted from the angry ocean outside the front windows. A few candles, and maybe hunt around for something strong and soothing to drink. If worse came to worse, she could take the new bottle of rum Harris had brought by, return to her bedroom, and drink herself into such a stupor that the storm would be no more than a minor irritation.

Another bolt of lightning sizzled by, followed by another crash of thunder, and Rachel dashed into the kitchen. "One more of those," she muttered shakily, rummaging through a kitchen drawer she could barely see, "and I won't answer for the consequences." There was an answering rumble from the sky, a dare if she ever heard one. Perhaps God was going to punish her for her sinful thoughts. She couldn't deny she deserved it.

No matches in that drawer, nor candles either. Slamming it shut, she pulled out the next one, shoving her hand into it without thinking.

Another bolt of lightning illuminated the dark, menacing figure that watched her from the doorway. Her hand caught on the wickedly sharp knife that lay point out in the drawer, and the thunder crashed about them like the judgment of God.

Rachel screamed, and then slumped forward in something very close to a faint.

Chapter Thirteen

Emmett was there to catch her before she fell. She felt the familiar warmth of him against her face, the scent of the hot tropical rain emanating from his cotton shirt, and her fingers clung tightly to his shoulders. His voice was low, caressing, ever so slightly mocking in her ear. "Was that an actual faint, kid? I didn't know you could be so gothic."

She nodded her head, then cradled it back against his neck. "You scared me," she admitted in a small voice. "I didn't hear you come in."

"I would have had to be a herd of elephants to be heard over this din." Another crash of thunder punctuated his point, and Rachel shivered uncontrollably. "It's all right, Rachel," he murmured gently, and his breath was hot and damp by her ear. "Nothing's going to hurt you."

She stood very still in the circle of his arms, afraid to move, afraid to breathe. One of his hands cupped her neck, the thumb absently stroking the delicate skin of her throat as he held her against his shoulder. The other was around her waist, pressing her slender, trembling body against his, holding her against the solid strength of him. Something seemed to flow between them, a tangible heat that started in the pit of Rachel's stomach, spread downward, and turned her shattered nerve endings to liquid fire. She could feel his strong, muscled thighs pressed against her, the broad back that sheltered her from the angry elements, the comforting shoulder where she could hide from the world. Her arms were around him, her fingers kneading the tight muscles of his back without her even realizing it as he tensed in her hold.

His heart was beating as rapidly as hers in the small, dark kitchen, and the breath that feathered her hair was coming more swiftly now. With a surprising gentleness the hand that cupped her neck reached around and caught her chin, forcing her to look up at him through the darkness. That closed, unreadable expression that usually haunted his hazel eyes was gone, banished seemingly forever. He was looking down at her with intent, white-hot desire, only distantly tinged with doubt.

"Rachel," he whispered in the rain-swept night. "What are you doing to me?"

Her eyes widened as guilt swept over her. Guilt, but no revulsion, no horror. Even that was denied her. She stood there, trapped in the shelter of his arms by his strength and her own weakness, as he continued to watch her out of passion-dark eyes. And then his head dropped, his cynical mouth moved to take hers, and she was mesmerized, waiting for the possession of his lips.

The streak of lightning was like the wrath of God exploding in the kitchen. Rachel tore herself out of the dubious protection of his arms with an anguished cry, panic and despair sweeping over her. She stared at him for a long, horrified moment, and then she ran from the room, her bare feet swift and silent on the rough wood floor.

She slammed the bedroom door behind her, leaning against it, breathless from fear and confusion. There was no way she could continue to deny it—she was in love with Emmett, desperately, unequivocally in love with him, and she wanted him more than she had ever wanted anyone in her entire life. And through some tragic twist of fate he seemed to want her too, no matter how forbidden such a longing was.

She had hesitated long enough, playing with fire, and now was in grave danger of being consumed in the conflagration. She had to leave, now, tonight, before the inevitable happened. She had no desire to play Antigone to her brother.

Ignoring the storm, the darkness, the throbbing pain of her lacerated hand, she began throwing all her clothes into the suitcase she'd dumped on her bed. They didn't all quite fit, and she left the remainder strewn about the pitch-black room before she zipped the bag. There was no sound from the room beyond, and she could only hope that Emmett, recognizing what had almost happened between them, was making himself scarce. She only had to make it as far as the Land Rover without seeing him. Uncle Harris could find a bed for her for the night, or Father Frank could provide even better sanctuary. And with the first plane tomorrow morning she'd be far, far away.

Yanking the suitcase off the bed, she ignored the pain in her hand. She flung open the bedroom door and headed toward the porch; the living room was lit by the soft glow of a kerosene lamp. Emmett was standing by the kitchen, watching her out of hooded eyes. "What do you think you're doing?" he drawled, that cool, mocking voice back in force.

"I'm leaving." She hesitated a moment too long, still mesmerized by him.

"Don't be ridiculous!" he snapped. "What did I do to send you storming off like a prima donna?"

"Nothing," she said. "You did nothing." She raised tear-filled eyes to his, no longer hiding all the misery and love she'd done her best to deny. "Don't you realize? It's me, not you. I have to leave." She all but ran from the door.

She had just managed to pull it open when he was there, slamming it shut with enough force to crack the windows. "You're not going anywhere." She was backed up against the wall, his arms on either side of her holding her captive against the hard wood. "You may not have noticed, but there's a storm going on, and the Land Rover doesn't have a roof. Not to mention that some of the roads are washed out. You're going to stay right here and we'll work this out."

He was too close to her—she could feel the warmth of his body penetrate her chilled bones. "No," she moaned. "I'll walk if I have to. Let me go, Emmett, please."

He moved a hand from its imprisoning hold on the door to run it exasperatedly through his shaggy hair. "Rachel, be sensible. . . ."

She took the opening he gave her, darting once more for the door. He caught her in an iron grip, yanking her against the wiry tension of his body. And then it was too late.

His head moved down, his mouth taking hers in a kiss that held the passion of a thousand years as his body molded against her trembling frame. His lips were hard and hungry as he fought against her resistance, and he pulled his head away for a moment, looking down into her desperate eyes with no pity at all. "Open your mouth, Rachel," he said.

And closing her eyes, she did, sliding her helpless arms around his body, pulling him closer against her yearning form. Just once, she told herself. Just this once. And she gave herself up to the searching demand of his kiss.

Once he'd gained her acquiescence he seemed in no hurry as he pressed her against the door. He took her mouth slowly, his tongue tracing random, delicate patterns on the soft, sensitive skin of her lip before delving between the ineffectual barrier of her small white teeth. She moaned softly, brokenly, as her tongue shyly caught his, and his murmur of approval sent a shaft of flaming desire shooting through her. And suddenly the tempo of the kiss changed, his tongue thrusting, taking, demanding her response, a response she found herself giving as she clung helplessly to his broad back.

His hands left the door to travel down the curve of her back, cupping her firm buttocks and pulling her up against him. The feel of him was hard and strong against her trembling hips; the lips that moved from her mouth to leave a trail of hot, damp kisses to her ear was one more demoralizing instrument of her destruction. Her knees were weak, her legs seemed scarcely capable of supporting her trembling body, and she wanted to sink to the floor, pulling him with her, pulling that strong, tough body over hers, into hers. She wanted him, all of him, completely, now and forever.

Her sudden panic took him by surprise. One moment she was trembling and pliant in his arms, in another she had shoved him off balance. He fell back, willingly enough, to watch her from a bare few inches away. She was leaning against the door, panting in panic and desire, her eyes wide with fear, looking like a trapped animal. "No, Emmett," she whispered brokenly. "For God's sake, you're my brother. No." And before he could stop her she whirled around and ran out into the rain-swept night.

As usual she'd chosen the wrong shoes. The high-heeled sandals buckled beneath her before she'd gotten halfway to the Land Rover, and she sprawled in the sand. She didn't take time to slip them off—a moment later she was on her feet and running again, soaked to the skin by the pouring rain, flinching in the face of the lightning that streaked across the angry sky. But the fury of the elements was preferable to the cottage, preferable to the wondrous shelter of Emmett's arms, preferable to—

The hand that caught her arm was iron, bruising her as it flung her around to face him. He looked brutal in the driving rain, his face grim, and the last tenuous bit of control snapped. She struggled like a wild animal, kicking, biting, hitting, crying helplessly. "No, Emmett. No, no, no!"

The other hand caught her arm, holding her tightly, the fingers digging into the soft flesh as he shook her until her bones rattled. "Stop it, Rachel!" he shouted over the noise of the storm. She ignored him, struggling to escape all the more, and he shook her again, more violently. "Stop it!" he yelled at her. "I'm not your brother!"

It took a moment for the words to penetrate. Slowly her struggles ceased, slowly she raised her head to look at him in a disbelieving stupor. "What did you say?" Her voice was hoarse, strangled.

There was no emotion on his face. The rain poured down on them, covering his set face in sheets of water, but he made no effort to wipe it away. "I said I'm not your brother."

She became very still, and she saw rather than felt his hands drop from their crushing grip on her arms. The marks of his fingers were white against the tan, and soon they'd be purple, she thought abstractedly. Raising her head, she looked at him woodenly through the pouring rain. "Who are you, then?"

What was one more lie among so many? he thought wearily. "My name is Jake Addams."

"Uncle Harris knows?" He didn't even have a chance to respond. "Of course he does. This was probably his idea." All traces of emotion had left her. She stood there, a cold, empty shell, watching the man who had lied to her out of bitter, unseeing eyes.

Now she understood the wariness that lurked about his unreadable face. "Come back to the house," he said, raising a hand to her and then dropping it in the face of her disbelieving grimace. "You've hurt yourself—it needs bandaging. I promise I won't touch you."

She looked down absently. Even the steady streams of rain couldn't wash the streaks of blood that had run in rivulets down her hand. She looked at him again. "If you did, I would kill you," she said very calmly. And slipping off the high-heeled sandals, she walked slowly back to the cottage, keeping well away from the man beside her, the only reality the feel of the wet, gritty sand beneath her bare feet. It was the only reality she wanted for the moment.

She stood in the middle of the living room, the thin cotton dress clinging wetly to her body, staring about her in blessedly numb disbelief. The man she had thought of as Emmett had disappeared after closing the door behind them, closing the storm out of the cottage, leaving a far more devastating storm trapped inside. A moment later he was back, bandages and iodine in his hand.

"Sit on the couch," he ordered in a subdued voice. She considered him, favoring him with a cool, untouched glare, and then complied. Her knees were scraped by the sand, and the thin sundress was soaking wet, the cold dampness making her nipples harden, pressing against the thin material. He knelt in front of her, and she could see his gaze brush her breasts, then look quickly away. She could only hope it bothered him as much as it did her. The glancing heat of his gaze only seemed to accentuate it.

"How did you cut your hand?" He kept his voice low, unemotional, as he washed away the blood. There was a moderately deep score on the tip of one finger, surprisingly small for the amount of blood it had produced.

"On a knife in the kitchen drawer." She suffered his ministrations stoically.

"I warned you about that. Sharp knives don't belong in kitchen drawers; they should be hanging up."

"I don't give a damn about where you keep your kitchen knives," Rachel said in that same cool, distant voice. "I want to know what happened to the real Emmett. Is he dead?"

The man sat back on his heels, eyeing her warily. "I don't think so."

"You don't think so?" Rachel echoed, lightly mocking. "Didn't it occur to you that he might show up, then? Denounce you and Uncle Harris and your cozy little scheme?"

"Believe it or not, that's what we had in mind. Why do you suppose we chose Kauai for Emmett's reappearance? It's the last place he was seen, and there have been rumors over the past few months that he's still here." His voice was more than reasonable.

"So you're doing this out of the goodness of your heart? To encourage the real Emmett to show up and claim his inheritance? I wouldn't have pegged you as a philanthropist," she snapped.

He looked up at her then. "No?" he countered coolly. "What did you have me pegged as?"

She opened her mouth to reply, then shut it again. She took a deep breath, reaching for that marvelous, unfeeling numbness that had washed over her at his announcement. It was fading fast, in its place a white hot anger so strong that it threatened to overwhelm her. "I think you'd prefer I spare you those kind of words, Mr.... *Addams*, was it? They wouldn't sound very fitting, coming from your little sister." She leaned forward, brushing the sand from her scraped knees, not even wincing at the stinging pain. "I'll take care of these," she said, holding out her hand for the iodine. The hand was trembling slightly, a fact the man opposite her couldn't help but notice. Mercifully he said nothing, merely placing the small red bottle in her outstretched hand.

She began painting her knees with the stinging red stuff, part of her welcoming the pain, giving the job her complete attention. "So tell me, what were you planning to do once my real brother showed up?" she queried with deceptive gentleness. "Bow out gracefully? And what if he never did bother to reappear? I don't suppose a man of your sterling character would have been even slightly tempted by the millions of dollars Emmett Chandler is heir to. It would be a simple enough matter to pass inspection, what with the major executor of the estate swearing you're his long-lost nephew, and the besotted sister ready to say the same thing. Or did such crass considerations never enter your mind?"

"I can't say they did," he replied, for once completely truthful. Her answering snort attested to her reaction. He was still squatting in front of her, watching her out of eyes as stormy as the windswept Pacific.

Rachel leaned back against the couch, ignoring the shiver that swept over her. The man in front of her saw it, but had the sense not to offer any assistance. Rachel was strung up as tightly as a spring, and if he so much as touched her without permission, she could shatter into a million pieces. "So tell me, Jake Addams, how did you get into this line of work? What have you been doing for the past few years?"

That drawl put an end to the check he'd been keeping on his temper. She recognized the combative light that flared in his eyes, and welcomed it. She didn't need his kindness or his pity—she was much safer with his anger.

"I spent six of the last eight months in prison." His voice was cool and controlled. "Before that I spent most of my time traveling." All strictly true, he thought wearily. One cardinal rule in this sort of game: Stick as close to the truth as possible, and you're less likely to get caught.

"Sounds productive," she scoffed. "And what was Harris going to give you in return for this impersonation? Besides Emmett Chandler's sister?"

"You forget, you arrived here unwanted and unasked," he snapped. "I tried more times than I can remember to get rid of you, so there's no need to act quite so betrayed."

"Isn't there?" she countered in a very low voice. He could hear the pain in her voice, and it cut through him like a knife. "What is Uncle Harris giving you?"

"Two hundred and fifty thousand if Emmett shows up."

"And if he doesn't?"

He met her gaze calmly. "One million if I can convince the other executors, impersonate Emmett for a year, and then manage to stage a convincing accident."

"Admirable. Quite a tidy amount of money for a drifter and a convict," she murmured. "It would definitely be to your advantage if Emmett stays lost."

"Not really. The quarter of a million is a sure thing, pretty easy to earn. Or it was, until you showed up," he drawled. "The full sum is a lot trickier. I've always been one to feel a bird in the hand is worth two in the bush."

"Since we're dealing with clichés, what about it takes a thief to catch a thief?" Another shiver swept over her damp, chilled body, and she sat upright. "You know something, Jake Addams?"

"What?"

"I don't believe you. Uncle Harris might, but now that I know just how deceitful you are, I don't trust you for a moment. If you're really doing this for something as simple as a chunk of money, then I really am your kid sister." She leaned back again, her triumphant expression at odds with the lost, lonely eyes.

"I can hardly tell you to believe me, can I?" He stood up then, stretching against the fitful kerosene light, the muscles working against the damp, tight jeans and the rain splashed khaki shirt. Her eyes followed the strong, tough lines of his body, and she realized she still wanted it. Boiled in oil, drawn and quartered, she reminded herself, to no avail. "You'll just have to decide what's the truth." She knew he was aware of her scrutiny, had probably deliberately stretched in front of her to remind her of what she'd been panting over earlier, she thought in disgust. Well, never again.

They both heard the engine in the distance, and they stayed motionless, listening as the car slid to a stop in the mud outside the cottage, waiting as the door slammed and a rain- and mud-soaked Harris pounded up the front steps and into the living room, shaking like a large, wet dog. His bloodshot eyes were soulful as they surveyed the inhabitants of the room, but he was too far into the rum to notice the tension.

"It is not," he announced, "a fit night out for man or beast. I thought I'd better come and check on my favorite niece and nephew and make sure they weren't swept out to sea. It's damned inconvenient that you don't have a phone, Emmett. I've told you—"

"Don't call him that."

Harris turned to eye his water-soaked niece with bleary surprise. "I beg your pardon, Rachel?"

"I said don't call him Emmett."

Harris turned to the man, an eyebrow raised. "What's she babbling on about, dear boy? Is she quite all right? The storm..."

"She's fine," He replied shortly. "She knows."

"Knows what?" Harris looked shifty, stalling for time.

"Knows what we've been doing here the past three weeks," he drawled. "Knows I'm not her brother."

"My dear boy, I have no idea what you're talking about," Harris maintained stoutly.

"She knows because I told her everything." His voice was implacable, and Harris Chandler's face fell in dismay.

"For heaven's sake, man, why did you do that?" he managed after a long moment. He snatched a quick glance at his niece's set expression, then turned back to the man. "There was no need to bring her in on it."

A bitter smile lit his closed face. "There was every need. You want a drink? Stupid question; of course you do. I could use one myself. What about you, Rachel?"

"No." She wasn't going to accept anything from him.

"You really ought to, you know," Harris attempted. "You'll catch your death."

"Your thoughtfulness overwhelms me." She bit the words off. "What have you done to find the real Emmett?"

Harris blanched before her sudden attack. "Well, we have tried, haven't we, dear boy?" he said defensively. "We tried to see your precious priest both today and yesterday, but he's been damnably elusive. He's our only lead."

"My priest?"

"Father Murphy. Word has it that he was seen talking with your brother sometime in the last few months. We can't get near enough to him to find out whether that's typical island rumor or something more substantial."

"I'll ask him." She rose, barely controlling the shiver that racked her slender body.

"Er...Rachel," Harris mumbled nervously, "what do you plan to do?"

"About what?"

"About me. Us. Our little plan? The bank won't take kindly to my machinations—I doubt they'd see them in the light they're intended. Are you going to expose us?" The man she had known as Emmett had paused by the door, and he was watching her out of calmly curious eyes, as if the answer to Harris's nervous question had no effect on his future whatsoever.

Rachel smiled coldly. "I don't know yet. I'll have to sleep on it."

"Uh...do you want a ride back to the hotel? I imagine I could find a room for you."

"There's no need, Uncle. I'm planning to stay right here." She moved toward her bedroom, picking up her abandoned suitcase as she went. She was gratified to see she had finally shaken some emotion out of Jake Addams's still face, though she still wasn't quite sure what it was.

"Here?" Harris echoed in a strangled voice.

"Certainly. If Emmett is ever going to show up, I expect it will be in the next few days, and I expect it will be to you that he'll make his appearance. I wouldn't put it past the two of you to do away with him when no one's looking. I intend to stick like glue. If my brother is on this island, I want to be sure I have a chance to see him before he goes up in smoke once more."

"Rachel!" Harris was shocked. "We wouldn't hurt Emmett. For heaven's sake girl, have some trust!"

Her laugh was short, ugly, and on the verge of tears as she made her way to her bedroom. Still the man she had thought of as Emmett stood there, leaning against the kitchen door, his distant eyes watching her. He stayed there until she closed her bedroom door, and then he turned and continued into the kitchen, pouring himself a drink strong enough to make even Harris blanch. And without a word he strode past his conspirator, out into the stormy night, and stood watching the ocean, his face a shuttered mask.

Chapter Fourteen

Great exits are one thing, she decided disconsolately. The problem was, if you forgot something in the drama of your departure, it was damned hard to go back and retrieve it. She stood behind her closed bedroom door, letting her eyes get slowly accustomed to the inky darkness, and wished to God she had commandeered the kerosene lamp. Let those two villains sit in darkness, she thought sourly. But it was too late—she wasn't about to make another appearance that night. She had had just about all she could take; one more look at Jake Addams's cynical, wary face and she would probably lose the tenuous hold on her self-control and...

What? she demanded of herself with a wry twist of her mouth. Throw herself on the floor and indulge in the strong hysterics that greatly appealed to her at the moment? Hurl herself at Emmett-Jake and try to wipe that unfeeling expression from his face? Tempting as the latter thought might be, Rachel already knew she wouldn't get far. She was strong, and reveled in her strength, but she was no match for his compact toughness. She would quickly find herself overpowered, and that would make things very much worse. She already felt painfully powerless and vulnerable.

Dropping her suitcase on the chair, she moved carefully across the tiny room to the rumpled bed, sinking down on it with sudden exhaustion. She had no idea what time it actually was—she hadn't bothered to look at a clock when she had woken up what seemed like a century ago. Besides, as far as she remembered all the clocks in the house were electric.

Looking out her window at the storm-tossed countryside was no help either. In the rain-swept darkness it could have been four in the afternoon or the morning. With a sigh she pulled the pillows into a pile behind her, resting her head against the iron bedstead. Sleep would be damnably long in coming; she resigned herself to the fact. She couldn't decide which was preferable to concentrate on: the stinging pain of her scraped knees and lacerated hand, or the more devastating injury to her heart and trust.

There was no sound from the room beyond, no whispering from the conspirators, no furtive movements, though Rachel wasn't certain she would have heard them anyway. The storm made an admirable cover for nefarious activities. They could always decide to drop her over the Na Pali cliffs, she thought idly. After all, the Chandler millions were more than motive enough for something as minor as murder. They may have already found Emmett, silenced him effectively, and...

No, she decided fairly. The man calling himself Jake Addams might be an amoral, cold-blooded jailbird, but he wasn't a murderer. When it came right down to it, she wasn't certain she believed he was amoral, or even a jailbird. And perhaps, she thought, a stray hand brushing her lips, not cold blooded either. He didn't need to tell her; he could have let her continue thinking she was desperately in love with her own brother. Exactly why did he tell her the truth?

If truth it was. One blessed relief in the whole matter: the moment he'd told her he wasn't her brother that burning overwhelming attraction died as swiftly as it was born. So much for eternal love, she thought with a tiny shrug of her shoulders. It hadn't borne up under such intensive duplicity, even if it had withstood the strain of incipient incest. The moment the words "I'm not your brother" were out, the fires that had threatened to consume her had died into cold, wet ashes, leaving her numb with pain and betrayal.

That icy numbness hadn't lasted nearly long enough, she sighed. It had turned into a white-hot fury in minutes, a white-hot fury that wasn't allowing her to think straight, to sort through the maze of lies and half-lies to find out what she really believed. She needed to replace that intense rage with a cool, deliberate anger that was strong enough to keep her from getting hurt again and reasonable enough to help her find the real Emmett.

Leaning forward, she pulled her knees up to her body, suppressing a small moan when the scraped skin protested against the movement, and reached for the cotton blanket at the foot of the bed. She draped it around her chilled, wet shoulders before leaning back. And what was the truth? Certainly not what the man had told her, she knew that much. The moment doubt had entered her mind a great many things had become clear. She was usually far from gullible, though she did her best to accept people for what they were. But she had been blinded by her delight in finding Emmett once more, blinded by her stupid infatuation for that . . . that con man.

She didn't believe he was in it for the money. Not that she suspected him of any humanitarian motives, either.

But now that the blinders were off and she could see him clearly she was developing a much-belated sixth sense about him. If his name was Jake Addams then hers was Mae West. And if he was out for money he never would have let her stay, never would have told her the truth without far greater provocation than her throwing herself at his feet.

The prison story didn't ring true either. Or maybe she just didn't want it to ring true, she thought, prodding her already lacerated self-esteem. *Are you looking for excuses, Rachel? So he doesn't look like a hard-core criminal who just got out of jail. Looks, as you very well know, can be deceiving. And the ability to deceive innocents like yourself is part and parcel of the trade.*

Was she making a mistake, staying on here? She was a lamb in a den of very experienced wolves who probably wouldn't think twice about devouring her if she got in their way. Uncle Harris had always been charmingly, blearily amoral. Jake-Emmett had stopped her from running off into the night, but if push came to shove and she was a real threat to him and a million dollars, would he feel any such compulsion? Would he feel any regret?

The windows rattled with the force of the wind; a bolt of lightning illuminated the room, followed by the inevitable roll of thunder. Rachel slid down against the pillows, wrapping the blanket more tightly about her. Where was Emmett? Was he watching all this, laughing at their ridiculous charades? She wouldn't put it past him—he had always had Henry Emmett's somewhat disconcerting sense of humor.

But if he was still alive, if he was there on the island, she would find him, with or without those two felons' help. She would also find out exactly whom she had been sharing a house with for the last few days, whom she had shared a bed with. What she would do with the information, she still hadn't decided.

It was a blessed relief, she thought, snuggling down further into the warm bed, that she no longer wanted him. Heavenly to be free from that aching, burning need that had threatened to consume her, wonderful that it had been replaced with a cool, calculated anger. Never again would she be vulnerable to him, never again would she shiver and tremble with wanting when he looked at her out of those unfathomable hazel eyes. Thank God, she thought sleepily, her hands reaching to delicately brush her bruised lips. She didn't even feel the brand of him on her mouth, couldn't even remember that shattering demand of his kiss. Could no longer feel the hard, strong imprint of his body against hers as he'd held her against the door.

All she knew was the raging storm outside, the sleepiness brought on by emotional exhaustion, and the warm, pulsing feeling in her body as, ignoring her mind's stern orders, it replayed that devastating embrace. And then she was asleep.

IT WAS VERY STILL and quiet when she woke up, and for a moment she lay there, huddled in the cotton blanket, trying to remember what was different.

Her first realization was a pleasant one. The storm had passed; the silence was only broken by the soft swish-swish of the palm trees, the cries of the birds, the distant sound of the surf. It was still very early—the sunlight pouring in her window had barely come over the horizon. She considered pulling the blanket back over her head, when the second wave of memory bit her. And then she was fully awake.

A hot shower, a cup of good coffee, she decided, before she faced the myriad problems this day would bring. She wouldn't even think about it till she felt more human, but heaven help Jake Addams if he got in her way before she was ready for him.

She needn't have worried. For the first time since she'd arrived, his bedroom door was tightly shut, and there was no sign of him lounging lazily on the front porch, none of that hideous stuff he called coffee sitting on the old gas stove. The power had come back on sometime during the night—the recalcitrant electric clock was moving merrily backward. Moving in a fog, Rachel started the coffee, wincing slightly at the pain in her finger, then wandered into the bathroom.

It was the longest shower she had ever taken, and she needed every minute of it to brush the cobwebs out of her brain. She could only hope she took all the hot water, and that Emmett . . . *No, damn it, his name is Jake. Maybe.* Anyway, she could only hope he wanted to take one too. A blast of cold water would do wonders for his sensibilities, she thought, scrubbing her scalp with needless energy.

There was still no sign of him as she headed for the front porch, mug of coffee in her hand. She had chosen her clothing quite deliberately, picking her briefest pair of shorts. They exposed every inch of her long, tanned legs, and hugged the round curves of her buttocks in what she could only hope was an enticing manner. It was cooler after the storm, but she still wore only an abbreviated halter top. She wanted to get some early morning sun, she told herself with righteous innocence. She also wanted to make him suffer.

Shaking her thick wet hair around her shoulders, she took a seat on the bottom step of the porch, took a deep, grateful swig of the coffee, and surveyed the morning.

It was absurdly beautiful. The bright sun was climbing in the deep blue sky, its glistening rays turning the wet sand into a field of diamonds. The tangled jungle that surrounded the cottage shimmered in the brightness; crystal drops of moisture beading the deep green leaves. It was a fresh, new world, just born from the raging torrent of the night before, and even the birds that wheeled about in the sky seemed younger, happier, more beautiful. Stretching out her long legs in front of her, Rachel leaned her elbows on an upper step, cupping the mug of coffee in her slender hands. Small hands, she thought, like all Chandlers. Why hadn't she realized when she'd noticed his beautiful, long-fingered hands? No Chandler ever had hands like that.

That was the wrong thing to think about, she told herself sternly, ignoring the sudden warmth that started just below the pit of her stomach at the thought of those hands. Don't think about his body, think about his lies.

That was easier said than done when the vibration of his footsteps could be felt in the small of her back. She heard the screen door open behind her, but she kept her face out toward the ocean, determined not to give him the benefit of her attention.

Of course, she hadn't expected him to ignore her. Without a glance in her direction he bounded down the stairs, heading straight out toward the ocean. He was wearing the faded cutoffs, most likely as a sop to her presence, she thought irritably, and unwillingly her eyes drank in the sight of his tanned, broad back and his muscled legs, with their fine covering of golden hair. He walked straight into the ocean, diving through the surf and swimming out, away from her, with single-minded concentration. She could see the muscles working in his powerful shoulders as he plowed through the waves, and a small shiver passed over her, one she tried and failed to attribute to her abbreviated attire. Taking another sip of her rapidly cooling coffee, she watched him out of unabashedly hungry eyes. Eyes that could always go carefully blank once he came out of the sea.

If he ever did. Rachel began to feel a stirring of unease as he continued to swim, straight out into the ocean, driven by worse demons than she had ever known. Her mouth went suddenly dry as he disappeared from view behind a swell, and her hand tightened unconsciously on the mug of coffee. What the hell was he thinking of, swimming out so far when the ocean was still rough from the storm? If he thought she would be able to save him, he had another think coming; her swimming abilities were definitely limited—nothing compared to the Olympic-style stroke he was using to eat up the distance. Was this his way of trying to get his own back? Was he going to disappear into the ocean, turn up a mile down the beach and fade into the tangled undergrowth? Or was he going to foolishly overestimate his capacity and end up drowning in front of her eyes? Damn the man, why wouldn't he come back?

He was only about twenty feet from the shore when she saw him next, and the wave of relief that washed over her was completely inappropriate for someone who cared as little as she did. She accepted it stoically enough. Maybe a tiny part of her did care. Anyway, it was only natural not to want to watch someone drown. Simple human courtesy. She wished she'd taken the time to get another cup of coffee while he was swimming; it would have given her something to concentrate on while he walked out of the ocean directly toward her. If she hadn't been so terrified that he'd disappear, she would have. Her temper wasn't improving as she squinted up at him through the bright sunlight.

He moved well, she had to admit that. His muscles were in all the right places and in the right shape, and if his body lacked the golden beach-boy prettiness that she was used to in California, it had a certain tough, battered grace that sat well on his forty years. Or was he forty? she wondered belatedly.

Looking up into his face as he crossed the sand, she was disconcerted for a moment. He looked like hell. His eyes were bloodshot, his chin stubbled, his forehead lined with what seemed like a very bad headache. His whole expression was bleak, cold, and distant, and he stopped a foot away from her perch on the steps, watching her silently. His body was glistening with seawater, sparkling in the sun, and she had a sudden, absurd longing to take him in her arms and tell him it was all right. Absurd indeed. He couldn't care less what she thought.

"There's coffee in the kitchen," she said finally.

"I noticed. I thought you might have added rat poison." He sounded tired, resigned.

She shook her head. "Too fast. I have a longer, slower revenge in mind."

His eyes swept over her scantily clad body, and heat followed in their wake. "So I noticed," he drawled laconically. "Do you want a refill?" Her empty mug was in plain sight.

A refusal sprang to her lips instinctively, and she swallowed it. Some sort of truce would have to be called if they were going to continue on here for a number of days. She wasn't going to go until she had picked both his and Uncle Harris's brains and done her best to find Emmett.

Her best bet would be to aim for a kind of cool impartiality. She held out her mug. "Please."

If she had hoped to fool him for even a moment, she was doomed to disappointment. The amused light in his eyes was unpleasantly mocking. "A cease-fire, is it?"

"For now. And an exchange of information," she added boldly.

"Sounds more and more promising. What have you got to exchange?"

Rachel leaned back against the steps, tossing back her damp mane of hair. It was a good feeling, to have even a small modicum of power over the man in front of her. "Get the coffee," she said lazily. "And then I'll tell you."

Unfortunately his cynical mouth widened in a smile, effectively wiping out her temporary feeling of victory. He didn't say a word; he didn't have to. His body language was eloquent enough.

She had a vague hope he'd take the time to change before bringing the coffee out on the porch, but the hope was in vain. Instead of taking his usual seat at the railing, he came and sat down beside her—at the far end of the steps, to be sure, but still too close for her peace of mind. The water on his body had dried in the early morning sunlight, except for a few errant drops in the thin mat of sandy-colored hair on his chest. It was all Rachel could do to keep her eyes off those drops. She was acutely aware of him, of his body sprawled next to hers, his long, bare legs stretched out beside hers. Perhaps her scanty shorts hadn't been such a good idea after all. It was more than slightly disturbing to be sitting there in the hot sun with both of them wearing a minimum of clothing.

"So what do you have to tell me?" His voice was a casual drawl as he eyed her over the coffee cup. His earlier bleak expression had disappeared, and Rachel had the uncomfortable feeling that it was her barely disguised reaction to him that had cheered him up. She resolved then and there to be as hostile as possible.

"You first. I don't trust you one tiny bit. If I told you what I know, you'd probably tell me it's useless information. You tell me what you know first, and then I'll decide whether it's worth what I know." She kept her voice cool and hostile, but her contemptuousness only seemed to increase his amusement.

"Sounds fair. We know Emmett was last seen here officially in 1969. He was growing dope on the north end of the island, hanging out with various transients, until the police caught wind of his whereabouts." The humor left his eyes for a moment, Rachel felt oddly chilled. "You remember the Cambridge bombings?"

She nodded, wondering why she suddenly felt so cold. "Of course. Emmett was involved in a student radical group connected to the bombings. He was wanted for questioning about the whole thing. Not that he probably knew very much. Emmett, as far as I can remember him, wasn't the most hard-core radical. He was more interested in theory than revolution."

"Theory's fine in its place," he said savagely. "A girl died in that blast."

"I remember," Rachel said softly. The girl had been one of the radicals, and Emmett's current girl friend. She had only been nineteen when she died, and sadly enough, Rachel couldn't even remember her name.

"The government traced him to Kauai, and Emmett went underground. He probably disappeared into the Na Pali cliffs area—they were always a good place for outlaws to hide. He hasn't been seen or heard from since, apart from rumor."

"Do you think he's still there?"

"He could be." He squinted out at the sun-gilded ocean, still choppy from the night's storm. "People have lived there for decades and never been seen. But I think it's more likely he's come back out and reentered life under an alias."

"Wouldn't he leave the island then? Why should he hang around here when this would be the obvious place to start looking?" she argued.

He shrugged, and Rachel's eyes strayed to his broad, bony shoulders. "He probably put down some roots during the last fifteen years. Hell, I don't know. I just have a gut-level feeling he's still here. Couple that with the fact that he's been seen by that priest, the gardener at the church, and a couple of taro farmers, and it's enough to go on."

"He might be married, with children," Rachel mused. "Most people are by the time they're forty." A sudden, horribly unpleasant thought entered her mind, one she tried to shut out by concentrating on her coffee.

"No," he said quietly.

"You don't think he's married?" She looked up curiously.

He shook his head. "No, I don't think so. But that wasn't the question I was answering."

"What question?"

"I'm not married."

"Who cares?"

"You do." He leaned back, very self-assured. "Anyway, I don't think your brother's married, but if he is, it won't make any difference."

She decided to ignore his earlier gibe. "Any difference to whom?" she queried.

He didn't answer. "So, what's your information? Admittedly, ours is pretty sparse, but then, Emmett's an elusive fellow."

The hell with it, she thought. "How old are you?"

He didn't even seem surprised at her sudden question. "The same age as your brother. Forty. Why?"

"And you've never married?"

The corner of his mouth turned up in a wicked smile. "Such curiosity, Miss Chandler. Yes, I've been married. Once, a long, long time ago, in a different world."

"What happened?"

"She disapproved of my profession and she divorced me. I think she's married to an accountant in Wichita."

Rachel tried to stifle a giggle at the incongruity of such a fate, failed, and almost choked in the attempt. "Well, I can't say I blame her. I wouldn't want to be married to a con man either."

"Is that what I am?"

"Aren't you?" She couldn't keep the curiosity out of her voice.

He smiled mysteriously, refusing to be drawn. "Quit stalling, Rachel. What is it you know about Emmett?"

The coffee mug was empty, the rising sun too brilliant to stare at over the ocean, and there was nowhere she could turn her gaze but at the man beside her. He's a liar and a cheat, she reminded herself sternly. Somehow this realization was sinking in with difficulty this morning. Maybe when he put a shirt on she'd have an easier time of it.

"Emmett's sent me birthday presents every year since he's been gone." She dug a toe into the wet sand, concentrating on the random patterns she was drawing.

"You mentioned that." He nodded. "It gave me a few bad moments. What has he sent you?"

"Butterflies." For some reason she scarcely hesitated to tell him something she had told no one else, something precious and private.

"Butterflies?"

"Silk ones, china ones, porcelain ones, silver ones. I used to love butterflies when I was young. I caught one once when I was five—a beautiful yellow and black one with delicate wings. My cousin Harold was visiting, and when I wasn't looking he impaled the butterfly on a pin. When I cried he pulled the beautiful yellow and black wings off it and threw them at me. I was completely shattered; I cried for days and days. Even when Emmett gave Harold a black eye, it didn't help. Ariel thought I was being ridiculous, but Emmett understood. Ever since then butterflies have been a special link between us."

The man beside her rubbed his rough chin thoughtfully. "Were there return addresses?"

"No. But there were postmarks."

"Better than nothing. Do you remember them?" He was suddenly alert, business-like, almost frighteningly so. What did he really want with Emmett?

"Not all of them. And I don't remember the years. The first was Kauai, and then there was Samoa, Australia, Rome, Paris." She hesitated, but he was waiting, his face intent. "The last one was Kauai again."

"I knew it!" His voice was low, triumphant as he leapt to his feet. "I could feel it in my bones." He disappeared into the house, leaving her staring after him. She considered following him, then decided against it. There was still one thing she hadn't told him, one tiny ace up her sleeve.

She was still sitting there when he returned, moving past her without a backward glance. He'd thrown on a rumpled pair of khakis, an aging blue T-shirt and his sunglasses, and the tattered sneakers were underneath his arm.

"Where do you think you're going?" Rachel demanded.

"To find that damned priest and shake Emmett Chandler's whereabouts out of him. I knew he was here, damn it, I knew it. And now that I've got proof I'm not going to let anything stop me."

"Stop you from what?" Her voice was cool, curious, and the man she thought of as Emmett-Jake only spared her a momentary glance.

"You stay put. I'll be back by the afternoon."

"The hell I will. I'm coming with you."

"Wanna bet?" he snapped. "Emmett might have been too much of a pansy to paddle that cute little bottom of yours, but I have no such qualms. Leave that porch and you'll regret it."

He meant it; Rachel had no doubts whatsoever. She also knew that if he put those strong, beautiful hands on her, she would be lost. For the moment discretion was the better part of valor. And retaliation would be deliciously easy. The moment he drove away she would search his room.

Smiling her sweetest smile, she gave him an airy wave. There was no way he would find Emmett that quickly, not after trying for so long. "Have fun," she said in a dulcet tone. "Give my love to Father Frank if you manage to catch up with him."

He was nobody's fool, and her sudden affability set warning bells buzzing in his head. But Emmett Chandler was first priority, and his infuriating, exasperating, delectable little sister could wait a few more hours. "Stay put," he said again. And with more than a few misgivings, he jumped into the rain-swamped Land Rover and drove away.

Chapter Fifteen

Rachel should have known that nothing would be as easy as it should be. She indulged herself for another ten minutes, legs stretched out into the sun, watching the sun-gilded violence of the ocean, still reeling from the storm, as she drained the last few drops of her now cool coffee. Even lukewarm it was better than Emmett's—Jake's—brew, and she had every intention of savoring it to the fullest. She had the entire day in front of her, more than enough time for a leisurely search of his room.

She finally rose, stretching her arms over her head with an inexplicably contented sigh, and headed into the dim, cool confines of the cottage. Only to find his bedroom door securely locked.

"It'll take more than that to keep me out, boyo," she said softly, taking pleasure in the sound of her self-assured voice in the stillness of the house. She had always been more than capable with her hands, and the hinges to that solid door were on the outside. It took her a few minutes to locate a decent screwdriver, another fifteen of swearing and sweating over the rusty screws, but at last victory was hers. Pushing the door carefully, she was able to squeeze through the opening and she stepped into Bluebeard's chamber.

She hadn't taken much notice of it the other night. It had been pitch black most of the time, and she'd been in too much of a hurry to catch up with her supposed brother to pay it much mind in the morning. With him gone it had held little interest to her. Now, however, it was a virtual treasure horde, albeit a far from neat one.

He hadn't slept well last night, that much was obvious. The sheets were pulled from the bed, half on the floor, and the pillows were punched beyond recognition in what appeared to be a fruitless quest for a comfortable position. Clothes festooned every piece of furniture, the ashtray beside the bed was full to overflowing, and crumpled packs of cigarettes littered the floor. Wrinkling her nose in disapproval, she knelt down and began scooping up the trash, then carried the full ashtray and the two half-empty glasses into the kitchen. He had done very well with the housekeeping in the rest of the house; only in his own room had he fallen short. And it wasn't really dirty—there were no cobwebs or dust. Just a casual sort of mess that for some reason Rachel found slightly endearing. She didn't trust a man who was too neat.

She cleaned quickly, efficiently, finding in it an obscure, possibly perverse enjoyment. She searched through every pocket, read every meaningless scrap of paper, dismantled the bed, the chair cushions, his seldom-used shaving kit, the even more disreputable pair of sneakers that lay hidden under the tangled double bed. She found things that amused her—antacids and a paperback novel with the dubious title *The Slaughterer*. She found things that infuriated her—a picture of a very pretty teenage girl and a package of condoms. And she found something that made her melt—the wilted flower she had worn in her hair two nights ago at the bar. She stared at it for a long, perplexed moment, and a part of her wanted to shut the drawer, replace the door on its hinges, and pretend she had never intruded.

And then her resolve hardened. She had probably dropped the flower when she'd come rushing in here like a fool to comfort him during his nightmares. There was little doubt he deserved every nightmare he got, and she wished him many more. She slammed the drawer shut with more force than necessary, moving on to the next one. His story still didn't ring true, and he was unlikely to be the one to enlighten her. Rachel had to rely on her own ingenuity to find out what was behind his game of charades, and she wasn't going to let her soft-hearted romantic streak stop her. It was ridiculous that she should feel guilty, she thought angrily. But as she searched on, the feeling of guilt increased. Until it was wiped clean by the contents of the bottom drawer.

Beneath the neatly folded jeans and the clean T-shirts was a packet of papers containing a passport, issued to a forty-year-old gentleman named Ben O'Hanlon. A man who bore an amazing resemblance to Jake Addams. Also included were various press passes, identifying Ben O'Hanlon as a member in good standing of the fourth estate. And a recent newspaper clipping, complete with grainy photograph, of the same ubiquitous face, and the headline, ''Reporter Released from Terrorist Captivity.''

Folding her legs under her, she sat on the floor, immersed in the story. Ben O'Hanlon, apparently, had been somewhere he shouldn't have been in one of the more repressive South American dictatorships. Someone took exception to his presence, and he disappeared. Only to show up, some six months later, in a more neutral country, where he was whisked back to the States. The account was irritatingly vague, with the promise that more information would be forthcoming from the State Department once O'Hanlon was debriefed, but in the meantime the former captive had gone into seclusion. There were rumors of a book deal, even a possible movie, but for the time being O'Hanlon was mum.

That explained some of it, Rachel thought, refolding the newspaper carefully. The night terrors, the hours he spent on the porch, out in the open air. Prison, indeed! And she'd been gullible enough to believe him.

But it still didn't explain what he wanted with Emmett. As far as she knew, the real Emmett hadn't even ventured near South America in the last fifteen years, or if he had, he didn't stay long. He couldn't be connected with Ben's imprisonment.

Ben. She had to admit she liked the sound of that. It fit him, far better than Jake Addams or Emmett Chandler. She wondered whether it was short for Benjamin or Benson. Probably neither—it had simply read Ben O'Hanlon on the passport. She no longer had any doubts; that was his real name. It had the good, solid ring of truth to it. And it was also more than obvious what he was doing, and it was nothing terribly frightening after all. The article had said he was a well-known investigative reporter, co-winner of a Pulitzer Prize, who'd been in South America doing research for a book on missing radicals from the sixties. He was interested in Emmett for purely professional purposes, and newspaper people were known for protecting their sources. He wouldn't turn a hapless Emmett over to the authorities on a whim.

Pulitzer Prize, she thought as she made herself a salad for lunch. She was traveling in fairly exalted company, even if his recreational literature ran along the lines of *The Slaughterer.*

Of course, there was no reason why he couldn't have told her what he was up to. Once she had tumbled to the fact that he wasn't actually Emmett, he had no reason to keep pretending he was someone else. And she wasn't exactly thrilled with his methods. Impersonation, bordering on criminal fraud, wasn't an admirable way to get a story. No, she wasn't quite ready to call a truce. Not when he'd followed his initial lies with another series of lies just as far-fetched as the first.

She cast only a cursory glance at the door still propped against the wall on her way back out to the porch. It was going to stay right where she left it, with his papers and passport lying neatly on top of his dresser. She was looking forward to his reaction, she thought calmly, setting her lunch on the porch railing. Maybe he'd exhibit the first ounce of shame. Too bad she wouldn't be here to fully enjoy it, but Stephen Ames was taking her out to dinner that night. And she had every intention of going, and rubbing Ben O'Hanlon's nose in it. Taking a sip of her ice tea, she tipped the chair back in unconscious imitation of the subject of her less than convivial thoughts. She was quite prepared to watch him suffer.

As it was, she barely had time to enjoy herself. She was already dressed in the slinky gold dress, her thick, sun-streaked chestnut hair in a loose bun at the nape of her neck, waiting on the porch for her date, when Ben pulled in beside the cottage. He sat for a moment, oblivious to his audience, his arms resting on the steering wheel, his head bowed as he rubbed a weary hand across his forehead. And then he looked up, directly into her limpid gaze.

"What the hell are you all dressed up for?" he growled, pulling himself out of the Land Rover with noticeable effort.

She smiled sweetly. "I've got a date, remember? Stephen Ames, Uncle Harris's friend."

He looked even more disgruntled. "Don't tell me you're still going through with that?"

"Of course I am. Why shouldn't I? I don't even have the excuse of staying home to watch over my long-lost brother. I think a night on the town would do me a world of good, particularly in the company of a charming young man."

"You don't find me charming?" His sarcasm brought an answering light to her eyes.

"Not particularly. But then, I have a peculiar attraction to honest men. You wouldn't know much about that in your line of work. It must be exhausting to be a con man."

He grimaced, stretching his arms over his head with weary, unconscious grace. "It was today."

"I take it you didn't get any further on your quest?"

"What makes you think that?" He was wary once more.

"Because I have little doubt you'd be crowing in triumph if you had succeeded in tracking down Father Frank and beaten Emmett's whereabouts from him," she said frankly. "So I can only presume that your day has been a complete waste of time."

He smiled then, that damnably infuriating smile that made Rachel want to kick him. "I wouldn't say that. Not a complete waste of time, not at all."

"And I don't suppose you're going to clarify that statement?"

Moving up the steps with leisurely grace, he nodded. "You're right. When is your gentleman caller showing up?"

"Any time now." It was a war of nerves. She could see by the tiny muscle working in his jaw that he was far from unmoved at the thought of her evening with Stephen Ames, but he seemed equally determined not to show her. She'd simply have to goad him further. She was suddenly desperate to have him lose that iron control he clamped down whenever she got too close. She hadn't seen him lose it yet, but with any luck the moment might be at hand.

"Fine." He slouched into the seat beside her, tossing his sunglasses onto the railing. They missed, falling over the other side into the sand. "It's just as well you're going out tonight; I could use some time to myself for a change."

She could feel him cast a surreptitious glance at her to gauge her reaction to the barely veiled insult. She smiled, unmoved. "A little solitude can be very pleasant. I had a lovely day today—got a great deal accomplished."

"Did you, now?" His voice was indulgent. "Like what?"

"Oh, this and that. I washed the dishes, sunbathed, did my nails, searched your room. Just boring stuff."

He turned his head slowly, staring at her out of wintry eyes. "You did what?" His voice was very soft and low, menacing, she thought.

She didn't pretend to misunderstand. "I searched your room. Honest as always, aren't you, Mr. Emmett Chandler Jake Addams Ben O'Hanlon. How did you get your Pulitzer Prize—making up stories and getting them printed?"

He rose from the chair slowly, and it took all of Rachel's willpower not to flinch. Ignoring her, he walked into the house to survey the damage to his privacy. The words that issued forth turned the air blue, and Rachel listened with profound admiration, storing away several nice turns of phrase for future use. It was little wonder he'd won a Pulitzer. The man was good with words, she had to admit it.

A moment later he was back at the door, looming over her like an avenging god. "I never thought I could sympathize with wife beaters," he said in a gravelly voice, making no effort to come closer.

"I'm not your wife."

"Thank God for small favors." His laugh was harsh. "Are you pleased with your efforts?"

"Quite," she said calmly. "Now at least I know what you want with Emmett."

The screen door opened, and he stepped out, directly in her line of vision, his expression dark and unreadable. "And what's that?"

"For your book, of course," Rachel scoffed. "You needn't think you can fool me any more; that newspaper article mentioned you were working on something about sixties radicals on the run. Emmett wasn't that important, but he was involved in the Cambridge bombings, and he is part of a fairly well-known family."

"Not to mention being heir to millions," he added dryly.

"I don't think Emmett intends to accept his inheritance."

"Don't you? Why not?"

"Because he would have shown up by now if he wanted it. He must have heard about the will—it's certainly gotten enough publicity. He never cared much for the money when he was younger, and I doubt if he's changed that much."

"Maybe he hasn't shown up because he figures all that nice money isn't worth the price he'll have to pay."

"He won't have to pay any price," Rachel retorted. "He didn't commit any crimes—his involvement in the bombing was only accidental."

"Then why hasn't he explained that very nicely to all the men who are interested? Why would Emmett Chandler hide out for fifteen years if he didn't have something to hide from?" His voice was coolly dispassionate, and Rachel once more came very close to hating him. But not close enough.

"I don't know. But I'll be sure to ask him next time I see him," she said pertly.

"Unless I see him first." His voice was cold and implacable, and Rachel felt a little shiver of fear cross her bare shoulders. Before she could reply, the sound of a high-powered sports car intruded on the far from tranquil silence. Both of them heard the tires squeal; the sudden blare of the horn was a violent intrusion.

Ben O'Hanlon's mouth turned upward in a cynical, weary smile. "There's the little gentleman now. Best not keep him waiting."

Slowly, deliberately, Rachel rose, moving past him, brushing his taut, waiting body with a deliberate, gentle brush.

"Bastard," she murmured gently. And ran down the steps to the car.

Chapter Sixteen

Ben O'Hanlon watched her leave. There was a pain in his gut, one that he refused to put a name to. His skin tingled from the light feel of her body as it brushed against him, and the scent of jasmine still lingered in the air. He drank it in appreciatively, then swore, turning away from the ocean, from the sound of the souped-up sports car disappearing into the tropical night. Now was not the time to go all sentimental at the thought of Rachel Chandler. Too much had happened today; he was coming too close to his quarry to be distracted.

He probably should have risked giving her his real name yesterday. It hadn't even connected, but then, she had only been twelve years old at the time. Why should she remember what was indelibly burned into his brain? It wouldn't have made much of a difference to the skinny adolescent she must have been.

He found he liked the idea, picturing her with a solemn face, those great dark brown eyes too big for her, her thick hair in two plaits down her back. She would have been a quiet, kind child, practicing none of those subtle cruelties children seem to revel in. Her children would be like that.

He moved back into the cottage, restless and on edge, and stopped for a moment as he caught sight of the damage done to the hinges of his door. For the first time a smile touched his lips. She was quite a surprise; he should have known she'd have enough ingenuity to get past a simple lock. Well, she had taken the door off; she'd have to put it back on for him. In the meantime he was damned well going to undress as usual, and if she was too squeamish, that was her own bad luck.

It was going to be a tough day tomorrow, one that he had better be ready for. He'd almost regained his strength after his enforced imprisonment in that hellhole that passed for a government prison, but whether he was up to a daylong climb up the Na Pali cliffs was another matter. He'd feel better about it if he'd managed to corner Father Frank, but the priest as usual had been damnably elusive. The gardener was second best, but in the end had probably proved more helpful. Emmett Chandler had been seen on those cliffs more than once in the last few months—hiding out in one of the many obscure encampments that lay hidden in the hills. Ben could only hope the gardener was as knowledgeable as he swore he was.

And then, as always, there remained the problem of Rachel. She had made it surprisingly easy, coming up with a perfect excuse for his pursuit. As long as she believed the latest variation she would keep relatively quiet. By the time she knew what he was really after, it would be too late. For Emmett. And for Ben and Rachel.

Not that there ever had been a Ben and Rachel, he told himself savagely, passing the vandalized door and heading toward the kitchen and a cold beer. There had never been a chance for them, not since the events of fifteen years ago. He was a fool if he hadn't accepted that simple fact yet. But then, when had he had any doubts recently about just how big a fool he was? It took forty years to get to his advanced stage of idiocy, and he only made it by sheer determination and hard work. And as a special prize for his efforts, he was awarded Rachel Chandler, with her melting eyes, tremulous mouth, and beautiful, long-limbed body. He had a feeling he was going to hate the scent of jasmine for the rest of his life.

It was one of the longest nights of his life. He managed to kill forty-five minutes packing a knapsack for the strenuous climb tomorrow. Another half an hour went for the dinner that he didn't eat, fifteen minutes per beer, and for a final twenty-five minutes he showered. He even shaved, telling himself it helped pass a boring night. By the time he left the bathroom it was nearly eleven o'clock, and Ben felt like nothing so much as a Victorian father. Where the hell was she? he fumed. She didn't even know Stephen Ames; she was just fool enough to be dazzled by his beach-boy looks.

Moving on restless feet, he paced out onto the porch. The clean white shirt was hanging loose around his bare torso, the faded jeans low on his hips. Leaning against a column, he stared out at the wine-dark sea, listening to the thick, tropical silence that pressed down around him. What if she didn't come home at all tonight? he thought suddenly. What if she spent the night with that swaggering idiot? The very thought sent such a shaft of white-hot rage through him that he shook with the effort to control it. If she tried anything like that he'd . . .

But what the hell could he do? He had no say in the matter, no rights over Miss Rachel Chandler. If she fell in love with Stephen Ames, it would only be for the best.

But she wasn't going to fall in love with Stephen Ames. He had been around women most of his life; he knew that she was well on her way to being in love with him, if not there already. For all her fury with him, her hurt, and her ultimate fear, she wanted him with every fiber of her being. Just as he, heaven help him, wanted her.

He heard the car's engine from way off. It wasn't the low, throaty rumble of Ames's Jaguar, and it wasn't the stately purr of Harris's Lincoln. It wasn't until the headlights glared at him, waiting with seeming patience on the porch, that he recognized the humble charms of Louie's Taxi Service.

The headlights were shining too brightly to enable him to make anything out. He remained motionless, listening, as the door opened and closed, heard the low murmur of voices, and then the taxi backed away, leaving them in darkness once more. He could barely make out her shadowed figure in the drive. There was something about her silhouette, the set of her shoulders, that alerted him.

"Rachel?" he said softly.

He heard her clear her throat. "I . . . uh, I think I'll go for a walk," she said.

"Where's Ames?" He kept his voice low, easy, so as not to alarm her. He could hear the pain and fright in her voice—one word and she would panic as easily as a cornered doe. If she took off into the tangled underbrush he'd have a hard time finding her on this moonless night.

"He . . . uh, we decided, that is . . . he stayed behind. I just got a taxi." Her voice was high-pitched with tension, and slowly, easily he moved down the steps, one at a time, edging toward her still, dark silhouette.

"What happened, Rachel?" Ben's voice was soothing, gentle, infinitely tender. She was almost in reach; if she tried to bolt for it, he could catch her in time. "Did he hurt you?"

She stood there, motionless, completely silent. And then the dam broke. She moved into the pool of light cast by the house, and he took in the ripped dress, the swollen mouth, the tears streaming down her face. "Oh, Ben," she murmured brokenly, looking up at him beseechingly out of those huge, pain-filled dark eyes. "Or is it, Oh, Jake, or Oh, Emmett?" Her voice was ragged with pain. "I don't even know what damned name to call you!"

He moved then, no longer afraid of her panic, pulling her into his arms with one swift, sure move, holding her tight against him. "Hush, Rachel. Hush now. No one's going to hurt you. Hush, love." Her body was stiff and tight in his arms, suffering his embrace, until suddenly, with one convulsive movement, a sigh left her body, and the stiffness with it, and she was relaxed, pliant against him.

"I warned you," she murmured against the comforting solidity of his shoulder. "I did warn you."

"What did you warn me, love?" he murmured, allowing himself to brush the tangled hair away from her tear-streaked face.

"That nice men were no good. No good at all," she whispered against him. "They smile and they charm and then they hurt you. I like bastards like you much better."

"I'm glad to hear it." He let his lips brush the cloud of hair. "So for all my transgressions I'm not quite as bad as Stephen Ames?"

"Don't," she gasped. He felt the shudder that passed through her body, and his arms tightened around her.

"What did he do, Rachel?" He kept his voice low and calm, all the while a dangerous rage building inside him. "What happened to him?"

She struggled for a moment in his tight embrace, shaking her head. And then she gave in. "I decided it was past time for me to come home. He didn't agree." Shivering slightly, she looked up at his shuttered face. "I don't think he's very comfortable."

A small smile curved his lips. "What did you do to him, wicked girl?"

"Kicked him, I'm afraid. He...he wasn't used to hearing no." She managed a rueful grimace. "He said it was my fault. I suppose it was. I shouldn't have bought this dress, shouldn't have dressed up like that, if I didn't mean to go through with it. But when he put his hands on me I just...just panicked."

"It was nobody's fault but his, Rachel; don't let anybody fool you. Whether he likes it or not, a decent man knows how to take no for an answer." He loosened his hold just a tiny bit, reluctantly.

"I'm afraid he...wasn't terribly decent," she stammered. "He said he liked a fight in a woman."

Ben loosened his hold, guiding her up the front steps with a gentle hand. "He didn't realize what he was tangling with," he said, ruffling her thick curtain of hair.

Rachel even managed a rusty-sounding laugh. "That's the truth. I don't know if he'd try anything like that again in the near future."

"Probably not. Where did you leave him?" His voice was studiedly casual.

"At the Winding Lei. Once I got free of him I just ran—I don't know if he's still there or not."

"I'll let you know," he said pleasantly. "You go on in, pour yourself a large drink, and wait for me. I won't be long."

"No!" She turned in a panic, grabbing his arm. "Don't do anything stupid. I got away from him in time.

He's just a stupid kid with overactive glands, and I guess I was sending him the wrong message or something. I'm okay, no harm done."

Ben smiled, a cool, gentle smile that was even more alarming, and one hand gently brushed her cut lip. "Go on in, Rachel. I'll stop in at the hotel on the way and send Uncle Harris to keep you company."

"No!" She was being propelled up the porch steps, across the porch, and into the living room. "You're not my brother; you don't have to defend my honor."

He made no response, and before she quite realized what was happening he had her ensconced on the lumpy living-room sofa, a worn cotton blanket around her, a very dark, very strong glass of rum and ice in her hand.

"Drink all of it," he ordered, tucking the blanket around her long, bare legs. She'd lost her sandals somewhere along the way, she noted with a distant anger. He was overwhelmed by her innocent vulnerability; angry and frightened and guilty that she could be hurt so easily. Reaching out a gentle hand, he smoothed the tangled curtain of hair away from her pale face. "And stay put. If you don't want your uncle, that's okay, as long as you promise not to leave this house."

"I don't want you going," she said in a small, weary voice. "Please, stay here."

For one long moment he was sorely tempted. Never had she looked more desirable. And never was she in greater need of not being desired. He doubted he could do that if he did stay, and beating the hell out of Stephen Ames would go a long way toward easing the hard knot of frustration that had taken to lodging permanently in his gut.

Kneeling down beside her, he cupped her chin in one strong hand. "I have to," he said softly, his thumb stroking the sensitive underside of her jaw. He wanted to kiss her so badly it hurt, wanted just to touch those sweet, soft lips of hers that he'd only begun to taste. Dropping his hand, he rose to his full height. "I'll be back." And he was gone into the night.

The silence grew around her, a beneficial silence, not a threatening one. Her hand tightened around the cold, tall glass of rum, and dutifully she brought it to her lips, taking a very large, determined gulp. The strong, fiery liquid burned its way down her throat, and she coughed, choking on the unexpected harshness of the drink.

Carefully she leaned forward, setting the half-empty glass on the floor. After the piña coladas Stephen Ames had been forcefeeding her all night, she didn't need any more rum to melt her brain. Too much had happened in the last week, more than she had had time to assimilate, and she needed to retain whatever remnant of a clear head remained to her.

She had found her brother, lost her brother, been tormented by the specter of incest, infuriated by being made a fool of, been moon-eyed by an ill-placed attraction, been lied to, suffered the dangers of flying, snorkeling, and sunburn, and to top it all off, had almost been horribly raped by a half-drunken playboy she should have known to steer clear of in the first place. And it was all Ben O'Hanlon's fault. When he returned from beating the hell out of Stephen Ames, she would tell him so.

Though she had to admit, the thought of him beating up Stephen Ames was irresistibly charming. She could only hope Ben would be the beater, not the beatee. Stephen Ames had quite an amazing set of muscles, and he was ten years younger than Ben. But he lacked a certain ruthless quality that Ben had in abundance. The same ruthless quality that made him able to lie to her again and again and again, she reminded herself. Maybe it would be nice if Stephen Ames managed to connect a few times before Ben mashed him to the ground.

Sighing, she pulled her legs up, under herself, and stretched out on the couch. She was too weary, too sad, and admittedly just a tiny bit too drunk to get to her bedroom. She would have to watch it: drinking too much rum was not the proper way to handle the stressful situations she kept falling into. Uncle Harris was enough of a drinker for the illustrious Chandlers.

Besides, she would be interested to see what Ben would do when he came home and found her there. It was a wicked temptation, but one Rachel was in no mood to resist at that point. Closing her eyes, she lay her head back down with a sigh. If she had any sense at all she'd get up and straggle back to her room. But then, she hadn't shown much sense in the last week; why should she set a precedent?

The night was still and quiet as she lay there, drinking in the sounds of the night birds, the rustle of the palms, the whisper of the surf on the dark sand in front of the cottage. With a distant feeling of wonder Rachel realized that she was perfectly content, lying there, waiting for Ben to come back. There was no anxiety, no resentment in the anticipation. Just a deep security that he was coming. Coming back, to her. And with a small, happy sigh she gave herself up to sleep.

Chapter Seventeen

It was very dark when Rachel opened her eyes. Dark and silent; even the omnipresent night birds seemed to have settled for the moment. Rachel's head weighed a thousand pounds as she lifted it to stare hazily at the illuminated clock by her bed, and she shivered. Never in her life had she felt so cold, so lonely, so alone.

Twenty-five past two. The middle of the night, in fact. She sank back into the pillow with a hopeless sigh. And then she realized where she was. And what she was wearing.

The last thing she remembered was lying on the sofa, dressed in her torn dress. Slightly drunk and blissfully awaiting Ben's return from defending her honor. At which time she had fully expected to be seduced into bestowing said honor on her slightly battered champion.

Apparently Ben had had other ideas, none of which included bedding Rachel Chandler. He must have carried her in here when he got back—her bedroom, not his. He had even managed to remove her clothes and replace them with a loose cotton nightgown. And then left her.

She sat up then, completely, furiously awake. A small part of her mind pleaded for sanity—he didn't want to take advantage of her; she'd been nothing but hostile to him in the last twenty-four hours. None of that made any difference. She loved him, wanted him, and had deliberately, if subconsciously, set up a situation for him to take her back into his bed. And he had ignored it.

Throwing back the thin blanket, her bare feet slammed onto the floor. Hell hath no fury like a woman scorned, she told herself grimly. It didn't matter if it was logical—at that point she was past logic. Ben O'Hanlon had effectively thrown her offer of love back in her face, and she wasn't going to lie in bed and cry about it. She was going to do something about it—a small, perfect act of revenge.

She slammed her door open, and the thin wood bounced against the wall. The living room of the cottage was dark and deserted, lit only dimly by the late rising moon. The dismantled door to his room still rested against the wall, and without a moment's hesitation she stormed in there, standing over his sleeping form like an avenging goddess.

Something should have softened in her, watching him. He slept the sleep of total exhaustion, his eyes shadowed, the golden lashes a fan beneath them. There was a cut on his cheekbone, a bruise on his temple, a raw scrape on his chin. Received from Stephen Ames during his defense of her, no doubt. Very carefully she leaned over him, the scent of her jasmine perfume tickling his sleeping nostrils. Very carefully she reached beside his head, took a pillow, and raising it high over her head, smacked him sharply in the face.

He was instantly awake, roaring in fury. "What the hell do you think you're doing?"

That was a little difficult to answer. Fortunately she still retained hold of the pillow. "Saying good-bye," she snapped, and swatted him again with the pillow.

This time he was ready for her. He'd already swung to the side of the bed, and he caught the pillow in time, yanking it out of her grasp before it could connect. Bereft of her meager weapon, unarmed in the face of his formidable anger, Rachel did what most Chandlers would do. Turned and ran.

He caught her on the porch, his hand biting into her arm, no doubt adding to the bruises he'd already inflicted, she thought angrily. "What the hell is wrong with you?" he shouted, shaking her. He was wearing dark blue jockey shorts, nothing else, and his chest rose and fell with the sudden exertion. She had to use what little self-control she had left to keep her eyes jerked upward.

"Nothing!" She fought back, remembering but ignoring that it would be a useless struggle against his implacable strength. "I'm leaving."

"Like that?" he asked derisively, and belatedly she realized she was standing there clad only in a light eyelet nightdress and bare feet.

"If you'll let go of me," she began with a noble attempt at icy calm, "I'll go in and change. Someone will bring the Land Rover back for you."

He eyed her in silence for a long moment, as if trying to fathom what was going on behind the cool face with the blazing eyes. "What's gotten into you, Rachel?" he finally asked, and his voice was treacherously tender.

It almost proved her undoing. "I just want to leave," she mumbled miserably.

"Why? I thought we were getting along better. I kept my distance, put you safely in your own bed like a nice little Boy Scout...." Something, a mere flicker in her dark eyes, must have betrayed her, for he let out a sharp, surprised breath. "That's it, isn't it? You're angry because I put you in your own bed?"

"You're demented!" she snapped. "Believe it or not, every woman in this world isn't panting for your dubious favors."

"Not every woman," he agreed. "But you are."

"You egotistical pig!" She doubled her struggles, but his hand slid down to capture her wrist, his grip gentle but unbreakable.

"I think you want me almost as much as I want you," he mused, and there was a disturbing, demoralizing light in his hazel eyes as he watched her.

Rachel felt a slow warmth begin spreading through her beneath the heat of his gaze. Now that the moment was almost at hand she had an absurd need to try to postpone it. "Don't be ridiculous," she said. It didn't help that her voice came out low and husky, that her eyes when she looked up at him were warm and vulnerable and filled with something very akin to love.

"Unless you only get turned on when you think I'm your brother," he added, and that hypnotizing, sensual languor that had filled her snapped.

"Damn you!" She reached up with her free hand to slap him in her sudden rage, but he was too fast for her. Before Rachel could even realize it, he'd pulled her into his arms, and she was crushed against the heavenly warmth of his chest, his strong arms around her, imprisoning her, holding her. She could feel his hot breath stir her cloud of hair, felt the brush of his lips against her temple.

"That's much better," he whispered, his lips taking tiny, delicious little nips of her skin as he moved down the side of her face to her sensitive earlobe, his tongue tracing the delicate curve of her jaw. "I can fight myself, Rachel," his voice drawled in her ear. "But I can't fight you too. Come to bed with me."

She opened her mouth to protest, to stall for time, only to have it silenced by his almost savage kiss. His mouth was hot and hungry on hers, demanding a response that she gave unthinkingly, even as its intensity frightened her. It was too late for second thoughts now, too late to back away. The fire that had been released in him found its match in her, and she melted against his tightly wired body, needing to absorb his tough strength into her very pores.

His tongue was a rough intruder at first, startling to her as it thoroughly explored all the soft and secret contours of her honeyed mouth. But even as her mind was wondering, her body was responding, her tongue meeting his. She gave herself up to the wonder of his mouth, lost in the miracle of it, not even aware that her wrist had been released, that she had slid her arms around his waist and was holding him tightly, as if afraid to let go for fear he'd vanish from her life, as so many others had done.

His hands were warm and strong on her back, molding her against him. She loved the feel of his warm, bare arms holding her, the strength of his chest through the thin cotton barrier of her nightgown. She was trembling with fear and desire and love—beyond anything she had ever experienced. The force of it was dark and terrifying, and she never wanted it to end.

She almost cried out in pain when he pulled back, looking down at her out of passion-hooded eyes. "Rachel?" he said hoarsely.

A quiet sigh left her. "Yes," she said. "Yes, yes, yes."

Ben scooped her up in his arms, holding her high against his chest as he carried her back into the cottage, past the shrouded, familiar shapes of the furniture into the night-dark bedroom. They were alone now for the first time. There was no Emmett, no Harris, no lies or masquerade or motives or revenge. There was just Ben and Rachel, together in the darkness.

Slowly, carefully he lowered her to the wide, rumpled bed, following her down with that strange, tough grace of his. Lying beside her, he pulled her into his arms, not moving, not saying a word as he held her, the warmth of his body soothing her fears, reassuring with tenderness and a mysterious communication. Her slender form was pressed tightly against his, and she could feel how much he wanted her through the soft cotton of his shorts. Almost as much as she wanted him, she paraphrased in her own mind with a smile. But this wasn't a contest, a competition. This was love, whether Ben knew it or not.

His tight, possessive embrace loosened, and gently he rolled her onto her back. Hovering above her, his hands worked with the tiny row of buttons that fastened the ruffled cotton nightdress, fumbling with them. "I didn't have any trouble getting this on you," he murmured, concentrating on the fastenings.

Rachel gave in to a long-denied impulse and ran a questing hand through his shaggy blond hair. "Maybe I'm more distracting when I'm awake," she suggested, raising her other hand up to gently stroke the side of his face.

"Could be." The last button gave, opening the gown halfway down. He made no move to strip it off; he just knelt there, watching her out of passion-dark eyes.

Rachel lay still, feeling strangely weightless against the soft cotton sheet, gazing up at him with mute longing. In the short time she had known him he had kissed her twice, slept with her, but never once touched her breasts. They ached for him, ached for the feel of those large, beautiful hands, and still he didn't move. She could feel herself harden against the thin cotton lawn of the nightgown; her breath was coming in rapid, shallow pants when at last he reached out his hands. To clasp her shoulders, his thumbs gently massaging the tense muscles.

His only response to her groan of frustration was an enigmatic smile as his warm hands slid down her bare arms, his long fingers gently kneading her tense, aroused flesh. They moved, to span her rib cage, and her pulse leaped. Leaning forward, he let his tongue gently trace the wildly beating pulse at the base of her neck.

"Ben." Her voice was agonized, tortured.

"Show me what you want, Rachel," he whispered against the soft warmth of her neck. In answer she reached down, caught his wrists, and brought them to her straining breasts. And then almost wished she hadn't as a wave of feeling stunning in its intensity washed over her.

Very gently his long fingers cupped the swelling peaks, his hands warm and caressing, slowly worshiping. The thin cotton covering was only an added stimulant, rustling against the aroused flesh, adding to the sensations that flowed through her. And then those deft, clever hands pushed the nightgown down, over her shoulders, and his hands were on her, the lightly callused skin a fiery demand on the warm swell of her breasts. Just when Rachel thought she could stand no more, his mouth followed, taking a slow, leisurely possession of one aching breast while his hand continued its wicked way with the other.

She wanted to reach out and touch him, but a strange, sensual lassitude had washed over her with the tender ministrations of Ben's hands and mouth. All she could do was lie there beneath his practiced, delicious onslaught, her body trembling with reawakened and entirely new sensations. His assault on her senses was total, and there was nothing she could do but surrender her body, her mind, her soul, to him.

The gown was pushed off her hips, and his mouth followed, reluctantly leaving the soft bounty of her breasts to blaze a heated, damp trail down her midriff, glancing off her navel, scattering kisses over her gently rounded stomach. He moved lower still, and she stiffened, suddenly shy.

"No, Ben, don't," she whispered.

He looked down at her through the darkened room. "Why not?" His voice was gentle.

She shook her head. "I haven't... that is, no one has ever..."

"Good," he said. His hands were cradling her hips, holding them gently, and before she could protest again, his mouth had found her.

She was completely unprepared for the sensations that swept through her. The pleasant lassitude, the drifting sensuality, and then the unexpected explosion that rocked her body, more violently than anything she had ever experienced.

Rachel called out for him, her voice tight in panic and wonder, and he came to her swiftly, holding her in his arms, soothing her, all the while murmuring gentle, meaningless words in her ear. She hid her face against the warm fur of his chest, breathing in the rich, warm sea and salt smell of him as her breathing shuddered to a more even rate. He kissed her then, his mouth lingering on her sweat-dampened temple, the arch of her cheekbone, the eyelids that had fluttered closed. And then he kissed her mouth, slowly, lingeringly, as she stirred in his arms, reaching out for him with sudden, renewed hunger. She almost cried aloud when he moved away.

But a moment later he returned to her, that frustrating, enticing scrap of cloth gone, and there were no more barriers between them. She reached out for him, desperate to encircle him in her strong arms, her long, slender legs, aching for him to complete the possession that had started days ago. He moved over her, his strong body a shadow above her, and she felt his long, hair-roughened legs between hers. He was ready, they were both ready, yet still he hesitated.

"Rachel?" It was a question, an entreaty. Even, she told herself, a declaration of love.

"Yes, Ben," she said, her eyes trusting as they looked up into his. "Yes."

He came to her then, with a slow, deep, strong thrust that penetrated to the very center of her being. She cried out then, from the sheer joy and wonder of it, surrounding him with a possession all her own.

How could anything so ancient and so universal still be so glorious? It was her last conscious thought before her body and her emotions took over, responding to the steady, powerful advance and retreat. She could feel the tension build, feel his body tremble with it, as she moved with him, accepting and losing as he completed and then withheld, and the storm began to build.

She wanted this to last forever, to prolong that final moment of reckoning. But Ben was too much for her newly aroused passion. Suddenly the velvet dark night split apart, her body arched, and she shattered. Moments later he was with her, gathering her back together, holding her through the star-pierced blackness as the storm washed over their sweat-damp bodies.

Was it a century later when he moved from her? He didn't move far—his hands still held her tightly, almost as if he were afraid to let her go. She knew how he felt;

she was just as afraid he might disappear if she didn't keep touching him.

With a deep sigh she snuggled up against him, drawing his arm around her waist. The feel of the wiry hair on his chest against her back, the warmth of his legs cradling hers, the soft stirring of his breath in her hair all contributed to an overwhelming sense of joy. Rachel didn't want to sleep—she was too happy. She wanted to savor every moment of it.

But once more her body betrayed her, and nestled in the comforting warmth of his body, she drifted off.

Chapter Eighteen

It was almost dawn when Ben awoke to look down at the sleeping figure in his arms. The thick eyelashes fanned out over her tear-streaked, tanned cheek, and her mane of chestnut hair tickled his nose. As he watched her he felt a tightening inside, one that came from an aching tenderness, not the fiery desire they'd shared earlier.

He'd never taken so much trouble with a woman in his life, he reflected. He'd always tried to make sure his partner shared in the pleasure, but never had he been so obsessed with someone else's responses, practically to the exclusion of his own. He had wanted to take her to heights she'd never known before, to show her the delights of her woman's body, which she sometimes seemed less than comfortable with, to give everything of himself to her and take nothing back. All that had mattered to him was Rachel and her pleasure. And yet somehow in that selfless giving he'd received far more than ever before.

If only there was some way to protect her, to remove her from the path of destruction he was about to blaze. But there was no way to spare her, he'd known that all along. And now that the inevitable had finally happened, it would only be that much more painful. For both of them.

The early morning light from his window was just beginning to penetrate the room. It must be after five; he was due to meet Tom Moko by the base of the Ne Pali trail by a quarter of seven. It was going to be a rugged forced march into the wilderness area of the cliffs in search of Emmett Chandler. They had to make an early start if they expected to be back by nightfall.

He no longer felt the certainty that he was going to find Emmett Chandler. No matter how big a bastard the man was, he couldn't leave his sister at the mercy of a man who had the strongest reasons for wanting to hurt her. Maybe he really was dead, had been for years? The Chandler millions were motive enough for anyone interested in a little blackmail. Who would know that better than him? It had been the only way to convince the gently avaricious Harris Chandler to help him.

And if Emmett was dead, what then? Sooner or later Rachel would find out who he was. And then that devastating light would go out of her eyes, and everything she felt for him would turn as cold and dead as yesterday's ashes.

He felt a small, almost imperceptible movement by his side, and he turned to look down into those warm brown eyes. Her mouth crinkled in a sleepy smile, and there was nothing he wanted more than to crush that mouth with his. "Tell me something," she said, her voice low and husky from sleep.

"Anything," he said rashly, suiting the action to the wish. Her mouth opened beneath his like a flower opening its petals to drink in the sunshine, and for a moment all was silent in the room but the rustle of the sheets as he pressed her back against the bed. He kissed her, slowly, leisurely, with a thoroughness that left them both wide awake. "What did you want to know?" he murmured against her earlobe, biting it gently with strong white teeth.

"Hmm?" His kiss had effectively erased all rational thought, and it took her a moment to regain a modicum of sense. "Oh, yes, I remember. I wanted to know if you were as tough and mean as you look." She was planting light, experimental kisses across the flat plane of his chest.

"No," he growled. "I'm tougher and meaner." Rolling onto his back, he took her with him, his hazel eyes laughing up into hers.

"I believe it," she said, sprawling gracefully across his body. "It looks like Stephen Ames managed to connect a few times." She ran an inquisitive finger gently along the scraped cheekbone. He didn't even flinch.

"You think I look bad, you should see Ames. On second thought, maybe you shouldn't. You're pretty damned squeamish."

Rachel let out a little squeak of dismay, accompanied by a wiggle that was completely distracting. "You didn't kill him, did you?"

"I did not. I never murder anyone during Lent. I just made sure he wouldn't try to force himself on some unsuspecting innocent again."

"And that's why you beat him up? As a public service?" There was just a hint of laughter beneath her stern expression.

"That was a major incentive," he agreed. "I was also suffering from an advanced case of frustration, and beating the hell out of that punk helped me let off a lot of steam. Of course I had no idea I wasn't going to have to spend another night going crazy from wanting you."

A small, secretive smile curved her mouth. "You almost missed your chance. When I woke up alone in my bed, I was ready to kill you."

"How was I to know you'd decided to forgive me? You can't imagine how hard it was to carry you in to your bed and leave you there alone. It was one of the most difficult things I've ever done, but I figured after almost being raped by that idiot jock, the last thing you needed was me."

She reached up her small, well-shaped hands and placed them on either side of his face, letting her thumbs gently brush his lips. And then her mouth followed, kissing him lightly. "I never needed you more," she said in a soft, shy voice.

A sudden shaft of guilt shot through him, and quickly he stifled it, summoning a mocking grin. "You looked pretty silly, racing out into the night in your nightgown and bare feet."

She let him change the subject with equanimity. "I was mad," she confessed.

"Do tell? And where were you planning on going in that outfit?"

She made a face, playing his game. "I don't know. I just wanted to get as far away from you as fast as I could."

There was a silence, and when Ben spoke his voice was curiously harsh. "Would you have left me?"

She looked down at his battered, dark face against the white of the pillow. "No," she said. "Would you have let me leave?"

"No," he said.

They gazed at each other for a long, silent moment. Ben had the odd, fanciful feeling that in that silence they'd told each other more than all their words had ever spoken.

"Could we make love, please?" Her voice was small, entreating.

"I thought we just did," he drawled, smiling, then sucked in his breath sharply as her hands moved down his chest, her gentle, inquisitive fingers exquisitely exciting on his warm flesh.

Smiling, she shook her head before dipping down to press her hot, sweet mouth against his chest. "No, we didn't," she murmured. "You made love to me magnificently, I might add. This time I want to make love to you, too." And her hand trailed lower, enticingly lower across his flat stomach, to catch and hold him.

Her eyes widened as she looked down at him. "Ben?" she whispered in muffled awe.

Leaning back, he smiled serenely, consigning guilt and Emmett Chandler and morning appointments to hell, where they belonged. "Have your wicked way with me, kid."

Pulling herself into a sitting position, she stared down at him, her brown eyes luminous in the haze of the dawn. Slowly she leaned forward, feathering her lips across the scrape on his cheekbone, the bruise on his jaw, the cut lip. She let her tongue gently bathe the wounded lip, following it with small, nibbling kisses. Then she moved her mouth down to the scar on his chin, the knife scar on his chest, the faint trace of an appendix scar on his flat belly.

"You've lived a rough life," Rachel whispered against the heated skin of his chest. "Do you mind that people have tried to kill you?" She let her hands trail up his sides, her fingers playing lightly on his ribs.

"I count it as a measure of my success," he replied in a slightly strangled voice as her tongue dipped into his navel. She was stretched out over him now, her mouth making a leisurely exploration of his stomach and chest, shyly touching, tasting, arousing, both him and herself. She felt suddenly, wickedly wanton, with no restrictions and no rules, only his body stretched out in front of her, wanting her.

Her hands were trembling as they slid up to grasp his shoulders, and her lips found the rapid, pounding pulse in his neck. She could feel his mouth at her temple, and his hands reached up to cradle her against him, strong and hard against her sweat-dampened skin.

"Am I allowed to participate?" he whispered in her ear, his tongue slyly exploring its delicate contours.

"Please," she gasped. Desire had swiftly outpaced her experience, and she was helpless in the grip of it. She needed him—her body was afire with longing, and yet she was unsure of how to tell him, how to move.

Ben had no such qualms. With deft assurance he pulled her over him, positioning her hips above his. His hand reached down and found her, damp and ready for him, and she trembled above him, her eyes wide and hungry.

"Do you want me, Rachel?" he whispered, his voice tight with desire.

"I want you."

"Show me," he murmured. She could feel his pulsing hardness resting just at the entrance of her overwhelming need, wanting her, teasing her, waiting for her.

All hesitation left her. Slowly she sank down, filling her aching body with him, joining them together with a sure, steady pressure. And when he was finally one with her, she collapsed against his chest, trembling with a thousand fly-away longings that threatened to tear her apart, unable to complete what she had started, needing him to regain control.

He knew without words. He held her for a moment, his arms cradling her on top of his tense, sweat-slick body. And then his firm hands caught her hips, holding them, as he slowly withdrew, then arched up to fill her again. Rachel's breath was coming in staggered gasps, her eyes were glazed, and the hands that grasped his strong shoulders were convulsive fists, her nails digging into him.

He could feel her tighten around him, feel the shudders that shook the body that covered his so sweetly. And suddenly he abandoned the control that was so crucial to him, pulling away and then thrusting into her, once, twice, six times, before her body went rigid in his arms.

All she could do was cling to him, tight around his straining body as wave after wave of midnight darkness clenched her body around his, brought muffled cries from her throat and tears pouring down her face. And as each wave began to die away another took its place, until she was gasping and sobbing and beating against his strong, trembling body. And with one last deep thrust he joined her in that final moment of life and death.

She collapsed against his chest, breathless, the spasms dying away with a stubborn reluctance. She could feel his strong, rough hands running along her back, holding her to him, at a wonderful variance with the heated passion they'd just shared. She could feel his heartbeat slow, feel his lips gently touch her temple, his breath warm on her flushed skin.

Sudden embarrassment made her attempt to shift her position, but his hands slid back down to her hips, holding her in place.

"Don't leave me." It was the breath of a whisper, a voice in the darkness that she may have only imagined.

But the tiny possibility that he might have asked it of her was enough. Putting her head back on his shoulder, she let the tension flow from her. Cradled against his heated, sweat-slippery body, she slept once more.

Chapter Nineteen

Rachel was alone when she woke up the next time. Bright sunlight flooded the room, penetrating even the sheet she'd thrown over her head sometime during the morning hours. She didn't need to open her eyes to know she was alone—as wakefulness slowly intruded she was conscious of a sense of incompleteness.

Throwing back the sheet, she pulled herself out of bed. Her nightgown was draped neatly over the chair by the bed—Ben must have picked it up when he got dressed that morning. She pulled it over her head, then caught sight of the white shirt he'd been wearing the day before. Reaching out a tentative hand, she stroked the thin cotton sleeve, imagining Ben still inside it. And then she pulled it on over her nightgown.

It smelled like him. Of the hot, blazing sun and sea water, and those vile cigarettes. And something else, something indefinably Ben. Hugging the shirt tightly around her slender body, she made her rounds of the bathroom, the kitchen for a cup of coffee, ending up on the porch, stretched out once more on the steps, her nightgown pulled up to her knees. It was warm enough to discard Ben's shirt, but that was the last thing she was about to do. She sat there, content, sipping on her coffee and watching the ever-changing blue-green waves.

So Ben had gone to the Ne Pali cliffs. It was in a brief note he'd left for her on the kitchen table, offering not much in the way of information. But she had begun to understand how he thought; obviously he had decided that Emmett was still hiding out somewhere in the wilderness area that had harbored fugitives for centuries.

She could have told him otherwise. When he was first on the run he might have gone into the jungle surrounding the jagged, magnificent Ne Pali Coast on the north side of the island. But Emmett had always been a man who liked his creature comforts—good food, a warm bed, fine wines. Roughing it in the jungle was all right in times of necessity, but after fifteen years the romance would have begun to pall a bit. She wouldn't be surprised if Emmett was in disguise as a stockbroker or an insurance salesman somewhere on the island, bringing in a very good living.

But if it made Ben happy to scramble over those rocky cliffs in search of a story, then she wished him well. Much as a major part of her longed for him, missed him, her more sensible side was glad he had chosen this day of all days to leave her alone. Because today was the day Emmett would come.

He hadn't missed a birthday in fifteen years, and he certainly wasn't going to miss one now, when she was so close. She turned twenty-eight today, and she was going to stay right where she was and await her long-lost brother.

Cradling the coffee mug in both hands, she leaned forward, squinting out at the sea as if looking for answers. She was conscious of a small, nagging, ridiculous sense of guilt for not having told Ben. Not that she owed him complete honesty in the matter of Emmett, far from it. And she wanted her first meeting with her brother in fifteen years to be uncomplicated by a roving reporter who also happened to be her lover. Her lover. She savored the phrase, reveling in the newness of it. She had had boyfriends, she had had a fiancé, she had even made a fumbling, adolescent form of love with them that was a world away from the passion-dark moments she had shared with Ben O'Hanlon last night. But she would never have called any of them her lover. Not like Ben. She hugged the thought to herself, along with his soft white shirt, and smiled out at the ocean.

Once she had Emmett settled in her own mind she could concentrate on Ben. After all, she had been a sister longer than she had been in love with Ben—first things first. With Emmett sure to come and Ben returning to her, life was taking on a positively golden hue. It was going to be a glorious day.

Rachel was in the kitchen fixing herself a very late lunch indeed when she heard him. It had taken the far side of starvation to drive her from her comfortable perch on the front porch steps, and even then she took a long hot shower before dressing in denim shorts and a pale blue shell. She still wore Ben's white shirt, holding it to her as some sort of talisman, a good luck charm. One she might need before the day was through. She was mixing the last bit of mayonnaise from the jar into a bowl of tiny shrimp when she heard the footsteps on the front porch.

She stopped—as did her motions, her breath, her heartbeat. Had Emmett finally decided to show his face? She had waited all morning, but there had been no sign of him. She still had no doubts that he would come today, she had always known it. *Please, dear God, let it be him.*

"I hope I'm not intruding?" Father Frank's rotund figure appeared in the kitchen door, and Rachel let out her pent-up breath.

"Of course not," she said warmly, wiping her hands on the sides of her shorts and moving forward to welcome him. She could only hope the crushing disappointment didn't show in her too expressive face. "You're always welcome, Father. What brings you to this side of the island?"

"I wanted to see how my young friend was getting along," he said, eyeing the shrimp salad with an appropriately soulful look. "And I hoped I'd get a chance to finally meet your brother." He glanced around the kitchen expectantly, as if waiting to see the supposed Emmett materialize out of the ancient cupboards.

"He's not here, I'm afraid. He'll be so sorry to have missed you—he and Uncle Harris have been trying to track you down for days now."

"I'm a busy man," Father Frank explained vaguely, his attention back on Rachel's lunch. "My parishioners are a far-flung group, and I've been particularly occupied these last few days, getting ready for my new assignment. But I've come at a bad time: I'm keeping you from your lunch."

With amusement banishing the last of her disappointment, Rachel took her cue. "Please, join me, Father. There's more than enough for two."

Father Frank didn't waste time with polite demurals. "I would love to, my dear. Tell me, is your brother due back sometime soon?"

She returned to the table and began dishing up the salad. "He's spending the day on the Ne Pali cliffs on some wild goose chase, and I imagine he won't be back till dark." She paused, handing him his plate. "And he's not my brother."

Father Frank appeared unmoved by this revelation. "Ice tea would be fine," he replied in answer to her proffered glass.

"You knew, didn't you?" she accused him, leading the way back out onto the shaded porch. Her tone held no rancor.

"Let's just say I suspected something of the kind. In my position one hears things, you know. It seemed more than likely that the Emmett Chandler who so conveniently showed up was not the same man who disappeared from here some fifteen years ago."

"Why didn't you warn me?" She climbed into the hammock, sitting cross-legged with her plate in her lap, the glass of ice tea balanced precariously. "Do you think it was fair letting me go off like that to a probable swindler?"

"Oh, I didn't think you were in any danger." He was disposing of the shrimp salad at a phenomenal rate. "I had asked a few pertinent questions of a few important people when he first showed up. I knew you'd be safe enough. Though I must admit I thought he'd get rid of you the first chance he could. I was hoping you'd put, if you'll pardon the expression, the fear of God into him, make him think twice about whatever he had in mind. If I had known at the time that he'd let you stay I might have tried to say something. Not that there was much I could have done. I had no proof, and the confessional is sacred."

"I knew it!" Her brown eyes blazed triumphantly. "You have seen my brother! He came to see you, didn't he? He always said he'd return to the Church someday."

"I'm afraid I can't say, Rachel." His plate was clean; he licked a finger, and reached out to pick up the last crumb. "The church is very strict in these matters."

Rachel smiled brilliantly. "I understand," she said. Of course he could say no more; he had said enough. Enough to assure her that Emmett was indeed alive and well and living in the islands. Her knowledge of her brother supplied the rest: He would come today, on her birthday. With that knowledge secure, she changed the subject. "When are you leaving for South America, Father?"

The priest made a small, apologetic moue. "Tomorrow."

"Tomorrow?" she echoed, distressed. "I thought it was going to be a matter of weeks." She felt curiously bereft at the thought of this friendly, understanding man disappearing from her life so quickly, when she had only just begun to know him.

"Things moved a bit faster than anyone expected. My orders came through, my replacement arrived early, and El Salvador was disposed to be welcoming. My superiors and I could think of no reason to delay. I'll be sorry not to see the outcome of your tangled situation, Rachel. I wish we had time to get to know each other better." He seemed genuinely sad, a sadness echoing Rachel's own.

"I do, too. But I can tell you what the outcome of my tangled situation is going to be," she said with impish certainty.

"Have you the gift of second sight from your Irish ancestors, Miss Rachel Chandler?" he queried with mock severity.

"Nope. From my Jewish grandmother." She stretched languidly, then jumped up as her glass of ice tea spilled in her lap. "Damn," she said, then looked guiltily at the cleric.

"*Damn* is a very handy word, Rachel," he said mildly. "I use it myself every now and then. Why don't we take a walk down by the water and you can outline your future? This will be the last time I get a chance to walk on the beach for quite some time. I doubt the beaches in El Salvador are quite as glorious."

Rachel hesitated for only a moment. She wouldn't miss Emmett; he would wait for her. Doubtless he would recognize the priest's ancient black Ford and know it was safe. She could walk with Father Frank with equanimity, knowing that Emmett would still come.

In answer she held out her hand to him. "I'd love you to come. I always liked fairy tales, hearing them and telling them." They started down the steps, the plump, black-garbed priest and the long-legged young woman. "Emmett is going to reappear today, and he and Ben will hit it off beautifully."

"His name is Ben?" They walked through the damp solidly packed sand, her bare feet and his shoes making a strange duet of footprints.

She nodded. "Ben O'Hanlon. He's a newspaper reporter—he even won a Pulitzer Prize. He wants to interview Emmett for a book on sixties radicals still on the run."

Father Frank looked profoundly disturbed, the afternoon sun glinting off his balding head. "I've heard the name," he said slowly. "That seems a lot of trouble to go to just for a story. Possible fraud, among other things."

"He's gone through worse. Before he came here he was imprisoned in South America for six months for sticking his nose where it didn't belong."

"Some of the South American governments, and I use the term loosely, have an aversion to reporters," Father Frank mused. "And you're certain that's what Ben O'Hanlon wants from Emmett Chandler?"

"What else could he want?" Rachel replied reasonably.

"What else, indeed?" Father Frank was concentrating on their footprints, and she couldn't read his expression. "So tell me more about your fairy-tale ending. Emmett and Ben will become good friends, have a series of interviews that will win him another Pulitzer Prize..."

"You're good at this," Rachel laughed. "How about a Nobel Prize while we're at it? Emmett will come back to San Francisco, giving up his inheritance to all the greedy aunts and uncles, and move near me. He'll be married, and give me five nieces and nephews to play with."

"Will you like his wife?"

"We'll be best friends. She'll even be matron of honor at my wedding."

"You're thinking of getting married?"

She nodded. "To Ben O'Hanlon."

This time he did look at her. "Does he know?"

"Not yet. But he will eventually."

"You love him." It was a statement, not a question, and his eyes were filled with deep concern.

"Of course. But I told you that days ago, when I thought he was my brother." She laughed ruefully. "You didn't give me much help that day. I wish you could have dropped a hint or two."

"I didn't know for certain. There was always a chance in a million that he really was your brother. And I still think I gave you the best possible advice. If he wasn't your brother, you had nothing to worry about, and if he was, worrying would have only given it added weight in your mind. By relaxing about the whole thing you would have negated its power over you, and soon enough you would have turned to someone more suitable."

"Maybe. I can't really imagine not loving Ben, even if he were my brother."

"Well, fortunately you don't have to deal with that. He's not your brother, thank heavens."

"Thank heavens," she echoed.

"So now that I know about your future, Rachel Chandler, tell me about your past," he suggested in a warm voice.

It was a real gift in anyone, particularly a priest, Rachel reflected, to have such a natural interest and compassion for perfect strangers. She had to marvel at his skill in drawing her out, even as she told him with traces of humor the saga of her twenty-eight years. He seemed particularly interested in the last fifteen of those twenty-eight, and how she had dealt with her brother's disappearance. Apparently he was satisfied that she had done all right, for when she came to the end of her rambling tale he nodded approvingly.

"Ben O'Hanlon will be lucky if he wins you," he said.

"He's already won me," she replied with a grin.

"Perhaps. I'm afraid you might find that things are often a little more complicated than they first seem. The course of true love has never, I repeat, never run smoothly."

"I've begun to catch on to that fact. Don't you think we've already had our share of complications?"

Father Frank shook his balding head. "I doubt it." Catching sight of her suddenly worried expression, he smiled, squeezing her hand comfortingly. "Don't worry, Rachel. You're a very resourceful, loving woman. I have no doubt at all you'll have your fairy-tale ending, even if you have to earn it with blood, sweat, and tears. It won't be exactly as you imagined, but I'm sure it will be close enough."

Rachel looked up at him for a long, silent moment. They were back at the cottage again, and she knew as well as he did that it was time for him to leave. "What time's your plane tomorrow?" she queried, stalling for time.

"Two in the afternoon. I'm flying to the mainland first, then on to El Salvador."

"I wish you weren't going."

He smiled down at her, the beneficial smile that was warmer than the rays of the Hawaiian sun. "I'll think of you often, Rachel. Take good care of Ben—I think he needs it."

"I will. And you take care of yourself." She went into his arms then, holding him tightly, loath to let him leave. His embrace was as strong, and they clung to each other for a long, emotional moment. When he released her and stepped back there was a deep sadness in his face, despite the smile, and Rachel could feel tears lodge in her throat and fill her eyes. For some strong reason it felt as if still another part of her life was being ripped from her, and a sudden desolation filled her.

"Good-bye, Rachel," he said softly. "God be with you." And then he was gone, swiftly, without looking back.

Chapter Twenty

Emmett didn't come. She should have known it; some-where deep inside she should have realized that it was too good to be true. She hadn't ever really had much claim to being psychic, despite her cheerful assertion to Father Frank there was second sight in her family. But that morning she had been so certain, so very positive that he wouldn't let her birthday pass without some word.

Probably just wishful thinking, Rachel thought as she wandered down to the water. She had wanted him to come so badly, had longed for it with every fiber of her being, that it had metamorphosed into not only a possi-bility, but a certainty. And she should have known by now, nothing was certain in this life.

Perhaps Emmett really was dead. For some foolish reason she had thought she would know if he died, that some small, silent part of her would die too if she felt his loss. But her instincts had been wrong about her birth-day; they could just as easily be wrong about that, too. He could have died any time in the last year, lost in some South African jungle, dead in a stockbroker's bed of an early heart attack. There was no guarantee that he was still alive.

Of course there was always the chance that a small package containing a silk or china butterfly was awaiting her in the Berkeley post office that was holding her mail. Emmett might be nowhere near Kauai; perhaps they had all been on a false trail. But somehow, comforting as the thought might be, Rachel didn't believe it for one minute. Either Emmett was near, or he was dead. She didn't allow for any other possibilities. And since he hadn't come, he must be dead.

What would Ben say when she told him? Or Uncle Harris, for that matter? They seemed so certain that Emmett was somewhere around, waiting to appear like some magician. They would believe what they wanted to believe, and she doubted that included her hazy feelings. She would be alone in coping with his certain loss, while Ben and Harris still scurried around, chasing ghosts.

The water was warm to her bare toes, and she dug them into the wet sand, squinting into the horizon. She wanted Ben, needed him with every cell in her body. She needed his arms around her, his strong body pressing against hers; she needed to hide her face against the warmth of his shoulder, to howl away her grief and abandonment. She needed someone to give her trust and love to completely, without question; she needed his mouth, his hands, his loins, his legs, his heart and soul. And she needed a love that he was far from ready to give.

It was late when Ben returned that night. Darkness had already enshrouded the small cottage, and a few solitary stars lit the inky black sky. Rachel was very quiet as she waited for him on the front porch, curled up in the hammock, her body folded in on itself. She should have known, she told herself with only a trace of bitterness. Things seldom go as they should. Emmett Chandler had forgotten his sister's birthday for the first time in fifteen years.

"What are you doing out here?" Ben was looming over her, exhaustion and something else shuttering his slightly battered face. She must have fallen asleep waiting for him—the moon was already beginning to rise over the whispering ocean.

She smiled up at him, at least half of her sorrow vanishing at the sight of him, unwelcoming as that closed expression was. "Waiting for you," she murmured. "Did you have a good day?"

A cynical smile curled his lip. "It was a waste of time. A wild goose chase, set up by someone with an interesting sense of humor. Possibly your priest."

"He came to see you today."

Ben looked unimpressed. "Sure he did. After sending me chasing over Ne Pali with his gardener. Did he have anything to say about your brother?" He threw his tired body into a nearby chair, stretching his legs out in front of him. It was hard to believe that the last time she had seen him that morning he'd been kissing her with that twisted, cynical mouth, that those hard, hazel eyes had been soft and warm with something akin to love, that he'd been stretched out over her love-flushed body, holding her....

Depression settled over Rachel, and determinedly she fought it off. No one had ever said Ben O'Hanlon was an easy man to get along with; the demands of a relationship with him would be extraordinary. So would be the rewards.

Pulling herself into a sitting position, she crossed her legs under herself, swaying back and forth in the canvas hammock. "He didn't say much," she admitted slowly. "He didn't seem very surprised that you weren't really

Emmett, but then, we expected that. We really talked more about me than about my brother. I guess Father Frank may have met Emmett in the last few years; he wouldn't say." Rachel's voice was doubtful.

"Why wouldn't he tell you any more?"

"He said it was information sealed under the confessional." She wanted to reach out and smooth the hair away from his lined brow; she wanted to kiss his eyelashes. She remained right where she was.

"That's as good an excuse as any." He sighed. "I guess I'm just going to have to camp on his doorstep and beat it out of him. I'm getting damned tired of chasing around after shadows."

A faint smile lit her face. "He won't be around for you to beat it out of. He's leaving for El Salvador tomorrow afternoon."

"El Salvador? Why the hell is he going to El Salvador?" Ben seemed to take it as a personal affront.

"Because he wants to, and his superiors gave him permission. I guess he feels he's needed."

A bleak look had settled over Ben's face, the dark shadows of memory haunting his eyes. "More likely he's got a martyr complex. What's he got to atone for?"

"Nothing!" Rachel snapped, beginning to get angry. "He just wants to help people. Is that so strange?"

"It is in my experience," Ben said wearily, leaning back and shutting his eyes. He was gray with exhaustion, the marks of Stephen Ames's defense standing out against the sweat-stained pallor of his face. "Especially risking your life to do it."

"Maybe you've had the wrong sort of experiences."

"Maybe I have," he agreed shortly. "Well, I'll give your martyr priest a nice, safe way to help people. He can tell me where and when he last saw Emmett Chandler. What time's his plane?''

She considered lying for a moment, then dismissed the idea. Ben O'Hanlon contributed more than enough lies to their tenuous relationship; she should do her best to avoid adding to the spider's web of falsehoods.

"Two o'clock," she said finally, leaning back in the hammock. "But you needn't bother. Emmett's dead." Saying the words out loud was surprisingly easy, considering how hard she had avoided them the last few hours. She could say it; she just couldn't accept it.

That caught his attention. "Why do you say that?"

She didn't answer him. "Why do you suppose I let you go off to Ne Pali without me?" she countered. "I knew you were leaving this morning...I could have forced you to take me with you."

"You couldn't have forced me to do anything I didn't want to do," he contradicted flatly. "All right, why didn't you say anything when I left?"

"Because I knew you wouldn't find him. If Emmett were still alive he would have come here today, not been roaming all over the cliffs."

"Why?"

"Because it's my birthday, and he hasn't missed one in fifteen years," she said in a quiet, pain-filled voice. "Until now."

Dead silence settled over the porch. "You didn't see fit to tell me that?" His voice was cold and still, and she wanted to weep for the double loss. That of Emmett, and the man who had loved her last night. In his place was the cold, hard man she had seen too much of.

"I wanted to see Emmett alone."

"You wanted to make sure it was safe to let me see him," Ben countered. "You still don't trust me." There was no surprise in his voice, no disapproval. Just a statement of fact.

Rachel opened her mouth to deny it, then closed it again. No lies, she told herself again. Much as she wanted to, she didn't trust him. Not yet.

Quietly she changed the subject. "What does it matter to you? Emmett is small potatoes compared to some of the other radicals still on the run. He just happened to be at the wrong place at the wrong time—he never did anything terribly criminal. It was just bad timing. Bad luck."

Ben's face was carved in granite, and he looked right through her, as if she were as inconsequential as the butterflies Emmett used to give her. "*Bad luck* that someone was killed? Wouldn't you say that's putting it mildly?"

"It was an accident. Emmett didn't know what was going on when he brought her there; he was just visiting friends."

"And he left her there, alone, to die in the rubble while he was off getting pizza." Ben's voice was rich with disgust.

Rachel stared at him. "How did you know that?"

"Know what?"

"That Emmett had gone out for pizza? That wasn't public knowledge."

"Reporters don't have to settle for public knowledge," Ben said with a harsh condescension.

"But what would it matter? Why should you remember a tiny detail like that?" she persisted. Something was wrong, horribly wrong. She could feel a dark feeling of dread begin to grow inside her.

"It wasn't a tiny detail. It cost an innocent nineteen-year-old girl her life." Something in her stunned expression must have penetrated his anger, and suddenly all temper had vanished, replaced by an extreme weariness. Running a tired hand through his rumpled hair, he took a step toward her. She remained motionless, staring.

"Look," he said, "let's not argue about it. I'm tired and in a bad mood. I'm going to take a shower. Have you eaten?"

She didn't say a word, just continued to stare at him. He swore then, a short, ugly word. "Listen, I'm sorry I snapped," he said wearily. "I'll be more human after I've had a shower and a drink. I'm sorry," he said again. She just looked at him.

The door slammed behind his retreating figure, and a few moments later she heard the shower running. Very slowly she moved from the porch railing, staring down at her hands with a detached air. They were trembling.

Rachel had only met her once, when Emmett had brought her home for a weekend that coincided with a demonstration at Berkeley. Rachel couldn't even remember her name. Kathy, was it? Cassie? Something like that. Nineteen years old, and she absolutely worshiped Emmett Chandler. Not for one moment had she left his side, and the eleven-year-old Rachel had been torn with jealous anger.

Krissy. That was it. Pretty, nineteen-year-old Krissy, who had done her best to get past an eleven-year-old's fearful jealousy by telling her all about her life and how much they had in common. They had both lost their parents when they were children; they were both devoted to their older brothers. Krissy's brother was a journalism student at Columbia, and they were just as close as Emmett and Rachel. She had told Rachel about their life, growing up with grandparents as loving, if not nearly as wealthy, as Ariel and Henry Emmett, slowly winning the young girl's interest and dissolving some of the barriers. The next day they were gone; two months later she was dead, and Emmett was on the run.

She moved through the house like a zombie, past the bathroom with the shower still pounding, past the dismantled doorway into Ben's room. The picture was where she left it, in his top drawer. She drew it out, and looked back fifteen years into Krissy O'Hanlon's face.

She hadn't even heard the shower stop, the door open, or the footsteps approach the bedroom. She could feel him there, staring at her, and slowly she looked up.

He had a thick towel knotted around his waist, and water still clung to the hair on his chest. His hair was damp and rumpled, and the hazel eyes that watched her were wary. At last she understood the reason for his wariness.

"She was your sister." Her voice came out hoarse and rusty-sounding in the stillness.

"Yes."

"And you don't want Emmett for any book, do you? You want to hurt him."

"Yes."

Each single syllable was like a nail in the coffin of her heart. She didn't even flinch before the pain. "Were you going to kill him? Or just turn him in?"

For a moment she thought he wasn't going to answer. Moving into the room, he took the picture out of her lifeless hands. "I was going to beat the hell out of him. And then turn him in. He wasn't worth the price I'd have to pay for killing him, no matter how much he deserved it. He's already ruined enough lives—I wasn't going to let him ruin mine."

"I think he already has," she said softly. He was so close, she could feel the heat from his body, smell the scent of soap still clinging to his damp skin. "And where did I come in? Or do I even need to ask?"

He said absolutely nothing, staring down at her with a shuttered, unreadable expression on his face.

A small, sad smile flitted about the corners of her mouth. "You lucked into the perfect revenge, didn't you? If I hadn't showed up so precipitously you would have had to make do with that rather mundane vengeance. But this must have been really sweet. You think Emmett destroyed your sister, so you very kindly returned the favor. I presume you weren't thinking of actually killing me, either? Just performing a neat, slicing, twisting murder of the heart and soul. Emmett's sister for yours. An eye for an eye, a tooth for a tooth. Very poetic."

Still he said nothing, his mouth a straight line, his hazel eyes bleak and haunted.

Rachel smiled again, the smile faint and distant, and drew herself up to her full height. "Would you care to deny it? Do you deny you took one look at me and the perfect revenge fell right into place?" Deny it, she begged silently. *Tell me I'm crazy, that you love me, that you don't want to hurt my brother.*

"No," he said, his voice flat and toneless. "I don't deny it." He looked as if he were about to say something else, and she waited, breathlessly, one last hope still clinging desperately to the threads of her being. And then he said the worst thing he could have said. "I'm sorry."

She slapped him then, so hard that her hand was numb. The sound of it was shocking in the still room, and she stared at him in distant surprise. She hadn't even remembered raising her hand.

She turned and walked away from him, out of the room, out of the cottage, her pace slow and calm. She was a few yards down the beach when something broke, and she began to run. She ran until her heart pounded painfully against her ribs, until her legs cramped, until her breath was a rasp in her throat, and still she ran. Until she tripped, sprawling facedown in the sand on the deserted beach.

She lay there, crying, crying for her flighty mother and the father no one had known, for Ariel and Henry Emmett, for her brother and for Krissy O'Hanlon, for all the people who'd left her and all the people who'd stayed behind. And most of all she cried for Ben O'Hanlon, who lied and lied and lied. And she cried for Rachel.

Chapter Twenty-one

Ben stood there, motionless, watching her walk slowly away from him, out of the cottage, out of his life most likely. He could still feel the stinging imprint of her hand on his cheek—she'd managed to connect quite soundly. His first instinct was to go after her, to try to explain.

Explain what? he jeered at himself silently. Explain that he'd dismissed the idea of using her shortly after it had come to him, explain that though he had every intention of crucifying her brother, he still wanted to salvage something of their relationship. Fat chance. Listen, honey, once I finish destroying your brother, why don't you and I go to bed together again? She'd take to that real well, he thought, yanking clean clothes out of his drawers.

Last night was a mistake, but then, everything he'd done with Rachel Chandler had been a mistake. Not that he'd been thinking at all, but if he had he would have hoped that making love to her would take the edge off the aching longing she brought out in him, would destroy the mystery of her attraction for him. It had done just the opposite. He wanted her more than ever, wanted her with those stricken brown eyes staring up at him, wanted her when she slapped his face, wanted her as she turned her back on him and walked away.

His gaze fell on Krissy's picture. Rachel was another innocent sister, destroyed by stupidity and possibly noble motives. Was he any better than Emmett Chandler, when it came right down to it? Even if he did think twice about it, he was more than ready to sacrifice Rachel for the sake of justice and revenge.

She couldn't get very far on foot, he thought, wandering out on the porch. Her footsteps led off to the left, in the direction of the point. No houses that way, just progressively rockier shoreline. She wouldn't get into much trouble out there; sooner or later she'd have to turn around and head back. And he'd be waiting for her.

With a sigh he sank down on the porch railing, lighting a cigarette. Sometime he'd have to give the damned things up, but right now he needed one almost as much as he needed Rachel Chandler. He inhaled deeply, and the scent of jasmine mixed with the strong tobacco. He swore then, sharply, and stared down the beach in the direction of her footsteps. The moon wouldn't be coming up till late; he hoped she wasn't afraid of the dark. She was afraid of so many things—airplanes and the ocean and storms. The one thing she hadn't been afraid of was loving him. Maybe he should go after her after all.

Don't be a fool, O'Hanlon, he told himself. The last thing she needs right now is you and your feeble excuses. If you can't give up going after Emmett, the least you can do is leave her in peace. For the time being.

Leaning back against the post, he took another drag on the harsh cigarette, then sent it spinning into the sand in disgust. He wouldn't go after her; he'd wait for her to come back, even if it killed him. He owed her that much.

RACHEL HAD MANAGED to pull herself into a huddled position against a small outcropping of rocks. The sea was rougher this far down the coast, the shoreline wilder. The crashing of the surf against the rocks drowned out the sound of her tears as she sat curled in on herself.

She would have to learn to carry tissues with her if she intended to indulge in periodic fits of weeping, she told herself numbly. Chances were tears would become a habit in the next few weeks. Who was she kidding: the next few months, or years. Now that the dam had broken, it seemed that she was going to cry forever, and the running nose that accompanied it needed more than the worn scrap of Kleenex she'd discovered in the pockets of her shorts. So she sat there, for what may have been minutes or may have been hours, and wept and sniffed and sniffed and wept. When she finally decided she had cried enough for the time being, she fell asleep, resting her head on the arms draped across her knees. Ben found her that way several hours later.

The moon had risen, casting eerie shadows behind him on the darkened sand, and he looked unnaturally tall, standing over her hunched figure. She looked up at him, but his face was in the shadows, and she couldn't tell what he was thinking. She didn't really care.

"Go away." It sounded neither childish nor petulant. Her voice was cool and neutral, despite the rawness left by her bout of tears.

"It's after two, Rachel. Come back to the house." His voice was calm, patient, even politely concerned, she thought savagely.

"No. I'm never going back there." Still in that cool, detached voice, she noted with satisfaction. Maybe once again she'd managed to turn off the pain of his lies.

Though she knew from bitter experience that the emotional anesthesia wouldn't last long.

"You can't spend the night out here, Rachel," he said in a reasonable voice. "The temperature gets quite cool this time of year, and you're not dressed for it." His eyes took in her long, bare legs beneath the shorts and the sleeveless shirt that exposed her tanned, chilled arms.

Damn him; in her misery she hadn't even noticed she was cold. "I'm staying here." Now she was sounding petulant, but she couldn't help it. A shiver washed over her body.

"No, you're not. I'm not going to let you." His voice was implacable, and he held out a hand to help her up. It was beautiful in the moonlight, one of the strong, large hands that had cradled her body last night, that had driven her to the edge of madness, and then past it to completion.

"Don't you touch me!" she snapped.

He dropped his hand. "All right. If you'll come back with me on your own accord."

"It's a little late for bargaining, isn't it?"

"I don't know, is it?" he said softly. "Come back to the house, Rachel, and I promise I'll leave you alone. When you wake up tomorrow morning I'll drive you anywhere you want to go."

"Just the airport."

He nodded. "The first plane out is ten thirty. Or there's a later one around noon, and one at two."

"Ten thirty will be fine." She scrambled to her feet, stumbling slightly from cramped muscles, and he put out a hand to steady her. She drew back as if burned. She didn't think she could bear it if he touched her again; that storm of tears wasn't far in the past, and it wouldn't take much to set it off again. The last thing she needed was to break down in front of him again. She didn't want guilt or compassion from him right now; she only wanted his love.

He seemed to hesitate. "Are you all right? I thought you might..."

"I'll come back to the cabin if you don't try to talk to me," she interrupted sharply. "Just keep away from me." Don't, she prayed silently. Take me in your arms and tell me it was all a mistake, that you wouldn't hurt my brother, that you wouldn't hurt me. I love you, Ben. Don't leave me like all the others did.

"All right," he agreed slowly, deaf to her unspoken pleas. "I'll follow you in."

And in complete silence they walked the full mile down the deserted beach back to the dimly lit cottage, Ben right behind her every step of the way. When she got to her bedroom door, he stopped, and she turned to look up at him, wishing she didn't have to, unable to help herself.

In the light of the cottage she could see his face now. Hours later there was still a mark from where she had slapped him, and the hazel eyes that looked down at her no longer looked wary, or mocking, or even guilty. They looked full of a tender longing that could only be called love.

It was the last straw. "Liar," she spat, turning away from him. A moment later she was spun back around, pushed up against her closed bedroom door. His hips ground up against hers, and she could feel him hard against her, wanting her. In self-disgust she accepted the heated surge in her own veins that answered him, and when his hands imprisoned the sides of her head, holding her still for the bitter strength of his kiss, she was powerless to stop her response.

Keep your hands at your side, she told herself through the haze of passion that swept over her. That way you won't be responding. But even as she did so her hips pressed back against his, her nipples hardened through the thin cotton that caressed his chest, and her mouth opened beneath his, allowing—no demanding—his entrance, and his tongue swept past the meager barrier of her small white teeth in a savage kiss of punishment and possession. It was that thrusting, demanding possession that she responded to, her arms betraying her by sliding up around his neck, her tongue catching his in a silent duel of rage and love. She was his, he was hers, and nothing would change that.

Suddenly he thrust her away, and she fell back against the door, staring up at him out of wide, shocked eyes. His own hazel ones were glittering strangely with passion and anger, and a shudder shook his tense body.

"Don't push me any further, Rachel," he said hoarsely. "Go to bed."

She felt lost, adrift. "But..."

"Don't even think it," he said roughly. "You can't seduce me into forgetting about your brother, so don't even try. I'm not going to give you any more cause to hate me than you already have."

"But I didn't..." She hadn't even thought of such a thing, but now that she did, it was a damned good idea. She craved his touch like a strong drug, and she might just possibly sway him....

"Forget it," he said. "Tomorrow I'll drive you anywhere you want me to. Go to bed, Rachel. Now." It was an order, clear and simple, one she had no choice but to obey.

He was right, she thought, disappearing into her bedroom and slamming the door behind her. She had reason enough to despise him. If she gave in to the unbearable longings that were sweeping her body and slept with him, knowing what he had planned for her brother, that hatred could very well take over her life and destroy her.

Except she knew perfectly well that she could never hate Ben O'Hanlon. She would have to try very hard during the next few months to summon forth the animosity required to get over the last week. Somehow she knew she was doomed to failure. Rachel didn't hate easily, and she didn't love easily. Ben O'Hanlon was fated to receive an uneasy mixture of both from her, probably for the rest of her life. It wasn't the most comforting thought to try to fall asleep on.

Chapter Twenty-two

When Rachel finally struggled out of the mists of sleep she forgot, for one blissful moment, where she was. Instinctively she reached out, subconsciously searching for the warm male body she'd slept with only the night before. Her hand encountered the edge of the narrow bed, and with it came reality and memory, flooding back in all their harsh ugliness.

It amazed her that she had slept at all, but she had, almost the moment her head had hit the pillow, sleeping the sleep of total exhaustion, both physical and emotional. She could be grateful to a less than generous fate for that much—she had the feeling she'd need all the physical reserves she could call on to get through the day.

Waiting for her at the end of it would be her large, untidy apartment in Berkeley and her job catering to the lost and hopeless of society. She'd fit in well, once she got back on her feet enough to join the walking wounded. What in heaven's name had made her choose social work when she went to graduate school? She must have known she'd need it herself some time.

She still hadn't gotten around to buying a decent bathrobe. Wrapping the sheet around her like a toga, she dashed into the deserted bathroom. With any luck at all she wouldn't have to face Ben until he drove her to the airport. She wondered what he'd tell Uncle Harris. The elder statesman of the Chandler clan could have no idea what Ben had in mind for the young heir; she could imagine his reaction when he found out who Ben really was. All the Chandlers had always avoided the press assiduously. Harris Chandler would very likely be drummed out of the clan for harboring a snake in his bosom.

The swift shower didn't help at all. Her large brown eyes were haunted as she stood in front of the mirror braiding her chestnut hair in one thick braid, and there were circles under them. She would return from her Hawaiian vacation looking even more drained than when she had left, albeit a great deal more tanned. So much for a tropical paradise. Next year she'd go to Kansas.

It was a quarter past nine by the time she dressed in the white linen suit she'd arrived in, slid her feet into the high-heeled sandals, and fastened tiny pearl studs in her small ears. Her suitcase, stuffed to the brim, stood by the door; her purse was crammed full of tissues. Last night had taught her a lesson—she had little doubt she was going to cry from Kauai to Oahu to San Francisco, and she intended to be prepared. Maybe that preparation would render her dry-eyed and stoic. Somehow she didn't quite believe it.

She wasn't going to succumb to temptation and try one last cup of his wretched coffee. It was half past nine— more than time to leave for the airport. Taking a deep breath, she grasped the porcelain doorknob with one shaking hand. If she could just carry off the next hour with some small trace of aplomb....

Sometime during the night Ben had put back the hinges on his door. She hadn't even heard it, but it remained firmly shut to her inquiring eyes. He was awake, she was absolutely sure of it. After a moment's hesitation she rapped firmly on the door. The only answer was a muffled grunt.

"I'll need to leave for the airport soon," she called out, sounding as businesslike as she could manage. Something akin to a growl answered her, and she nodded, satisfied. She would wait on the porch until he appeared, savoring the last few moments of the dream she'd lost in her tropical paradise.

It was still and quiet out there, with the early morning sun blazing off the gently rolling waves. The palm trees that edged the beach swayed in the gentle trade winds, and the salt smell mixed with the flowering bush by the side of the house. Rachel sat there, stony-faced in her misery, drinking in the sights and sounds and smells around her. Damn him, couldn't he hurry? A few more minutes of this and she'd throw herself at his feet.

The door opened beside her, and she looked up expectantly, then blinked. He was dressed in his bathing trunks and nothing more, and the sight of that tanned, tough hide of his nearly upset what little amount of equilibrium she had left to her.

"You're driving me to the airport like that?"

He shook his head. "I'm not driving you anywhere. I'm going for a swim."

"But you promised!" Rachel wailed.

"I changed my mind." He was watching her, his face still impassive.

She looked up at him in complete bewilderment. "Why?"

"Because I don't want you to leave me," he replied quite simply, and walked past her, down the steps, and into the sea.

She stared after him, openmouthed in astonishment. And then belatedly she reacted, jumping to her feet. "Wait a minute," she shrieked after him, but he was already knee-deep in water and making no effort to turn around. "Wait just a damn minute, Ben O'Hanlon."

He continued his forward stride, his muscular legs slicing through the surf, and she scrambled down the stairs after him. "You come back here," she yelled. "You can't say something like that and just walk away from me." But apparently he could. His back was broad and imposing, and a moment later he dove into the water, his body skimming through a wave with perfect grace.

"No!" she shrieked, and ran into the water after him. She was knee-deep before she kicked off the sandals, and still she plowed onward, the sea water soaking into her elegant linen suit. The skirt was too narrow to swim in, even with its thigh-high split, and the water was colder than she expected. He was swimming away from her as rapidly as he could, and determinedly she plowed onward, using her arms to push through the water. A cold wave slapped her in the face, and she choked for a moment before opening her mouth to call him again.

"Damn you, Ben, come back here!" she shrieked. "I'll follow you to China if I have to. You can't get away with this. You . . ." A stronger wave slapped her in the chest, toppling her over, and she went under, her mouth still open in outrage.

When she struggled to the surface she had swallowed what seemed like several quarts of salt water, and she was thrashing about in an impotent fury when two strong arms wrapped around her, pulling her up out of the water. Ben's hazel eyes blazed down into hers.

"What the hell do you think you're doing?" he demanded, holding on to her with needless force, his fingers biting into the slender arms now covered with wet linen.

She felt forlorn, bedraggled, and suddenly very uncertain. "I don't want to leave you either," she said in a very small, meek voice.

The look of dawning delight in those wary hazel eyes was worth everything: the shattered pride, the wrecked suit, even her prodigal brother. And then he kissed her, his mouth cold and wet and salty and absolutely delicious. She couldn't get enough of the cool, clean taste of him, and a shiver of pure delight ran through her as her tongue eagerly explored the magical cavern of his mouth.

He misinterpreted that shiver, and his grip on her tightened for a moment before he swung her up in his arms, striding with her out of the heavy surf toward the cottage. "You're out of your mind, do you know that?" he said roughly. "Chasing after me with this ridiculous suit on. You could have drowned, do you know that?" All during this tirade he was holding her close against his chest, and she could hear the slow heated beats of his heart.

"No, I couldn't have," she murmured, resting her head against his cool, damp chest. "You would have saved me."

He looked down at her for a moment before climbing the porch steps, making no effort to put her down. "You can't always count on that," he said grimly.

"I know." Her voice was very gentle.

He didn't release her until they reached his bedroom. Kicking the door shut behind them, he slowly lowered her feet to the floor, his mouth reaching for hers again, with light, hungry little kisses as his hands went to the near impossible task of stripping the sodden linen from her chilled body. Rachel was shaking too much to help him, shaking from the cool dampness of her clothes and from something far more elemental. She tried to deepen the kisses, but he proved frustratingly elusive, darting away before her tongue could reach his, as the linen jacket landed on the floor, followed by the ruined silk blouse.

Ben hesitated for a moment when he got to the thin wisp of a bra, and his hands cupped her chilled breasts, warming them, his thumbs gently brushing the softly rounded undersides. She moaned softly, and his mouth followed, his breath heated against the cold flesh. The bra fell apart at his deft touch, and then his lips closed over one turgid peak, his tongue gently circling, touching, tasting her cool, wet skin and turning it to fire and ice. She was an inferno by the time he got to the other one; all the while his deft hands were loosening her waistband and sliding the narrow, wet skirt down over her hips. It landed in a pool at their bare feet, and she was standing there, clad only in the peach silk panties she'd worn when he'd walked in on her days ago.

His clever, sensitive hands trailed down the taut skin of her stomach to rest lightly on the elastic waistband of the bikini panties. "I've fantasized about these for days now," he murmured in a low, sexy drawl. And dropping to his knees in front of her, he pressed his mouth against the thin silk, his hands cupping her round buttocks.

She could feel the damp, moist heat of his breath through the thin, wispy cloth, and an answering warmth and moistness flowed from her. Her knees felt weak, and she reached out to steady herself, holding on to his tanned shoulders as he knelt in front of her. Her fingers were digging into his smooth flesh, clutching him helplessly as his mouth moved slowly, exploringly over the silk-covered mound. And then she was back in his arms again as he lowered her to the bed just behind them, his body covering hers with leisurely grace.

He was so strong, so hard against her. Reaching down between them, she ran a wondering hand over him, exulting in the power of his arousal. With measured deliberation she traced his hard contours, exploring the length and breadth of him, until he groaned against her ear, rolling onto his back. Taking her hand in his, he slid it just inside the waistband of his swimming trunks. It was all the encouragement she needed. Her hand moved lower, and her mouth followed, showering small, tasting kisses on him as she slid the trunks off his narrow hips. She kissed his thighs, his knees, his calves, his feet, reveling in the salt-sea taste of him, the roughness of the hair beneath her tongue, the warmth of his sun-heated flesh. And then he was reaching down, pulling her up and over him, enfolding her against the tough, solid warmth of him, holding her in a grip so tight it was painful as one hand caught her neck and held her still for his hungry mouth.

Rachel closed her eyes beneath the slow, sensuous onslaught, her heart, her breasts, her body clamoring for him. His hand released her head to trail downward to her hips, slipping the peach silk panties off with a practiced ease that should have disturbed her. And then his hands slipped between her legs to find the heated core of her. With a touch both deft and sure, he brought her the final steps toward readiness.

She reached out for him then, her touch less practiced but no less stimulating. Liquid silk was flowing from him, proclaiming his readiness, and the fierce desire in Rachel's loins flamed out of control. She arched against him, a low, inarticulate cry in the back of her throat. And then she was on her back and he was over her, around her, in her, filling that aching emptiness that had longed for him with a slow, sure, driving thrust that sent her suddenly rigid, her body clenching around his as pure sensation took over. He held her, not moving, as the spasms rocked her body, cradling her tightly until they began to die away.

And then he did move, beginning the sweet, slow rhythm of love, the ebb and flow as timeless as the ocean outside them on the bright sunny morning. Rachel was lost, floating, adrift with the universe, tied forever with the ocean and the land and the man in her arms, who was bringing her back to the edge of fulfillment and taking her beyond, time and time and time again. Until she was weeping against his sweat-slick shoulder, clinging to him helplessly. "Don't leave me," she whispered brokenly against the damp skin. "Come with me."

And when the next wave hit her, she felt his body tense in her arms, heard his muffled cry, and they were there together, lost and found, flung out into the gently rocking ocean of eternity. She was content to cling to him through the storm, safe in his arms at last, reveling in the feel of his strong frame as it shuddered against hers. She felt as old and wise and powerful as the earth, as warm and fertile and serene. For a brief moment in time they were the only two people in the world. Soon enough reality would intrude, hearts would be broken, trusts betrayed. And lies. Without doubt, more lies. But right now it didn't matter. Nothing mattered but the man in her arms, his breathing hoarse and ragged, his damp forehead cradled against her neck. Clinging to him fiercely, she pressed her lips against his damp, blond hair and smiled.

Chapter Twenty-three

It was a long time before Ben stirred, moving away from Rachel to stretch out on his back, head and shoulders propped up against the bunched white pillows, and his eyes met hers for a long, pregnant moment.

She rolled onto her side, lazily, her body warm and tired and completely satisfied. She smiled up at him, a tentative, wondering smile, and a sigh seemed to leave his tense body.

"Come here," he growled, pulling her up against him, cradling her head against his strong shoulder. She settled there quite happily, reveling in the feel of his hand stroking her skin, holding her with a tenderness she wouldn't have thought him capable of.

"I'm not going to forget about Emmett," he said, his voice low and implacable above her ear.

"I know," she whispered.

"You'll hate me even more." Why was he torturing both of them? he wondered wearily, pulling her slender, warm body closer against his. She'll know it soon enough.

A small shake of her head stirred the hair that flowed across his chest. "No, I won't. I can't hate you, Ben. No matter how hard I try." He felt her mouth move, the light feathering of her lips against his shoulder, and the raw tension that never seemed far away began to fill him again.

He had his choice: He could stay in bed and love her again, keep her there until they were both sated, if such a thing could ever happen, and then love her some more. Or he could get up, put a stop to an affair he should have had the sense to never begin. It was already too late for them—there was no need to compound the damage. He needed to remove her from him, physically and emotionally. To keep her here would only make things worse.

But first he would give in to temptation one more time. No matter that it would only make the parting more difficult, no matter that he was prolonging the agony. Molding her slender body to his, he ducked his head to catch her mouth in a slow, drugging kiss that ripped away the last of their defenses and left him totally aroused once more.

He heard her cry of protest when he pulled away, but he didn't stop, didn't turn, heading into the bathroom without a backward glance. He knew if he did, he wouldn't leave her—ever.

Rachel lay there, bereft, for a long, sorrowing moment. She would have to get used to that feeling, she told herself. No matter how much she loved Ben O'Hanlon, there was no future for them. They both had their blood ties, bound inextricably with the past, stronger even than what they shared. He couldn't sacrifice his sister for her, she couldn't sacrifice her brother for him. They were at a standstill, with nothing but pain on all sides awaiting them.

The linen suit was destroyed, probably beyond repair. She doubted she could ever bear to wear it again anyway, and scooping up the sodden pile from the floor, she dumped it in the wastebasket before padding barefoot out into the living room. She could hear the sound of the shower—Ben shutting himself off from her again. The sunlit sea beckoned, and she didn't even hesitate, walking naked out the front door and down the beach, diving into the sea, welcoming the cold, salty waves with a lover's embrace.

The buoyancy of the sea water was suddenly liberating. No longer was she afraid of jellyfish, sharks, and the myriad other denizens of the deep she had always imagined lurked beneath the blue-green surface, ready to pounce. She dove, she surfaced, she dove again, at one with the elements and the ocean, a naiad reveling in her sea world, filling her mouth and eyes and heart with the water from which all life had sprung. She swam until exhaustion weakened her, and then she struggled slowly back toward the shore.

Ben was waiting for her on the front porch, dressed in faded jeans and a denim shirt open around his hips. She emerged from the sea with unselfconscious grace, tossing her wet curtain of hair back over her shoulder as she moved toward him, no overt sexuality in her nudity, just a clean, healthy body moving freely toward him. He had never wanted her as much.

When she came even with him he smiled faintly. "There's still hot water if you want to take a shower before you go."

She handled it well, not even flinching. She knew as well as he did that she had to leave, and leave soon. She shook her head. "I want to go back to San Francisco with some of Hawaii still on my skin." She knew a moment of regret—she had washed every trace of him from her—she would have preferred to savor the lingering smell and feel of him. She had given it up to the ocean, and yet somehow it was right.

"Get dressed and I'll make us some lunch." He didn't touch her—his hands clenched with the effort not to—and it was only from years of experience at hiding his feelings that he managed to keep his face cool and remote.

A tiny, sad smile lit her face again, recognizing his withdrawal. "All right. Maybe if I hurry we can still make the two o'clock plane."

"We'd really have to push. The three o'clock will be time enough." Or the four o'clock, he thought silently. Or maybe they could snatch one more day. Tomorrow would be soon enough, wouldn't it? *Don't be a fool, O'Hanlon. Let her go.*

Ben's idea of lunch wasn't much better than the dinner he had cooked the first night she arrived. Dried bread, soggy tuna fish, and damp potato chips wouldn't have enticed even a normal appetite. Ben and Rachel barely touched it.

She was perched on the counter, her long legs swinging freely. Her two dresses were ripped and filthy beyond repair from the vagaries of the last two days. That left shorts, and a loose cotton tunic. It would be freezing when she landed in California, and she couldn't care less. The remembered warmth in Ben's eyes as they lingered over her long, browned legs would dispel the chill.

"You'll tell Uncle Harris good-bye for me, won't you?" she said finally, putting her uneaten sandwich down beside her.

He nodded, his hand reaching for a cigarette. It hovered over the package, then pulled back without taking one. "I'll tell him."

"Are you going to tell him who you are?" she questioned, curious. "He doesn't have any idea, does he?"

"He thinks I'm a small-time swindler named Jake Addams, out for all the money I can get, no questions asked. And no, I'm not going to tell him who I am and what I want. He might try to stop me." His eyes dared her to avoid the flat honesty in his voice. "I'm still going to do it, Rachel." Why did he have to keep reminding her? he thought belatedly. Or was he reminding himself?

"I don't think it's going to matter," she murmured, leaning back against the wall and pulling her bare feet up under her. "Emmett's dead."

"You don't really think that."

"Yes, I do. My heart may not believe it, but my head certainly does. And I think it's time I learned not to trust my heart." Her voice was without inflection, but Ben winced anyway.

"You think he's dead because he forgot your birthday?" he scoffed.

"When you put it that way, it sounds juvenile, but yes, that's part of it. I also think that he wouldn't ignore Henry Emmett and Ariel's death, that he wouldn't just abandon me...." Her eyes met his for a long moment, and then she plunged on, "abandon me to the wolves without a backward glance. He has to know he's heir to the whole fortune—there's been massive publicity and a thousand private detectives looking for him over the past fifteen years and there's never been a trace. He vanished off the face of the earth."

"What makes you think he's heard about the whole mess? He may be living a comfortable life in Connecticut, working on Wall Street and raising two point three children."

A sad smile lit her face. "Five children. That was part of my fantasy; I want lots of nieces and nephews." She shook her head. "No, he's not doing that. He would have heard about it—the case of the missing heir even made the cover of *Newsweek*. He would have had to be in a monastery to miss it...." The words were barely out of her mouth when it happened. "No," she choked in a barely audible whisper.

"What is it?" She heard his voice from far away, through the sudden roaring in her ears and the blackness that threatened to engulf her. She could feel his hands catching her arms, shaking her, and she looked up dazedly. "What is it, Rachel?" he demanded again, and without thinking she blurted it out.

"In a monastery..." she repeated in shock. "He's Father Frank."

"That's impossible!" Ben snapped, his eyes blazing down into hers with sudden intensity. "You've seen him any number of times in the last few days. How could you have not recognized him?"

She tried to shake off the fog that enveloped her. "I haven't seen him since I was twelve years old. That's a long time for a child. And he had hair to his waist, a full beard, and he was skinny as a rail. Father Frank is cleanshaven, fat and balding. And he's a priest, for heaven's sake. I never even thought of him as a possibility."

Ben's voice was low and deadly, but Rachel was too caught up to recognize the danger. "Rachel, are you sure?"

She looked up then. "*Sure?* Of course I am. Why do you suppose he never let you and Uncle Harris see him? I may have been too young to remember him, but he couldn't trust you two to be as obtuse." Her voice was filled with bitter recriminations. "Damn him. Oh, damn him to hell."

"When does his plane leave?"

Ben's stillness finally penetrated, and Rachel suddenly was calm. "I won't tell you."

He said nothing for a moment. "You don't need to. It was the two o'clock flight, wasn't it? I still have time to catch it."

She beat him to the car, snatching the keys from the ignition and clutching them tightly in her fist. "No, Ben," she begged. "I can't let you do it. Let him go, please."

"Give me the keys." His voice was cold and implacable, terrifying to a much braver person, but Rachel shook her head.

"No, Ben."

"I don't want to hurt you, Rachel. But I will." He was moving closer, slowly, menacingly. "Give me the keys."

She shook her head again, trying to back away, when one long arm shot out and caught her wrist. He did it quickly, efficiently, grinding her bones together until she cried with pain, dropping the keys into the sand.

There was no regret on his face, no anger, no sorrow. Just a blank, implacable determination. Turning from her, he climbed into the Land Rover and turned the engine on swiftly.

She was beside him in the passenger seat by the time he started moving, clinging for dear life to the frayed and tattered seat. He didn't say a word, didn't look at her, keeping his attention on the twisting highway as he raced down the road.

"You don't really want to do this, Ben, you know you don't," she said calmly, reasonably. "You don't want to hurt me, and you don't even want to hurt Emmett. He's spent the last fifteen years helping people, serving people. Don't you think that atones for whatever sins he may have committed? Krissy's death was an accident, a tragic accident. Emmett didn't set out to hurt her, you know that as well as I do.''

The wind was whipping her hair about, the wet strands stinging her face, but she pushed onward, determined to drive some sense into him. ''She wouldn't have wanted you to hurt him, you know. She was in love with him. If you hurt him, you'll be betraying her trust, her love for you....''

''Shut up, Rachel,'' his voice came suddenly, low and feral. ''If you don't, I'll push you out of this car.''

An answering flare of anger wiped out the last trace of her fear. ''You will not. Don't you bully me, Ben O'Hanlon. You may be perfectly willing to destroy my brother, but you aren't going to hurt me if you can help it.''

''I'm about to hurt you,'' he grated, pressing down further on the gas pedal. She hadn't realized the old Land Rover could travel so fast. ''I'm about to hurt you quite badly, and I could stop if I wanted to. I don't.'' His voice was bitter.

And suddenly she knew he would do it. He would destroy both their lives with that one act of vengeance, destroy hers and his own. Father Frank wouldn't survive the circus of publicity, even if the charges were dropped. And the repercussions from the church would be awesome—entering the priesthood under a false name was a definite sin. If he even really was a priest.

''Don't worry, Rachel,'' Ben drawled viciously. ''The Chandler millions will probably be able to buy his way out of any kind of sentence. He'll be free to spend all that money and provide you with your nieces and nephews.''

"Then why bother turning him in?" she cried.

"Because there's a chance in a million that he won't get away with it. I have the power of the press behind me; I'll crucify him on every editorial page I can get to. Maybe for once money won't triumph." He cast a sideways glance at her as he slammed into the airport parking lot. "And then you can hate me to your heart's content for what I did to your poor innocent brother."

"Do you think that's why I'm trying to stop you?" she cried. "I don't give a damn about Emmett—or not much of one, at least. He lied to me, he abandoned me—like all the others, like you're about to do. For God's sake, I've only seen him three times in the past fifteen years. I didn't even recognize him when I saw him."

He had paused, halfway in, halfway out of the Land Rover at the beginning of her impassioned speech. "Then why are you going to so much trouble to stop me?" he snapped.

"Because of what this will do to you. To me. To us. It's you that I care about. I don't want you to turn Emmett in because it will destroy us both. Ben, I love you." There were tears of entreaty in her eyes, and he looked down into them for a long, tense moment, disbelief and something else in his hazel depths.

And then he was gone, turning and running into the terminal without even a backward glance. Failure and despair washed over her for a long, numbing moment. And then she was after him, chasing barefoot down the tile-floored corridor, weaving through the chattering crowds of tourists.

She saw the broad back, the familiar, black-garbed figure of the priest at the same time he did. She wanted to scream, "No, Ben," but something kept her silent, doubling her speed. She could feel a sick panic rise in her stomach, anguish ready to burst her heart. She caught up with them just as Ben reached the priest, grabbing his arm and whirling him around to face them.

The strange, bespectacled face stared at them in complete bewilderment. "May I help you?"

Ben dropped his arm. "You're not Emmett Chandler!" He cast an accusing glare at Rachel's pale face.

"No, I'm not. I'm Father Gruning. I'm afraid I don't know Mr. Chandler—I'm new here to the islands. I was just seeing my predecessor off. Is there any way I can help you?" The man was obviously flustered by his sudden encounter, but he managed an affable smile.

"Father Frank has left already?" Rachel demanded.

"Just a few moments ago. I'm sorry, had you planned to see him off?"

Ben's face was grim. "We had hoped to. We had an important message for him."

A relieved smile lit Father Gruning's swarthy face. "Oh, well, that's no problem. He'll be staying over in Los Angeles for a night. We can get in touch with airport security and they'll pass the message along."

Rachel's heart screamed no, but her mouth was silent. She stood there, unmoving, brown eyes huge in her pale, haunted face, and waited for the words to come that would end everything.

Ben stood very still. He could feel the tension and panic radiate from the slender figure beside him, feel her love and despair washing over him in waves. Drowning him, washing him clean of the bitter twist of pain and rage that had eaten away at him for fifteen years. Emmett Chandler had destroyed many lives that day so long ago through his thoughtless idealism. How could he think he was any better when he was about to destroy just as completely and far more ruthlessly?

Krissy was long gone, a gentle, worshipful child who had lived far too short a time. Would she worship him any longer if she knew his unceasing quest for revenge, which he'd self-righteously labeled justice? He doubted it. And somehow, as he tried to conjure up the reproachful figure of his innocent younger sister, all he could see was Rachel, her huge eyes watching him, waiting for him to destroy their lives. And he couldn't do it. Krissy was dead, and it was past time for him to let her go. Rachel was alive, beside him, and the choice was clear.

There was a long, torturous pause. Rachel looked up to see Ben's eyes on her, distant and unreadable. And then his mouth twisted in a wry, self-mocking smile. "I guess that won't be necessary," he said, taking Rachel's limp hand in his icy one. "I imagine he'll be in touch this time next year."

Father Gruning didn't pretend to understand, just nodded cheerfully. "I'm sure he'll be sorry he missed you."

"I'm not so sure of that," Ben drawled, his grip tightening on Rachel's hand.

"That reminds me. . . . You wouldn't by any chance be Rachel Chandler?" the priest inquired.

"Yes." The word came out strangled and rusty.

Father Gruning beamed. "Well, this is convenient. Father Frank left a package for you. He said to tell you he meant to give it to you yesterday, but he forgot. I have it someplace. . . ." He was rummaging through his pockets, finally coming up with a small, gaily wrapped package no bigger than a pack of cigarettes. "Here it is. Well, that saves me a trip. Though I wouldn't have minded—anything for Frank. We were in seminary together, fourteen years ago, and a kinder, more decent guy I have yet to meet. I'll miss him," the priest sighed, pushing his glasses further up on his nose.

"Did he pay you to say that?" Ben drawled.

Father Gruning looked startled, almost dropping the package before placing it in Ben's large, outstretched hand. "I beg your pardon?"

Ben's smile was faint. "Just kidding, Father. Good luck in your new parish." He turned and moved away, still holding Rachel's numb hand tightly in his.

"Oh, if Frank should get in touch, should I give him your regards?" Father Gruning inquired distantly.

Ben managed a wicked, mocking grin. "Do that, Father. Tell him Ben O'Hanlon wishes him well. Come on, Rachel."

He didn't say a word as they made their way back out of the terminal, only relinquishing his hold on her hand when he started the car. He dropped the small package in her lap, put the car in gear, and started driving.

He didn't stop until they reached the secluded beach where he had first taught her how to snorkel. He put the elderly Land Rover in Park, leaned back against the seat, and draped his hands across the steering wheel. His tough, graceful body still radiated tension, and she sat there, unmoving, not knowing what to say, what to do to break the silence.

And then he let out a deep sigh, and with it the anger and tension seemed to drain from his body. He turned then, a warm, free smile reaching his hazel eyes. "I love you too," he said simply. And she went into his arms, as sweetly and trustingly as a child. Or a woman in love.

They held each other for a long, healing eternity, and the relief and love flowed between them like the tide. She wanted to move even closer to him, and she shifted, pressing against his enveloping warmth, when the small package on her lap slipped to the floor. Slowly, reluctantly he released her, nodding toward the small package. "Aren't you going to open that?"

She stared at it, curious and a little afraid. She didn't want to bring Emmett back between them, but the soothing hand on the back of her neck reassured her. "Go ahead, Rachel. It's okay. It'll be another butterfly, won't it?"

Her fingers were clumsy with the ribbon, ripping the paper nervously. "It should be. For fifteen years he's sent them to me." She dropped the top of the box onto the seat beside her, staring in wonder inside the box. "Oh, Ben," she whispered.

He looked down. Nestled in the box were two crystal butterflies, dancing together in a perfect flight of love. Trust Emmett, he thought wryly. Reaching out, he put his arm around Rachel's shoulders, drawing her against him.

She came happily, resting her head against his chest, the butterflies still clasped loosely in her hand. "I guess Emmett approves," he said softly.

She looked at them for a moment longer, a smile lighting her face. "I guess he does." And then she closed the box, putting them away, turning a look of such love and joy on him that it took his breath away. "Let's go home, Ben."

"Yes," he said. "Let's go home."

Epilogue

It was Rachel Chandler O'Hanlon's twenty-ninth birthday, a cold day in April. The dirt on the winding gravel drive scrunched beneath her heavy boots as she climbed back up to the house from the mailbox, and the wind bit through the heavy woolen sweater she'd filched from her husband that morning. The small package was there, regular as clockwork, postmarked El Salvador.

"Did it come?" Ben poked his head around the corner of their rambling, always-under-construction house. He was in the midst of adding a mysterious wing of rooms off their bedroom and, as always, refused hired help, making do with the intermittent visits of newspaper friends. He looked tough and lean and fit in his faded jeans and flannel shirt, and she smiled brilliantly at him.

"Of course. Direct from El Salvador."

He moved forward onto the deck, untying the nail apron and dropping it on the railing. "I really wondered whether we'd ever hear from him. For months I've been expecting a letter, a message, something. But not a word, even when Emmett Chandler was declared legally dead and the inheritance split among your family."

"I wasn't surprised," Rachel said serenely. "He isn't Emmett any more, he's Father Frank. There'd be no reason to get in touch with us. Besides, he probably thinks you still might turn him in.''

"Don't tempt me," he growled. "Open it up." He slid an arm around her in spite of his gruff tone, watching with interest as she tore off the heavy wrappings.

"Oh-oh," she murmured, looking into the box.

Ben grinned. "A baby crystal butterfly to match the two larger ones. Do you suppose he's trying to tell us something?"

"Well, he is a priest, you know. It's his duty to encourage people to procreate," she replied, keeping her eyes averted. It was something she had wanted so very much, she'd been afraid to bring it up, and now Emmett, with his usual lack of timing, had done it for her. She could only hope the ensuing discussion wasn't going to ruin her birthday.

"That reminds me," Ben whispered in her ear, that slow, sexy drawl, demoralizing as always. "Would you like your birthday present?"

She smiled up at him. "What is it? A table saw?"

"I thought you liked the belt sander I gave you for Christmas?" he protested.

"I did, I did. Even if you use it more than I do. But twenty-nine is getting perilously close to thirty, and I'm feeling a little ancient this morning. I hope you have something to make me feel more youthful."

"I have just the thing. We're going back to the cottage on Kauai for two weeks." His hand was kneading the small of her back in that way of his that never failed to make her knees weak.

"Ben!" she turned an overjoyed face to him. "When can we go?"

"I thought next week. The book's coming out on the fifteenth, and I wanted to make myself scarce when it did. A lot of people are going to be pretty unhappy with the way I portrayed the American government in the sixties. And they're not going to be much happier with the radicals. I thought it would be a perfect time to go back to the cottage—there are a lot of things I still want to try there."

"Like what?"

His hand had slipped lower, beneath the waistband of her jeans, and she leaned back against him, sighing.

Turning her around, he pulled her into his arms, pressing her hips against his. "Like making love on the beach. We never did, you know."

She made a face. "Sounds uncomfortable. All that sand ground into your skin."

His grin was a savage slash of white in his tanned face. "I'll be on the bottom," he said, biting her lower lip with a sudden, darting move.

"That sounds like an offer I can't refuse," she murmured against his mouth, her arms encircling his waist. "Why the sudden interest in the great outdoors?"

"I want to make babies with you by the ocean," he whispered, and her heart leaped. "Lots and lots of babies." His mouth trailed damp, nibbling kisses along her cheek, ending with her delicate earlobe. His teeth sank in, lightly, and she moaned. "What do you think I've been building?"

"Another bathroom?" she murmured dazedly against his hair.

She felt his slight headshake. "A nursery. That is"—he pulled away, looking down at her with a smug grin—"if you want one."

He knew her far too well. "I want one," she said. "Can we make babies in the ocean, too?"

"We can only try," he murmured wickedly. "And I promise to have the house finished by the time you're three months along."

"Sure you will," she said, knowing of old how long it took him to finish anything. It wasn't that he didn't work hard; he was just easily distracted. With Ben's arm tightly encircling Rachel's waist, they strolled back into the house, heading for one more distraction. Her forehead was wrinkled with concentration, and he paused outside the doorless entrance to their bedroom to look down at her.

"Penny for your thoughts," he queried, cocking his head to one side.

Reaching up on tiptoes, she brushed her mouth against his. "I was just wondering whether we could make babies in the hammock." And she joined him in his shout of laughter before tumbling onto the unmade bed.